Just Friends

Elizabeth Grey

SNOWFLAKE
PUBLISHING

Please visit www.elizabeth-grey.com **to sign up to Elizabeth Grey's newsletter and for more information on her books.**

Facebook: www.facebook.com/elizabethgreyauthor
Twitter: www.twitter.com/elizabethjgrey
Instagram: www.instagram.com/elizabethgreyauthor

Just Friends - The Agency #1

Published 2017
ISBN-13: 978-1976074080 : ISBN-10: 1976074088

Set in 12 pt, Times New Roman.

Cover designed by Elizabeth Grey Art & Illustration of South Shields, Tyne and Wear, UK.

Copy Edited by Kia Thomas Editing of South Shields, Tyne and Wear, UK. www.kiathomasediting.com
www.twitter.com/kiathomasedits

DEDICATION

For Chris,

My best friend and soulmate – who never ever stopped
believing in me.

ACKNOWLEDGEMENTS

Phillippa Chippendale – thank you for showing me what a friend is, and for teaching me that only some people's opinions are important – the rest is just noise.

Andrea Grey – my very-nearly-almost sister – thank you for your continued support, advice and encouragement.

Kia Thomas – I will never ever stop being grateful that I know you. Thank you for telling me straight! A (secular) miracle happened the day I found you in the schoolyard.

Kara Grande – my friend over the pond who cares so much about all the really important stuff. We will win back the world one day.

Sharon Wilson – no words to describe how much I enjoy laughing with you. We will always have our curry and Pimms nights.

Joanne Philpot – I was so proud you struggled through the swears! Thank you for having the best pre-school in town and for looking after my children so I could write.

Mum – thanks for telling me I'm brilliant. You'll have a paper copy one day. If it helps you cope chapter 26 was ghost-written (not really though).

Dad – you're not allowed to read this, but thanks for the other life stuff!

Massive thanks to those who read the first draft of this book and encouraged me to keep going: Lynne Thompson-Hogg; Natalie Jewitt; Alison Imrie; Alison Chisholm; Rachel Oliver; Chris Grew & Lindsay Hodgson.

TABLE OF CONTENTS

Dedication
Acknowledgements
Mailing List

1

IT'S ONLY TAKEN THREE MONTHS, two weeks and five days, but here I am – in Stuart Inman's Notting Hill bedroom, wearing underwear that screams "sex goddess" and a spray tan that shrieks "never again!"

Thankfully Stuart is too busy burying his head in my cleavage to notice my tangerine armpits and stripy inner thighs. He's also groaning and purring and nuzzling and . . . okay, I'm not really sure what he's doing down there, but I hope he tries another move soon. I can think of much better things I'd like him to do to my boobs than use them as a pair of earmuffs.

Ah, good, he's heading north now. I look into his deep blue eyes and remind myself why I'm here. Stuart Inman is hot. Think Matt Damon in an action movie: all blonde and ripped and gun-toting. Matt Damon, that is, with the gun-toting. Not Stuart. The only thing Stuart totes is a rather feminine Burberry man-bag.

He backs me up against his bedroom wall and I run my fingers over the taut muscles of his fabulous chest. Then I feel his lips brush against mine, his tongue darting in and . . . oh, sweet Jesus, what the . . . ?

Breathe. Close your eyes, think of England and for heaven's sake, just breathe . . .

What in the name of all things holy was that? If it was supposed to be a kiss, then please don't let him kiss me again. Talk about disappointing. Has he been practising his make-out skills with a bathroom sponge? I've kissed a few men in my life, and most of them have been far less confident, successful and drop-dead gorgeous than Stuart Inman, so how is it possible that he kisses like a half-starved pufferfish devouring a shrimp? Ugh . . . no. Just no.

I run my fingers over his abs, trying to avoid his hungry mouth. So what if he's a crap kisser? We can work on the finer details later. The important thing right now is sex is happening – my eight-month-long drought is coming to an end and my velvet-touch, thirty-function, silicone Rampant Rabbit can hop off into the sunset and do one.

His hands move over my body as he lowers me onto his bed. I look into his eyes, his cheeks dimpling as he smiles seductively. I should be kissing him, feeling him, touching him until we're both sweaty and panting for more, but my stupid brain decides to torture me instead: *Stuart kisses like a pufferfish. Stuart kisses like a pufferfish. Stuart kisses like a pufferfish* . . . and . . . oh no, he's nuzzling my boobs again . . . and oh my god! What the hell was that? Why are his pants stuck to my stomach? Oh shit, he has, hasn't he? He's shot his load. He rolls onto his back with a thump. "I'm sorry . . ." he whimpers.

I don't know whether to laugh or cry. Where's my Matt Damon action hero gone? Why does the fittest client I've ever worked with have less knob control than a horny teenager who's just discovered Pornhub? What did I do to piss off the gods of shagging this time? Come back, my beloved Raunchy Rabbit, I miss you already.

He turns to face me, but I don't want to look at him. Yes, I'll admit, I'm a coward. I can't think of anything good to say, which, given words are my livelihood, is pretty pathetic.

"You're just so hot. I'm sorry. I couldn't help it." He removes his sticky pants to reveal an appendage that

11

could accurately be compared to a half-eaten Walnut Whip – sad, shrivelled and hollow. He crosses his legs in an attempt to hide his shame, and sadly, it doesn't take much to hide *it*. How on earth didn't I notice that before? I usually check out a guy's bulge before I commit. Jeez, this must be the most desperate for sex I've ever been in my entire life.

"It's okay. Maybe next time?" I say, with the kind of insincere politeness a politician would be proud of.

"I can still go on. Just give me a minute," he says with an enthusiastic tug to his manhood, and my stomach lurches. Do I want to have sex with a Matt Damon lookalike if he's only packing a chipolata and kisses like a pufferfish sucking on a sponge?

Ten seconds later, he's sliding his hand into my knickers and frantically rubbing away at what I'm sure he thinks is my clitoris, but of course, it isn't. The gods of shagging wouldn't be that merciful. I simulate a few polite moans and consider following through with a fake orgasm, but as he's jabbing the inside of my leg with the elbow of the hand that's futilely attempting to transform the chipolata into a frankfurter, I can't take it anymore.

Mission abort! Mission abort!

"Okay, stop. Just stop," I say as I squirm out of his grasp.

He removes his hand from inside my underwear and frowns at me. "What's up?"

"Um . . . that's not really doing much for me. Sorry."

"What do you mean? What's wrong with you? I always get girls off doing that."

I feel my eyes pop. "Really?"

"Yeah, really," he replies with an eye roll and way too much attitude. All of a sudden I have too many

12

words, but as none of them are kind, I swallow them down and start putting my clothes back on.

Stuart tuts, gets up and pulls on a robe. I leave his apartment as fast as I can and head towards Holland Park Tube, flagging the first taxi I see on the way.

***

At times like these, a girl needs her best friend, so I direct the taxi driver to the heart of the West End and make my way to Ethan's Soho penthouse. I check my watch – it's 1:15 a.m., but it's Friday and he said he was hosting a get-together with the lads tonight, so he might still be up. If he is, I hope he's alone.

I say hi to Gus, the doorman of Ethan's building, before taking the lift to the top floor. I listen at the door – silence, thank goodness – and ring the buzzer. And then I ring again. And again . . . until finally the door opens to reveal a bare-chested Ethan clad only in tartan pyjama bottoms, his usually perfectly styled dark hair sticking up in a hundred different directions and the aroma of beer lingering on his skin.

"Vi?" He rubs at his eyes. "What time is it?"

"Um . . . late—"

"Are you okay?" he interrupts, panic rising in his voice.

"Yes, of course. I just . . . I'm sorry. I didn't think you'd be in bed yet. I'll go. We can talk tomorrow." I turn on my heel, feeling stupid for coming over in the middle of the night.

"Wait," he says, his voice still gravelly with sleep and his Scottish accent more pronounced than usual.

I turn around. He's looking at me as if I've grown an

extra head. "Why are you looking at me like that?"

"Just wondering what you've done this time."

I scowl at him, and he beckons me into his apartment with a knowing grin. I head straight for the open-plan sitting/eating/sleeping room to find his very stylish bachelor pad has morphed into a students' union den – empty beer bottles, pizza boxes, lad mags, overflowing ashtrays, women's underwear . . . Whoa! What?

"Do you have a woman in here?"

"No, of course not," he says, pulling a t-shirt on over his head.

He looks confused. I don't want to ask, but the question is begging. "Have you had a stripper in here?"

"Eh? What are you talking about?" He looks absently around the room until his gaze finally settles on the skimpy fuchsia-pink pair of knickers sitting proudly on the coffee table. "Ah. Those are here courtesy of Max."

I dread to think. Max is my other best friend, and he was Ethan's roommate in halls at UCL. We've all worked together at Barrett McAllan Gray, London's most prestigious ad agency, for the last three years. Max is a designer; Ethan and I are a creative team – he's the art director and I'm the copywriter.

"Did Max have a woman in here?"

Ethan laughs. "Yeah, sure. Max had sex with a woman in my apartment and we all sat around and watched. Actually, now I think about it, that sounds like a fun night."

I stifle a giggle. "You want to watch Max having sex?"

"Ew, what? No. I didn't say that. In my mind there would be two women . . . and you know . . . I'd get to do stuff too."

14

I stare at him open-mouthed, wondering why my life is plagued with teenage men.

He exhales in defeat. "Okay, I did say that, didn't I?"

I tumble onto his grey sofa in a fit of giggles, hugging his favourite Beatles *Yellow Submarine* cushion. "Yep, you did. But I knew what you meant."

He slumps down next to me. "The knickers are Ruby's."

"Oh my god, no. Ruby and Max? My Ruby? My trainee and therefore my responsibility? Please tell me he hasn't." Ethan shakes his head, but I'm still questioning Ruby's sanity.

"No, it's not like that. It was Will."

"Will? That's not much better. He's horrible with women."

"No, you don't understand. It was a dare. She doesn't know we have them."

I stop laughing. We've been here before and it doesn't end well. The last time Max and Will pranked each other it ended up with a written warning from the CEO. "Ethan Archibald Fraser, confess your sins now. Have you and your merry band of fuckwits done anything gross, cruel or in any way misogynistic to poor Ruby?"

He nods his head and burps. A cloud of rotten-beer belch fills the air. "I would have to plead guilty on all three counts."

"Oh my god, why are you such a dick?"

"Don't call me that."

"What? A dick? I could call you a lot worse."

"No, don't call me Archibald. I know I'm a dick."

I prop the giant cushion behind my back and make myself comfortable. "Just get on with the story."

Ethan contorts his face into an aggravated scowl and

moves closer to me. I smile inwardly because I can tell he's trying not to laugh. He also has an unmistakeable glint of mischief in his eye, reminding me why we've been inseparable since the day we met: we get each other, trust each other, laugh at the same things, and as a result, we're the best advertising creative team in the city.

"Max has a thing for Ruby, apparently. He heard she needed help decorating her bedroom, so he volunteered. Will found out and teased the shit out of him. Mohammed joined in, it escalated, and the guys ended up betting Max he couldn't steal an item of clothing from her bedroom drawers." He points at the pair of knickers and chuckles. "Max won, so Mohammed owes him fifty quid."

"Let me get this straight – Max stole Ruby's knickers to win a bet? That is so disrespectful. I'm disappointed in Mohammed. You, Max and Will are a trio of shits, but Mohammed has always been a gentleman. Was he here tonight?"

"No, he's left."

"Left what?" I ask in confusion.

"Barrett McAllan Gray. Didn't anybody text you tonight? He pissed off a client – nothing major – but Will had a real go at him after you left work this afternoon, and he walked. Said he wasn't working with a sociopathic megalomaniac any more. It turns out Mohammed's flatmate works for the Daily Mail and he's landed a great copywriting job there already."

"Oh my god!"

"I know. I'm going to miss Mohammed. He was a good laugh."

"No, I mean, oh my god, the Daily Mail hired someone called Mohammed? What's up with that?"

He laughs and runs his fingers through his short, feathery hair. "So, I take it things didn't go too well with Stuart."

"It was a disaster," I reply, not meeting his gaze. "No, it was worse than a disaster."

Ethan raises an eyebrow and his smile fades. "Worse than your date with Eugene from Public Relations?"

Oh flip, I'd forgotten about him. After an unbelievably great evening – at The Ivy, no less – Eugene somehow slipped in the gents' toilets, cracked his head open on a urinal and had to be stretchered out. "Yes, it was worse than that. Much worse."

"Oh hell," he says. "Well, I always thought Stuart was a tube."

"A what?" I twist my face in confusion. "You thought he was an underground train?"

"No, a tube's an idiot – Scottish slang."

"You haven't been anywhere near Scotland for sixteen years. Speak the Queen's English, for goodness sake."

"Hey, I'll always be a proud Scotsman. Now, are you going to tell me what Stuart did, or are you just going to insult my vocabulary?"

I inhale deeply for courage. "You have to promise not to tell anybody."

"Of course," he says, and being a good Catholic boy who never goes to church and doesn't believe in God, he crosses himself for good measure.

"I don't know where to start, so I'm just going to blurt it out, okay?"

"Um . . . okay."

"Okay." I take another deep breath. "So, despite being blessed with the body and good looks of a demi-god, Stuart Inman is a crap kisser, he's hung like a

17

gerbil in a blizzard and he shot his load before I even got my knickers off."

Ethan covers his mouth with both hands and starts to turn purple.

"Don't you dare bloody laugh!"

He laughs. Actually, he doesn't just laugh. He wheezes, shrieks, coughs, splutters, almost chokes and then runs to the bathroom saying he needs a piss. It takes a solid five minutes for him to compose himself and I can hear him laughing the whole time he's in there. When he finally emerges he apologises, whilst trying not to laugh, and then he sits down and proceeds to start laughing again.

"It isn't funny. I'm totally mortified, and we still have to work with Stuart. I pretty much told him he was a shit shag and ran away. This make me a horrible person, doesn't it?"

"Um . . . yeah, a little bit," he says between giggles. "I'm sorry, but who'd have thought it? Now I know why he drives that ridiculous Porsche."

"I won't be able to look at him ever again without replaying it. And seeing, you know, *it* . . . oh, crap. Life is teaching me a lesson here. Can you remember when I passed that law last year after Eugene? 'Never screw around with people you have to work with.' Why didn't I stick to it? We have to see Stuart tomorrow night at that blasted awards show. Or rather you do. I'm not going. I can't face it."

"Oh no you don't. No way are you getting out of the AdAg Awards. You've been trying to find an excuse not to go for months. In fact, I wouldn't be surprised if you orchestrated this whole Stuart thing deliberately."

"You think I shrank Stuart Inman's penis to get out of going to the AdAg Awards?"

18

"Stranger things have happened."

"Have they? Where was that then? In darkest voodoo-magic land?"

He shrugs, but his expression changes back to pity again. "Do you want to sleep here tonight?"

The mention of sleep suddenly makes me feel exhausted. I shuffle down on the sofa, curl up into a ball and nuzzle my cheek into Ethan's super-comfy Beatles cushion. "Thank you, that would be nice."

"You can have my bed if you want."

"That's okay. I'll be fine here."

"Okay, I'll get you a blanket."

He disappears over to his bedroom, which is around the corner of his L-shaped open-plan studio. He returns with a dark-orange knitted throw and drapes it over me. Then he perches at my feet and rests his hand on my curled-up knee. "I *am* sorry about tonight," he says softly.

"Even if Stuart's a tube?"

"Yeah, sure. I mean, you can do much better than him, but you deserve to find a guy you can be happy with."

"Thanks, Ethan. I just hope I haven't screwed things up for you at work."

"Well, if you need advice from an expert, just pretend it didn't happen and go on as normal. That's what I do. And I have a lot of experience sleeping with clients, and co-workers, and—"

"And the models we hire. And actresses. And the woman who scrubs the office toilets."

"That only happened once, and Kiki is a very lovely girl."

"She doesn't speak a word of English."

"She speaks the language of love."

I groan and turn over as he laughs and pats my knee.

"Look at it this way, Vi. The fact Stuart shot his load before the main event means you must be pretty damn hot in bed."

I play along. "Maybe I am, but after tonight I'm closing the well. It's the only way. I have to start obeying my law, so I'm not just swearing off dating men I work with; I'm swearing off all men, everywhere. I'm going to enjoy being single until I'm at least thirty."

"Well, that's a shame," he says with a chuckle, tucking the blanket around me. "And just for the record, you are hot. You're the hottest woman I've ever met."

What the hell? My stomach flips, and I have no idea why it's flipping because Ethan and I joke like this all the time. I close my eyes and listen to the sound of his feet padding over to his bed, followed by the creak of his mattress as he climbs in and gets comfortable. And just for a very brief fraction of a moment I imagine joining him.

My eyes fly open in surprise. I must be really bloody hard up if my brain is thinking about my best friend in this way. Thanks a lot for breaking my brain, Stuart Inman!

I push it out of my mind and fall asleep to the strangely comforting sound of traffic mixed with spring rain falling on the windows.

2

TONIGHT IS THE HOTTEST DATE in the advertising world's calendar, attended by all the big names in the industry. Every young, ambitious creative in the city hoped to get an invitation – everyone, that is, except me. Ethan and I have been nominated for Best Advertising Campaign of the Year, but I couldn't care less about it. I work in advertising because it's challenging and it pays the rent. I'm not here for accolades, so while my "rivals" are slipping into their newly purchased designer dresses after spending the entire day throwing money at hair stylists and beauticians, I'm hiding out in my basement flat hoping that my admittedly rubbish excuse for skipping the show is deemed acceptable.

My mantel clock ticks past the number seven and my stomach leaps – I'm almost home and dry. I daren't look at my phone in case there's a barrage of abuse waiting for me, so I snuggle into my sofa, wrap myself up in my purple velvet blanket, delve into a brand-new tub of strawberry cheesecake Häagen-Dazs and settle my laptop on my knee. I flick between the half-dozen open windows and curse the fact that I can't focus on anything but last night's embarrassing Stuart episode. The reason I'm hiding out is because I didn't handle it like a grown-up and I'm ashamed of myself.

A ping from my inbox calls me away from Candy Crush, which can only be a good thing given I've been stuck on Level 374 for . . . ooh . . . probably the last seven and a half years and I need to give up for the sake of my blood pressure. Another ping, another message.

Apparently Selfridges are having an in-store sale all next week. As I have neither the time nor the inclination to go up west to be poked and prodded by crowds of people carrying armfuls of shoes, I'll be giving that a wide berth. But in far more interesting news, my next email tells me that the British Museum is starting a new exhibition on the Rosetta Stone in July. I'll admit to being more than a little bit excited about this. I've been a tad obsessed with Ancient Egypt ever since I was seven and I learned to write my own name in hieroglyphics at school: snake (V) – leaf (I) – wheat (O) – lion (L) – reeds (E) – bread (T). I'm just about to pay in advance for a ticket when there's a knock at my door.

I know it can only be one of two people – the only two people who ever come to my apartment – Ethan or Max. Yes, Barrett McAllan Gray is my life and the people who work there are my family. That should tell you everything you need to know about my actual family.

A second knock on the door lets me know that my visitor is very impatient. "I'm coming," I call as I unlock the door, and I open it to reveal Ethan Fraser dressed as James Bond.

"You look pretty," I say with a chuckle.

He rolls his eyes and twists his mouth into an exasperated pout. He thinks I'm teasing, but I'm not. He does look totally drop-dead gorgeous. He stands at my door dressed in his tux, his shoulders broad, his blue eyes sparkling and his dark hair impeccably styled. My stomach repeats the strange somersault it did last night. Jeez, I wish it would stop doing that.

He walks into my flat as if he owns it, spins around and fixes me with a glare. "What the fuck's got into you?"

"Excuse me?" I say, narrowing my eyes.

"Do you think I'm buying your bollocks excuse for not going to the awards show tonight? How stupid do you think I am?" His accent, which usually has a lovely, soft David-Tennant lilt, has advanced to "shit-faced Glaswegian on a stag do". This means he's angry. He always gets more Scottish when he's angry.

My hands go to my hips. "Are you calling me a liar?"

"You're damn right I am. What kind of shitty excuse for missing an event like this is 'I'm on my period'? In case you didn't receive the memo, we've both been nominated for our work and we come as a team. Recycling a sick note you used for getting out of PE when you were thirteen doesn't even scratch the surface of convincing."

I swallow hard. I honestly thought I could play the crampy-and-bloated card and both he and Max would sign it off as woman stuff and run a mile in the opposite direction. "I just don't feel well."

"I don't believe you, Vi. I know you hate these awards, and you said last night you didn't want to face Stuart."

Why does he have to be right and reasonable all the bloody time? It makes it so much harder to lie to his face. I decide to change tack – a bit of humour might save my bacon. "Well, there's only one way to prove to you I'm not lying, and I don't think you'd want to go down that road . . ."

He screws up his nose and I feel my mood lift when I see his trademark smirk tug at the corners of his mouth. See how well I know him? All it took was a spot of random vulgarity. I watch his smile grow wider until his cheeks dimple. "Well, you know some men like to visit when—"

"Oh my god, stop talking!"

He laughs a filthy laugh, and I know we're back on track. "Okay, Vi, time to come clean. What's going on?"

"I don't know. I just . . ." I exhale in defeat because I know the game's up. Maybe it would have been easier to tell the truth from the start. I walk into the sitting room and he joins me on the sofa, narrowly missing the empty Häagen-Dazs tub.

"Was that your dinner?" he says with a smirk. He's always ribbing me for my lacklustre eating habits. I cook and eat like a ten-year-old, which means I can make a cracking sandwich and little else.

"No, just a pick-me-up."

"Look, Vi, I'm not going to the awards without you." His expression is etched with disappointment. "Please come."

I sigh and curl my legs up on the sofa underneath me. I hate disappointing him. "Okay, I admit I'm hiding from Stuart, but there's more to it. You know I hate all that pseudo-celebrity awards-show stuff. I mean, our job is hardly important to world peace or the advancement of mankind." He registers my prattle with an eye roll. I knew he wouldn't see things the way I do long before I opened my mouth. He's my best friend and he knows me better than anyone else in the world, but he still doesn't understand me the way I wish he could. "I keep out of the spotlight for a very good reason. You know I don't like that kind of attention. I thought you got that about me?"

"I do get you. I just didn't think you'd spoil this for the rest of us."

"Ethan, you're being unfair. You can have a good time without me. You don't need me to be there."

"We're a team. We did this together. Of course I need you."

My heart misses a beat as my eyes lock with his. His pleading is making me waver. "You should leave now or you'll be late."

"It's not even half past seven, and the awards don't start till nine. We'll only miss the pre-show dinner. We could grab a kebab from that Lebanese place you love on the High Street and eat it on the way. Come on, Vi, please. We did an amazing ad and we had a great time working on it. I want to share this with you."

I sigh again. I know I've lost. "Okay, give me fifteen minutes."

"You're coming?" he asks, beaming a huge smile.

"Yes, on the condition I sit nowhere near Stuart Inman."

"You're on."

I head to my bedroom and start trawling through the dresses in my wardrobe. I pull out something black. It's plain, calf-length, slightly floaty but elegant all the same. No idea where it came from or when I last wore it, but at least it's ironed. I match it up with a silver sequinned bag and strappy shoes. I have no time to do anything but backcomb my long dark hair into a wispy side bun, and then I start with the make-up, my signature look being classy, understated and natural, but with a splash of red lipstick. The red is necessary when your alabaster skin tone would make a polar bear look like he's got a suntan.

"You look . . . amazing," Ethan says when I walk back into the room. He drops the magazine he's been flicking through and stands to greet me. My stomach cartwheels and I feel like I'm seventeen.

"You owe me big time for this," I say as I pick up my mobile and keys and pop them into my bag.

"Fine. The kebab is on me."

"It'll take a lot more than that, but it's a start," I say with a jokey scowl, pulling on my coat. "And no garlic."

I open the door and he walks out into the corridor before me. "No garlic, eh? Who are you planning on getting off with tonight?"

"Shut up, you idiot."

***

It's after nine when we arrive at the Grosvenor Hotel on Park Lane. In hindsight, we probably shouldn't have visited the Beirut Grill, but when a man's gotta eat, a man's gotta eat, and Ethan can't function on an empty stomach. More to the point, given tonight's free bar, he can't drink on an empty stomach. I've seen the evidence – two years ago, at the annual agency summer party. He barfed on the pavement outside and accidentally painted my white shoes a permanent shade of red-wine.

By the time we take the two empty seats at the Barrett McAllan Gray table, we've missed dinner and two awards have already been declared. Oh, and I've just noticed an oily kebab stain on my dress. Could the night get any worse? Of course it could, and I fully expect it to. Shit, I need to stay positive and look on the bright side. *I don't live in a cardboard box. Bacteria aren't eating me alive. I don't live in a cardboard box. Bacteria aren't eating me alive.*

Ethan greets the other seven guests seated around the table and makes our apologies – or rather he lies his arse off. Apparently there were roadworks in Kilburn which blocked up my road into the city for two hours. I look around the table at the familiar faces, skipping Stuart, who I can't bear to make eye contact with, and I wonder who's buying it. The clear answer is nobody.

Max is sitting to my right. Or to be more accurate, Max slouches to my right with the posture of a giraffe who doesn't have enough space for his legs. At a gangly six foot four, my lithe German friend's enduring life struggle is to be comfortable. Just ask Debra in Facilities. She's provided him with six expensive ergonomic chairs for tall people over the years, and he hasn't come close to finding the chair of his dreams. Max and Ethan are wearing identical tuxedo suits, but while Ethan looks like he's working undercover for MI6, Max looks like he's off to see the wizard. His muddy-blonde scarecrow hair is wild and unkempt, while his thin, patchy beard looks like it's been drawn onto his face by a four-year-old. I try to catch his eye, and he responds with one of the filthiest looks I've ever seen him give anybody – including the one he gave to the intern who tripped over and landed a pile of canvasses on top of the miniature model of a Spitfire he'd spent two months making. Why is he so pissed off we were late?

"I'm pleased you could make it, Violet. We were beginning to worry," says Malcolm Barrett, our CEO and owner of the agency's bushiest moustache. Malcolm has bouncy blow-waved grey hair and a body that seems too small for his skin. He's always been a great boss to me, but he's as popular as swine flu with everybody else. Malcolm knocks back his glass of wine and glares at Ethan. "I must say your being this late doesn't look good."

"Yeah, well, it couldn't be helped," replies Ethan without making eye contact. This kind of exchange between them is usual. It's common knowledge that Malcolm and Ethan loathe each other.

"What have we missed?" I ask with fake eagerness, attempting to move the grey cloud on.

"You've missed dinner," says Stella Judd, our formidable head of Creative Services. "My lamb was so undercooked I half expected it to skip off my fucking plate, so you've had a lucky escape." I'll admit to having a bit of a girl-crush on Stella. She's beautiful, brilliant and brave, with a platinum-blonde razor crop, the dress sense of royalty and an aura that exudes power. In contrast to her stately appearance, she smokes like a chimney, swears like a sailor and couldn't care less if anyone has a problem with either. I've never met anybody like her.

"MRT won Best Print Ad for Hurly Gurly, and Diablo Brown won Best TV Ad for AirCat," says Daniel Noble, the lead account director for Quest – our current biggest client. Daniel is smart, good-looking and confident, and he could sell a glass of water to a drowning man. I realise that MRT's art win means Max lost in his category. I hope that's the reason for his mood, rather than our lateness. I make eye contact with him again and he looks as though he's still thinking of ways to kill me. I peek under the table to see if I can see an axe.

"I personally thought the Hurly Gurly ad was top-notch," says Ridley Gates, who, as usual, looks like he's just stepped out of a 1990s Brylcreem advert. Whenever I'm in the same room as Ridley I'm struck by how slimy he looks and what a slimeball he is. He's writing his own rules of rhetoric – visual onomatopoeia. Easily one of the least popular people at BMG, Ridley is the head of Client Services and Malcolm's loyal number two. "I think MRT definitely nailed 'adventure' much better than we did with the Quest for Life print ad. We should let that influence the Quest Living launch."

"Sounds like a great idea, Ridley," says Stuart, Quest's representative, seemingly unaware of the agency politics and the fact that artist Max looks fit to explode at Ridley's comments. "The board is keen that Quest Living delivers something distinct from the main Quest retail brand."

"Of course," says Ridley. His stiff, dark hair looks like it's been moulded to his head tonight, reminding me of a Ken doll. "Daniel and I will get to work on it right away."

I fill up my glass from one of the bottles of wine in the centre of the round table and I sense I'm being watched. I've tried to ignore Stuart's assistant, Carly Hayes, so far, but we finally make eye contact.

"I love what you've done to your hair tonight, Violet," she purrs as she scans the full length of my body, casting a disdainful glance at my dress. "I wish my stylist could achieve that tousled, just-got-out-of-bed look on me."

My hand wanders subconsciously to my hair and I feel a sharp twinge of insecurity in my gut. I catch Stuart smirk, and my blood starts to boil. Has he told her about last night? If he has, I'll bet my life savings that she's been given the director's cut as opposed to the official highlight reel. Argh. She's horrible and I curse myself for letting her get to me.

The music in the Grosvenor's ballroom starts up to herald the announcement of another award. I lean over to Max, squeeze his arm lightly and whisper, "I'm sorry." His frown slowly melts away and a tiny upwards twitch of his mouth reveals the faintest hint of a smile. I decide he'll be good by the end of the evening as long as I keep the wine flowing, so I reach for a bottle and top up his glass.

***

As the giant screen in the ballroom starts to play the video showcasing the eight nominated campaigns in our category – Best Advertising Campaign of the Year – it hits me that there's a good chance we might win and, if we do, I'll have to go up on stage and – panic – I don't want to. I haven't written a speech, and I don't ad-lib. I'm not a great talker. I write, therefore I don't need to speak.

I turn to Ethan and whisper into his ear. "If we win, I'm not going up there. You'll have to do it."

"How about we both go?" He leans in so close that I can feel his breath on my neck. It still smells of onions and grilled lamb.

"How about no, *we* both don't," I whisper back.

He leans even closer, places his hand gently on top of my hand and, as if to run the gamut of inappropriate physical gestures, he lets his thumb trace – no, caress – circles onto my skin. "We're a team, so we're doing this together."

I expect him to pull away after he speaks, but he doesn't. He leaves his hand in mine and . . . Jesus . . . what the hell is happening? I swear my ovaries have just leapt into my womb and danced the cha-cha. Has the Stuart Inman disaster turned me into a sex-starved desperado?

"And the AdAg goes to . . . Barrett McAllan Gray for their Quest for Life campaign for Quest plc, art director Ethan Fraser and copywriter Violet Archer!"

Oh. Shit. And. Hell.

Ethan is still holding my hand when he takes to his feet, so I have no choice but to follow after him. My pulse is racing, my legs are wobbling, my head is pounding and I have no idea how I climbed the stairs onto the stage, but suddenly I'm here and, surprisingly, I don't want to crawl into a hole and die. The applause quietens and we're presented with the award, which looks like a huge pile of glass vomit on a brass stick, and then Ethan turns to me, smiles and mouths, "You're doing great." He walks over to the microphone, delivers a short impromptu speech – with jokes – and the audience erupts into laughter. Sadly, I can't process his words because my brain has created white noise which has blocked out everything but the fact that he is still – wonderfully yet terrifyingly – holding my hand.

I mutter a "Thank you" to the room after Ethan finishes speaking, and we walk back to our table.

And then he lets go of me . . .

And my body deflates.

I sit down to cheers and claps from around our table. Malcolm strides over, bypassing Ethan, and congratulates me by planting a kiss on my cheek. Max is on his feet and clapping, as are Ridley, Daniel and Stuart. Stella smiles proudly and offers us a strangely elegant "You both fucking nailed it!" And Carly? Well, Carly looks like she's just chewed on a wasp, which makes the trauma of the evening totally worthwhile.

As the awards finish and we move on to the aftershow party, I realise the AdAg Awards have given me something more than a lump of engraved glass.

It's given me the realisation that something has shifted in my relationship with Ethan and I don't have a clue what or why that is.

3

AS WE WALK INTO THE converted warehouse venue that the agency has hired for the aftershow party, I feel like I'm walking onto the stage of Cirque de Soleil. No expense has been spared: there are acrobats swinging from trapezes hanging from the ceiling, glamorous stilt-balancing servers dressed as clowns, and an enormous ice sculpture of a circus elephant. The entire left side of the venue has been transformed into a casino while opposite, an actual fairground carousel is lit up with dozens of strings of fairy lights. The casino zone has been claimed as the guy hangout, and as for the carousel – what do you get if you mix intense spinning with a free bar? Not rocket science, is it? Whoever thought that was a good idea should be given the job of scrubbing the puke off it at 3 a.m.

As we pass the dance floor, I notice that a couple of my more adventurous colleagues appear to be devouring each other whilst having sex with all their clothes on. A girl I don't recognise has her leg wrapped around the waist of Jack from IT. She's so far gone I wonder if she realises his hands are up her skirt. I watch as she drags him into a corner and leaps into his arms, gyrating against his crotch like a monkey scratching its bottom on a baobab tree. I figure she knew.

"Ha, looks like the kids are having a good time," says Ethan.

Max looks around the venue and his face contorts

with disgust. "It's like an advertisement for syphilis in here."

I laugh. "An ad for syphilis? Wonder if we could win an AdAg award next year for knocking out one of those."

"Well, get your mobile out and start filming because – holy fucking shit – take a look at where Jack Shipley's hands are now." He links his arm in mine and covers his eyes with his hand.

I don't want to look, but I can't help myself. I momentarily worry about Gyrating Girl's safety, but she's vanished and Jack has turned his attentions elsewhere. Yep, there he is with his hands down his own pants. The rest of the IT department seem to be amused and iPhones are engaged, so it's a dead cert that Jack's antics are being uploaded directly to Instagram. Could he be any more disgusting? He helped me recover a corrupted file on my external hard drive yesterday, but now I know where his hands like to visit, I'll be asking for a new keyboard on Monday.

"Ah, here she is, the star of the show." I feel Malcolm Barrett's hand on my elbow as he guides me to a group that includes Quest's representatives and our executive team. Carly Hayes is the only person in the group who seems to be wearing a slapped arse for a face. "Quentin Hibbard, may I introduce you to our most talented creative, Miss Violet Archer?"

I smile warmly, but inside I'm cringing because yet again Malcolm has completely ignored Ethan. I shake Quentin's hand as a stilt-wearing clown bends down and offers all of us flutes of champagne, as well as an eyeful of her cleavage. I'm impressed by her balancing.

Quentin Hibbard is the chairman and founder of Quest plc, and a well-spoken, silver-haired man whose face is etched with the lines of age and importance. "Lovely to meet you, Miss Archer. I must say we have been delighted with the work you've done for us, and we'll definitely be sending more work your way. You've got such a great feel for my company's vision. If you don't mind, I want to publicise your win across all of our social media platforms, and I think both PR teams should join forces to get this headlining in the press first thing on Monday. Do you agree, Malcolm?"

Malcolm nods and a wide smile beams from under his bushy grey moustache.

Quentin puts his hand on my shoulder and gives it a friendly pat. "Very well done, young lady, very well done."

He's old school, so I brush off the "young lady" as sweet rather than patronising. Ditto the literal pat on the back. "Thank you, and please, call me Violet," I say before tugging at Ethan's jacket and shoving him in front of Quentin's nose. "This is Ethan Fraser. He's the art director on your account. Every single one of your ads originated from inside his head. All I do is find the words to bring his ideas to life."

Quentin politely shakes Ethan's hand, but his expression is stiff. What on earth has Malcolm said to him? Ethan's face is flushed pink and he's clenching his jaw tight, so I know he's even more irritated than I am.

Stella Judd steps forward, her close-fitting silver sequinned dress perfectly reflecting the shiny platinum of her hair. "I know I speak for everyone at Barrett McAllan Gray when I say that Ethan is the most talented art director in the city. He's responsible for creating all of Quest's print and TV ads, and I'm very lucky to have both him and Violet headlining my

35

Creative department." Stella scowls at Malcolm as if he were a tomcat who's been caught pissing on her flowerbeds, and she's not finished yet. "Did you not mention Ethan to Quentin, Malcolm?"

Malcolm's smile remains fixed to his face, but his eyes are telling a different story. "Yes, of course, but we both agreed the Quest for Life campaign really took off after Violet's slogan went viral."

Stella takes a sip of champagne as she shoots him an ice-cold glare. "Well, I'm very pleased to hear you haven't deliberately overlooked the contribution of one of our most gifted employees, Malcolm. Because if you had, that would make you a bit of a prick, wouldn't it?" Her voice is even, balanced and commanding, and I make a mental note that Stella is who I'd like to be when I grow up. I don't know anybody else who could pull off roasting their boss so spectacularly.

Malcolm clears his throat and downs his drink, shooting Stella a death stare as he walks away, his loyal viper Ridley Gates slithering behind him. Stella is now centre stage. She takes another flute of champagne from the nine-foot-tall clown and spins around to face us all. "Well, that was fun," she declares before tucking her arm into Daniel Noble's and giving him a wink. "Ah, look, my friend has made it over from New York. Daniel, I want you to meet him. Hope to catch up with you all later. Gentlemen, ladies." She leads Daniel away to another group surrounding a tall, good-looking black man with a neat beard and a sparkling smile.

The group breaks down into a myriad of different conversations. Ethan slowly drifts off into the crowd, leaving me and Max alone, so we do what we always do at parties – plant ourselves close to an anonymous wall and take root.

"You know what I think?" asks Max, moving in close and lowering his voice to a whisper. "Stella's going to do a bunker."

"I have no idea what you're talking about. Bunker?"

"Yes, a moonlight bunker."

"Again, not a clue."

"What's the matter with you? You're not usually this stupid. She's leaving BMG."

"You think so?" English is Max's second language, but I'm only reminded of that fact when he delivers one of his trademark lost-in-translation gems. "It's 'bunk' and 'moonlight flit', by the way."

He dismisses my corrections with a wave of his hand. "You know who that guy is, don't you?"

"Nope." The American does look slightly familiar – tall, handsome, shaved head, neat goatee, passing resemblance to Samuel L. Jackson – but I can't quite place him.

"How long did you spend in New York?"

"A year."

"And you don't recognise the CEO of the agency you worked for? That's Dylan Best of BEST Advertising, you cornflake."

"Is it?" I squint in his direction and wonder if I might need glasses. I worked at BEST after I completed my master's at Harvard. Maybe I've blanked out everything to do with New York because my time there was so miserable. "I have a terrible memory for faces, Max."

We stand in silence, not really knowing what to do with ourselves. "Erm . . . do you want to dance?" Max says.

I laugh. "I'd rather stick pins in my eyes."

"Good. I can't dance to crap music. It's like a school

37

disco in here."

I notice that he's already lost his bow tie and one button off his shirt. I can't help but smile at his peculiarity – at our peculiarities. We're the nerds of Barrett McAllan Gray, two square pegs who'll never fit into a round hole no matter how hard we try.

"So why were you late tonight?" he asks. I lower my eyes, not wanting to talk about my earlier silliness. "Violet, I know you weren't held up in traffic – I checked the roads."

"You checked the roads?" I'm surprised, but I shouldn't be. One time I missed a flight to Edinburgh due to traffic on the M25. We were booked in at a conference and Max had to go on ahead without me. He'd managed to call seven hospitals by the time he was called to the boarding gate.

"Yeah it's easy. I have this app on my iPhone. It's called RouteChecker. Do you want to see? You should get it—"

I grip his arm. "I'm good with the app, Max." There's silence as he waits for me to speak. I run my fingers awkwardly around the rim of my champagne glass. "I didn't want to come," I say finally. "I hate attention, and . . . well, things didn't go so well with Stuart last night."

Max doesn't ask for details. He knows who I am, he understands me and he respects my need for privacy. All he does is nod his head and smile kindly.

"Ethan talked me round. He told me I was spoiling the night for everybody."

"That's not fair. I'll kick his arse for saying that to you."

"Thanks, but he was right."

Max places his hand tenderly on my arm. His

balding head shines fluorescent pink under the venue's circus lighting. I wonder when he'll start shaving what's left of his hair; he's starting to bear a passing resemblance to Doc Brown from Back to the Future. "You think about these things too much, you know?"

"Yeah, yeah, I know. I'm the world's worst overthinker of everything. How do I stop doing that?"

"Don't fixate, don't worry, don't fret. Just switch off and go with the flow – have faith that everything will turn out okay in the end. And tonight turned out better than okay, didn't it? You won a freaking AdAg award, for Christ's sake!"

I laugh as I glance over to the table where I dumped the hideous chunk of glass on a stick. "Yeah, I guess I did okay. I just wish . . . sometimes I wish I could be a different person. I'd love to be able to enjoy myself at big events like everybody else, instead of having my head jammed full of thoughts I don't want to think about."

"Hey, stop that. I'd have nobody I'd want to talk to if I didn't have you. You've met my friend Marek who I go clubbing with, haven't you? He's not exactly troubling Mensa, is he?" He motions over to the dance floor, where Ethan is delighting the rest of the creative team with his very own version of the Macarena. "It's great to be a thinker. He isn't. Just look at him. What does he looks like?"

I watch him having a blast, surrounded by people cheering him on, and my heart sinks because I want to join in and have a good time too, but I don't know how. "Don't you think life is easier his way?"

Max opens his mouth to speak, but almost chokes when he's slapped on the back by Will Thornton. "There you two are," he says. His East-End accent is chirpier than usual. "Have you seen Ethan over there? Talk about a suck-up!"

I look over to the dance floor and laugh at Ethan teaching his moves to Stella Judd and Dylan Best. I wish I could bottle and sell his confidence, not to mention his people skills. Stella laughs uproariously at Ethan. He's lucky to have her as our department head, seeing as how Malcolm hates his guts. To Stella, Ethan's the golden boy – the shining star in her creative empire.

"Do you think Best from BEST is trying to poach her?" asks Max, repeating his conspiracy theory.

"Nah, he was her bloke a few years back. Someone said he featured between marriages three and four." Will tosses a handful of salty bar snacks into his mouth, then his dark eyes flash with an idea. "Hey, maybe she's selling him Ethan. He'd go to the States in a flash. He already thinks he's too good for BMG."

"Oh, for heaven's sake, could you be any more jealous?" I say.

"Ethan would never leave London," Max protests.

"Yeah, but don't worry if he does go. I'll be your partner." Will winks at me, his lips peppered with salt and grease. "If I have to stare over a desk at someone for ten hours a day, I want somebody better looking than Mohammed next time. So, Violet, it's either going to be you or Ruby Sloan."

"You know I'm spoken for, and you can have Ruby over my dead body." I like Will – he's smart and funny, but he's also a pessimistic pain in the arse. "Oh, and speaking of Ruby, I need a word with both of you about the great knickers robbery and how it could be interpreted as sexual harassment."

Will laughs. Max looks worried.

40

"All down to Mohammed." Will tosses another handful of snacks into his mouth and waltzes off.

Max clears his throat nervously. "And on that note, I need to pee. Jesus, this is a long night. I'll be right back." He disappears into a swarm of black suits. Left alone, I've got no idea where to put my useless body. I consider staying put and waiting for Max, but judging on past performance it could take anything from three to three hundred minutes for him to actually get back to me, and there are decent odds on him not returning at all. He's as flaky as a redhead with sunburn.

I decide that if I'm going to stand around looking useless, I may as well check my phone as I'm doing it, but I left it in my coat pocket. Damn. And I can't remember where the cloakroom is. Oh well, searching for it will kill some time.

I leave the main room and find myself in an empty corridor with a fire exit at the end of it. I choose a door randomly and walk inside the room.

Then I freeze.

And I don't mean I just stand still in the room. I mean I stand still, looking stupid, with my mouth wide open as if I've just caught Santa coming down the chimney. But this isn't a jolly-fat-guy-bringing-me-presents kind of surprise. No, this is a shit-there's-an-elephant-in-my-sitting-room-and-it's-just-taken-a-crap-on-my-carpet kind of surprise.

I'm standing in front of Carly Hayes and a rather dishevelled Ridley Gates. They're both pink and sweaty, and Carly's gold dress is pulled so high over her hips that I can see her knickers. When she sees me, she adjusts her clothing and her brown eyes burn into my skin. She looks spaced out, and I figure she's high on something other than having just had sex in the side room of a converted warehouse. Ridley's wedding ring catches the light as he buttons up his shirt, and I have an overwhelming urge to punch him. I've met his wife; she's beautiful and kind and doesn't deserve to be married to such an unspeakable shit.

I spin around and walk out of the room as fast as I can, but as soon as I'm through the door I'm pulled back by my shoulders. I turn to find Carly glowering at me, her gold dress merging seamlessly with the dark peach skin of her overly made-up face.

"What the hell do you think you're doing?" I ask her, my voice raised in anger.

"I'm making sure you keep your mouth shut," she spits back at me, flicking her coarse mane of dark, bristly hair extensions behind her shoulder. I notice how ridiculous her acrylic-lashed eyes look. False eyelashes are supposed to look natural – not like they've escaped from the Insect House at London Zoo.

"I don't think you're in any position to issue threats," I reply calmly.

"Oh, and what position do you think I'm in exactly?" asks Carly, her tone laced with venom.

"I think that's obvious."

"Really? God, you're pathetic. No wonder nobody likes you. You act like you're so much better than everybody, with your self-professed intelligence and your ridiculous Snow Queen act. Why don't you ask Stuart Inman's fiancée how much better than me she thinks you are?"

I feel as though I've been struck by lightning. "His what?"

Carly's eyes flash with pleasure. "Oh, didn't you know he was engaged when you fucked him? Stuart and Adele have been together for four years now.

They're due to get married next year."

"I . . . didn't . . . know . . ."

I feel sick to my stomach. This is the second time I've been in this position. The first time I was partly responsible for breaking a family apart. Do I need to run a background check on every man I date? Clearly my married-cheating-bastard radar is seriously off-kilter.

"So, I think we're clear. Keep quiet, or I make life very difficult for you."

My chest heaves and I struggle to breathe, but I'm not going to let her have the last word. "Is that supposed to be a threat?"

"Yes it is, and I don't care, because I don't like you. I've seen how you look at me. You have such a ridiculously high opinion of yourself, but all you are is a leech, feeding off Ethan Fraser's success."

She storms off and I can't speak. All I can do is stare after her as she walks away.

Ridley appears from behind me, his shoulder slamming into mine as he walks past, almost knocking me to the floor. I steady myself against the wall as he spins round and says an insincere "Excuse me." His grin is as wide as his face.

I forget about my phone and walk back to one of the bars for a glass of water, wondering if now might be a good time to sneak off home before I kill somebody. Who decided revenge is self-defeating? Happiness is the best revenge, say the people who create internet memes. Or is it success?

Yeah, well, fuck that. The best revenge is revenge.

It's just a shame I'm totally crap at plotting. The only scheme my brain is throwing up is utterly ridiculous. I mean, how the hell do you infect somebody with elephantiasis of the vagina?

4

I RUB MY BROW AS my foggy champagne-brain knocks me to one side. Jeez, how much have I drunk? I promised myself I'd go home over an hour ago, but all I've done is drink fizz like it's going out of fashion. I hop off the barstool, but the heel of my shoe hits the ground at an angle and I tumble into someone.

"Whoa, sorry, Daniel. Um . . . are you having a good night?"

Daniel Noble is tall, blonde, fit, and very good-looking. I've always thought he bears a passing resemblance to Daniel Craig, but with less muscle. "Yeah, great. Well, aside from having to listen to the bravado in Captain America's corner over there."

I look over to see that Stella and Dylan Best are still joined at the hip. "Did you know I used to work for BEST?"

"No, I didn't." His eyes light up with interest. "How long were you in New York?"

"A year. I had a great time. New York is an amazing city to work in."

"So I've heard. Why did you leave?"

Stupidly, I falter and look at my feet.

"Ah, I know that look. A guy?"

"Hmm, you could say that."

Daniel takes a sip of whisky. "Can I get you anything?"

"No, thank you. I think I've had enough for tonight."

He smiles knowingly and his rugged jaw dimples. "So, you got us a fabulous win tonight.

Congratulations. You must be very proud."

"Thank you. And it wasn't just my win. Ethan's too, remember."

"Of course." He inclines his head slightly. "What on earth is it with Malcolm and Ethan?"

"You know, we have absolutely no idea. Malcolm was already hating him when I started at BMG."

"He's probably jealous. Ethan's a talented guy, and Malcolm? He's out of his depth to the point of being a liability. He's done well riding his father's name and legacy, but the agency would be on its knees if it weren't for Stella. She's been covering Malcolm's arse with the board for years."

"Really?" I like a bit of office gossip and I'm eager to hear more, but I also feel torn. Despite being an ass to everyone else, Malcolm has always been good to me, in an Obi-Wan Kenobi mentor kind of way. Not that Malcolm possesses the advertising world's equivalent of Jedi powers. The only force that's strong in Malcolm is the ability to piss people off.

"Suffice it to say he's the most inept executive at BMG, and considering Ridley Gates is my line manager, that's certainly something."

I'm about to tell him Ridley is infinitely worse than Malcolm, but as I turn to speak, I notice that Daniel is looking at me in a way he never has before. In fact, his eyes are staring so intently into mine that I feel myself blush and look away. I hope with everything I have that he isn't looking at me in *that* way, but I think he is.

"You know, there might be another reason why Malcolm Barrett heaps praise on you but ignores Ethan." He leans in so close I can almost taste the spice of his cologne – black pepper and a hint of nutmeg.

"Oh, and what's that?" I ask with a certain amount

of trepidation.

He pushes himself forward until I can feel his breath on my neck, the smell of whisky tingling my nostrils. "Maybe he sees what I can see."

Oh, shit, I think he *is* hitting on me. "I'm sure it's just a personality clash . . ."

He laughs as he swirls the whisky around in his glass before taking another sip. "I'm not talking about Ethan. I'm talking about you. You're smart, you're talented, you understand clients' needs effortlessly, but you're also so much more than that. How many creative teams do you think I've worked with over the years? I know more than enough to see there's something very special about you."

"Well, that's very kind of you to say, Daniel, but—"

"Have dinner with me tomorrow night."

"What?" I gasp, and every word I have ever known deserts me. Daniel smiles, and his blue eyes sparkle under the bright fuchsia and gold lighting of the bar. I allow myself to feel flattered at being asked out by BMG's most eligible bachelor, but at the same time this is hellishly awkward.

"I'd be honoured to get to know you outside of work." His voice is steady and filled with the self-confidence of a salesman closing a deal.

"I'm sorry, Daniel. I don't think that would be a good idea." I lower my voice to a whisper and hope with everything I have that I'm doing the right thing, but thankfully he doesn't look disappointed. Instead, he continues to talk to me as if he's negotiating with a prospective client.

"Why not? Hit me with your reasons because I bet I can counteract them."

"Okay, let's start with because I don't date men I

work with – colleagues or clients."

He raises his eyebrows. "I may be speaking out of turn, but I heard you went on a date with Stuart Inman." I bristle, and he notices my discomfort immediately. "I'm sorry. I shouldn't have said that. I was out of line, please forgive me."

"It's fine. I . . . um . . . admit my workplace-dating rule was implemented very recently, and Stuart Inman was a factor in that."

"Oh, I see," he says in surprise. "In that case, not mixing work with pleasure is a very good rule to have. I suppose there's no chance I can persuade Malcolm to fire you before tomorrow night."

I shake my head and laugh. He's taking this well. I'm impressed. "No, I don't think there's any chance of that."

"Okay. Well, I'll keep my offer on the table in case you ever change your mind. Have a great night." He stands to leave, and I realise I like him. I wonder if I'm certifiably insane for letting him walk away.

My watch says its half past midnight: time to head for home. I pick up my stupid glass vomit-on-a-stick trophy, find my coat in the elusive cloakroom and nip through a convenient side exit. But I can't even get that right – I walk into a dark alleyway instead of the street outside.

And then I'm hit by a truck. Not a van. Not a tow truck or a tipper truck. Those vehicles would cause some pain, but they wouldn't make my heart plunge to my feet, shattering into a hundred shards of broken glass. No, I'm hit by an articulated lorry filled with nuclear waste and a great big steaming pile of shit.

I don't know why it's hurting me so much to see Ethan with his arms wrapped around another woman,

48

but I quickly realise it isn't the act itself that has blasted my internal organs out of my body – it's the person his drunk, blind-stupid, sex-obsessed brain has chosen to do it with. In a venue full of beautiful and successful women, why the hell did he have to pick her? I tell myself I have no ownership over him – *we're just friends* – but my body feels like it's bleeding out. My head is dizzy and my chest aches as the sound of my pulse rings in my ears.

I watch their bodies slam together, my view partially obstructed by a neat row of wheelie bins, and I try to choke down my horror. He burrows his mouth into hers, his hands moving all over her body, pushing up that same gold skirt that Ridley Gates pushed up earlier tonight. His hands move to her thighs as he sways to the muffled music, his body pressing her into position like a clam to a rock, her lips placing soft kisses onto his neck . . .

Am I doomed to walk in on Carly Hayes every single time she has sex?

I stumble backwards from the scene, my breathing louder than the wind, and I find my way onto the street, where I almost trip over a group of people who have popped outside for a cigarette. "Get out of my fucking way!" I yell at a guy with curly red hair and a rubbery face who does his best to steady me by grabbing my arm.

"Hey, we were just standing still here. You walked into us."

I raise my head and glare at him. "Hey, ask me if I give a fuck."

Jesus, what's wrong with my language? Could I be any ruder?

I head for the taxi queue at the front of the building,

my arms wrapped protectively around my body as the cold spring night bites into my skin. I can't even bring myself to stop walking to put my coat on.

"Where are you going? You can't leave now!"

I turn around to see Max sitting at the bottom of the stone steps leading from the main entrance, his long legs stretched out in front of him. He's dressed only in his shirt and trousers.

I stand shivering before him, and I can't think and I can't feel and I can't see because my eyes are clouded with water. I daren't blink because I don't want to cry in front of him. "I'm going home, Max . . . you should go home too."

Max's green eyes glaze over with concern. He tries to stand up, but he's drunk, and probably high, and he flops back down again, his gangly limbs buckling awkwardly underneath him. I reassure him that I'm fine, and he relaxes, takes a lighter from his pocket and fires up a cigarette. He takes a long drag and exhales, filling the air with an aroma I recognise as something other than tobacco.

"Max, for crying out loud. You know that stuff's illegal, right?"

"Yeah, but I'm pissed and I have it. I don't know how I have it actually. I can't remember buying it."

I sit down next to him and slot my arm through his. "Just be as quick as you can with it and get back inside before somebody sees you. There are clients here tonight, for Christ's sake."

"It'll only take five minutes. Do you want a puff?"

I look at him and briefly contemplate it – smoking Max's dirty cigarette might dull the pain, after all – but I politely decline.

"Where's your jacket, Max?"

He starts to laugh and his eyes grow comically wide. "I have absolutely no fucking idea."

"Please tell me your mobile and house keys aren't in it."

He looks as though he's going to be sick. "Oh fuck." Then his head snaps up and he points a finger in the air as if he's just had a "Eureka!" moment. "I know, I'll call my jacket to find out where it is. I freaking love you. You're really, really, really smart."

"And you're really, really, really high."

He puts his arm around my shoulder and plants a kiss on my forehead. "I am, and I'm happy . . . and Jesus, you're freezing cold. Why is your coat crocheted with wool? There're holes all over it. Is that the fashion? I'd be a gentleman and give you my jacket to put on, but I've lost the bloody thing."

"Well, let's get you on your feet and we'll go find it. But first, finish that joint." I squeeze him close as the wind picks up, blowing leaves, rubbish and cigarette butts around our feet. He stubs the remainder of his joint out on the ground, and it joins the swirling debris.

"Are you going to tell me what's up?"

My insides churn as the memory of ten minutes ago resurfaces, but I decide to lie. "Nothing. I'm fine."

"You came out of the party looking like you'd seen one hell of a scary-looking ghost. What happened?"

I can't tell him. I don't want to. I huddle closer to him, ignoring his question.

"Is this about Ethan? I saw him go outside with Carly before I left. They looked to be, um, getting to know each other." He whispers the words so tenderly, but they still manage to knot my stomach. I keep my head down, refusing to look at him. I close my eyes and will the tears to stay put, but two free themselves and roll down each cheek, leaving wet streams behind them.

"Violet?" Max places his hand on mine, locking our fingers together. "It's okay. I know."

"What do you know?" I'm confused. Is he talking about Ridley shagging Carly? Or our argument? Or Stuart having a fiancée?

"I know you're in love with Ethan."

I almost choke on fresh air. "What? Max, you're way off the mark there. I'm not in love with Ethan . . . I mean, I love him, of course I do. He's my best friend – same as you – but I'm not *in* love with him."

Max stares at me, his eyes burning through my skin. He doesn't believe me.

"Max, I'm being honest here. I'm not in love with Ethan."

"Okay, I'm sorry. Why are you so upset then?"

Good question. Why am I so upset?

"I've just had a horrible couple of nights *and* I've just found out Stuart Inman has a fiancée. Max, you know what happened in New York. I would never, ever do that again. Not intentionally."

"Oh my god, the bastard. I'll kill him!" He stands up with fists already balled, but as soon as he's upright he starts to sway and I have to tug him back down before he falls. He puts his arm around me again. "None of this is your fault," he says, resting his head gently on mine. Another tear escapes and he catches it, smoothing the wetness off my skin with his thumb.

"What's wrong with me, Max? I'm not stupid, so why do I always date lying, cheating bastards? I turned down a lovely guy tonight because I don't trust myself and I made a stupid law swearing off men, yet I'm so sick of being alone."

He sighs and squeezes me tighter. "If you were less

52

smart, less talented and less beautiful then I'd fall in love with you myself."

His weird logic makes me smile. "Max, that makes no sense."

"I know, but it's true. You're too special for just anybody. You need to fall in love with someone who makes you thankful you are who you are, because who you are is amazing."

"Thank you. You're a sweetheart." I give him a kiss on the cheek. "You won't say anything, will you? About Stuart."

He bats my arm playfully. "Of course I won't say anything. What do you take me for?" Then he grabs my sequinned handbag from the step next to us, opens it up and pulls out my mobile.

"Now, give my jacket a call. I'm freezing my balls off sitting out here."

***

We head back to the party, but Max can barely stand, so I leave him in a chair while I head back to the cloakroom. Ten minutes later I give up the hunt for his jacket. It isn't in the cloakroom, and I've tried calling it from five different locations with no response. I return to Max with the sad news, but he's disappeared. The seat I left him in is empty and . . . oh, for the love of god, no . . . I can hear raised voices.

I shut my eyes for a moment, my heart thudding in my chest as I decipher the shouts and the swearing – some of which is in German. Then I decide to kill him.

I track the commotion to one of the bars, where a throng of people are crowding around Max and Stuart.

53

"You fucking piece of shit. You mess with my friend and you get me in your face!"

"Max, Max, just calm down," says Stuart in a patronising tone, which is not a great idea given Max has the temper of a tired toddler, and that's when he isn't pissed and stoned.

"Leck mich am arsch. Fick dich!"

I have no idea what he's saying, but some of the audience must know German profanities because they're laughing and cheering him on.

I charge through a fence of suits to get to Max just as he's stepping closer to Stuart with his fists bared. "Max, don't you dare!" I yell, but he takes no notice. He might be an imposing six foot four, but he's built like a lamppost. I've seen Stuart naked, on the other hand, so I know he could throw a weighty punch if he had to.

"Max, for crying out loud, what are you doing?" I shout again.

"Giving this piece of shit what he deserves."

Stuart holds his hands up and laughs. "Okay, I get what's happening here." He turns to look at me. His skin is reddened, but his demeanour is surprisingly composed. "Violet, if it makes you feel any better, Adele and I are having some problems and—"

"Max, no!" I scream . . .

. . . but it's too late.

He lunges at Stuart, grabs him by the lapels of his jacket and attempts to head butt him. Thankfully he misses and they both land in a heap on the floor. A group of guys, led by Will, manage to stop laughing for a moment to help them to their feet. Will looks at me and hand-signals that he's going to remove Max from the scene of the crime. I sigh in relief.

With Max ushered away, that should have been an

end to it, but as I turn to go home, Stuart calls after me. "I'm sorry about last night, okay? I was telling the truth about Adele, but if I knew you were going to be a crap shag anyway I wouldn't have bothered."

The best way to describe what happens next is to liken it to a demon possession. I lose control of my brain and my hand grabs the first thing I see: a full glass of white wine. Before I have a second to think, I've already thrown the contents of the glass over Stuart's head.

And the audience erupts with cheers and a round of applause.

"What the hell? You psycho-bitch!"

"Poor Stuart – prematurely wet again," I say to a chorus of laughter. "That's for Adele."

My audience is laughing so hard now that one guy high-fives me, and a lady in a swishy burgundy evening dress shouts, "You go, girl!"

And still Stuart is unrepentant. "Yeah, well fuck you! You're off my account!"

"Fuck you! And your teensy-tiny pathetic little penis."

The last word is mine.

Embarrassing?

Hugely, but at least I'm going home with a smile on my face.

5

I THOUGHT I'D PACED MYSELF last night, but as I lie face down on what I hope is my bed, my mouth is screaming for water as if I've been passed out in a desert for days. I wonder why there's a camel standing in my bathroom doorway holding a very tempting pitcher of iced water. "Come get it if you're that thirsty!" it says, then it starts to baa. Do camels baa? Maybe it's a sheep. Or maybe it's my cream bathrobe hanging on the back of the door. I clamp my eyes shut and try to focus on my head, which hurts all the way down my back and into the balls of my feet. Is that thudding even in my head? Is it in my ears?

I flip over and stare at a familiar ceiling. Great news! At least I'm in my flat. I don't know how I got here, but at least I'm here. I can't remember drinking that much. Perhaps it would be wise if I swore off alcohol as well as men, and I make up a new law to avoid absolutely bloody awful work parties too.

More thudding. I pull a pillow over my head and try to ignore it. My mouth is as dry as the dust on my mantelpiece, but there's no way I'm getting up for a drink. I can live with the thirst. Meanwhile, my stomach is on a roller coaster and it's looping-the-loop while the rest of me has broken down and is waiting for a technician to arrive.

I close my eyes as I respond to the thudding by wedging part of my pillow into my ear and wrapping the rest of it around my head like a scarf. Then it all comes back to me and I wish I was dead. The ache in my heart and the sinking feeling in my stomach. The relentless nagging in my brain from the memory that's clawing at me like a vulture pecking at a partly decomposed corpse. After the feelings comes the avalanche of memories. Finding Carly and Ridley together, our argument, Stuart having a fiancée, Ethan having sex with Carly behind the wheelie bins and finally, humiliating Stuart in front of an audience of agency clients and colleagues.

All in all, not my most favourite of nights.

Yet more thudding. My senses are jolted and my brain finally connects. The thudding isn't inside my head; it's at my door. I might be in my bedroom, but my body is on the moon and I don't think I have the strength to get up. I push up onto my palms and discover that I've been mummified in my sleep. I'm still wearing my party dress, but it's twisted around me like a bandage and my left boob is wedged through the armhole. Jesus Christ, what a night! I glance at my clock, which is streaked gold with ... with what? Sunlight? The time reads half past five in the morning.

I stagger to the door, repositioning left boob as I go, and the thudding gets even louder – each bang feels like nails are getting knocked into my skull with a sledgehammer. My shoulders burn with tension as I wonder who it could be. It's early ... far too early.

I cautiously open the door to reveal Max and Ethan. Or rather, the ghosts of Max and Ethan, because the human beings I see before me bear no resemblance to my best friends.

Max has his arm draped over Ethan's shoulder. His legs are loose, but they're holding him up, and his green eyes are dull and lifeless. He still doesn't have his jacket, and his shirt is unbuttoned and untucked around his middle. He also – amazingly – has on only one shoe. One flaming shoe, for Christ's sake. How the hell does a man lose a shoe on a night out?

"What's happened? Please, tell me what's happened." I can barely speak the words as I take in Ethan's appearance. His brow is creased with deep lines, and his eyes – his bright blue eyes which are usually sparkling with life – are clouded with sadness.

I move out of the way as they crash into my apartment and stumble through to the sitting room. Ethan releases Max from his hold and he clatters down onto my sofa, bewildered and speechless. I immediately go to him, resting my hand on his arm, and look over to Ethan, who stands hunched in front of me. His skin is red and blotchy, and his eyes are dragging me down with him into whatever misery is plaguing them both.

"What's happened?" I say again. "Guys, please talk to me. You're really starting to scare me here."

Ethan opens his mouth, but nothing comes out. He swallows hard and tries again. "It's Quentin Hibbard. He's . . . dead."

"What? Is this a joke? Please tell me you're joking, because you've crossed the line in bad taste if you are." I look at Max and wonder if he's capable of pulling something like this off. I don't even have to think twice about Ethan because tormenting people is one of his favourite pastimes, but Max?

"He had a massive heart attack," says Ethan. "Dropped down dead in front of everybody. He even hit his head on a table as he went down – there was blood everywhere."

"Oh my god, that's awful," I say. We'd only met Quentin for the first time tonight, but he seemed a lovely man.

Ethan stands at the back of the room, and my shock fades into horror as I'm confronted by the extent of his anguish. There's more. I can see it in his eyes.

"And Carly's in hospital. I don't know if she'll make it. We thought you'd know what to do," he adds, his voice crushed with panic.

"What? How? What happened to her?" My heart is beating so fast that my legs begin to shudder, and the involuntary movements make my teeth chatter. I know what catastrophe looks like. I was seventeen when I saw it embedded in the eyes of my parents. Tonight I'm seeing it again.

Ethan sits down in my armchair. I watch him stretch and rub at the tension knots in his neck. "We don't know what happened. It was after the paramedics had left with Quentin's body. Max was upset because he'd lost his house keys and his iPhone, so I offered to help him look for his jacket. We checked all the rooms for it, then we found her . . . I thought she was dead. They took her away, but it doesn't look good. They think she passed out and then was sick and choked on it. I rang the hospital on the way over here and she's still unresponsive. They have her in ICU."

I desperately try to gather my thoughts as my brain throws up question after question. Quentin is dead and Carly is in hospital. This is sad, and I need to feel something but . . . Jesus, what am I feeling? I can't describe it. Am I feeling anything? How should I be feeling? I hate this woman. I cursed every bone in her miserable body, but I didn't make any real effort to get to know her either. What's the etiquette for this? Someone I hate with passion and potency is fighting for her life in intensive care. What should I say? How should I feel?

This is bad. Did I do this? I spent a long time thinking up ways to get revenge on her, so is this karma?

No. Just no.

I don't even believe in karma. There's no supernatural force evening up random scores. My mind twists itself into knots as I try to find the correct emotional response, but I come up cold.

Oh god, I'm a horrible person. I'm a sociopath. This officially makes me a sociopath. Is this what being a sociopath means? Or does the fact I'm worrying whether or not I'm a sociopath mean I'm not a sociopath?

Max is still totally lost to me, so I turn to Ethan with what I hope are the appropriate platitudes. What do you say to a man who's just shagged someone you hate now that she's in danger of losing her life? "I'm sorry . . . This is awful . . . I . . . I don't know what to say." It's all I can manage, but it's the truth. I really don't know what to say.

Ethan studies my reaction, his grief-stricken eyes scrutinising my blank expression. "I thought you hated her."

What the hell? Is he sensing my inner turmoil and sticking the boot in? "I do hate her, and the feeling is mutual, but that doesn't mean I wish this upon her." Shit, I did wish it upon her, didn't I? I can clearly remember a rush of excitement after I imagined her contracting elephantiasis of the vagina.

Ethan looks across the room at me, his brow creased and confused. "I'm sorry. I shouldn't have said that."

"I'm going to be sick." Max jumps to his feet and crashes through my sitting room, through my bedroom and into my en-suite bathroom. I've never seen him

60

move so fast, and I'm relieved when I hear the toilet seat clunk up before the noise of his body retching up vomit ricochets around my apartment. I hope his aim is as good as his timing.

"You stay here, I'll go check on him," I say.

I have an overbearing feeling that our world has changed forever, but my brain still can't articulate my thoughts. I tell myself I need to just focus on one person at a time and Max seems to be in the most urgent need.

I walk to the bathroom and it's as if I'm functioning on autopilot. I force my mind to shut down everything but my priority, and my priority is helping him. This is why they came to me – I'm good in a crisis because I can separate emotional responses from logical ones. Last night's wine-throwing incident aside, of course.

In the few moments it takes to get from sitting room to bathroom, I have imprisoned my own guilt and I'm focused on the task at hand – keeping Max and Ethan from flying off a cliff edge. Only when I have all the facts can I fix it. It's how I operate. I focus, I analyse, I formulate and then I fix. Like a real-life Bob the Builder.

Max is sitting on the floor in front of my toilet when I get to him. His arms are draped around the bowl and his legs are tangled up in a bath towel. It looks like a scene from Trainspotting, and the jet-black circles under his eyes are testament to the drink and drugs he's been pumping into himself all evening.

I fall to my knees. The stench of vomit wafts over my senses as I get close to him, making my stomach lurch. I look him over to see if he splashed when he puked, but he looks clean. Ah, but my toilet isn't. I lean behind him and flush. When I turn back, I notice his

61

chin is bleeding, and he suddenly looks very old. How has he aged a decade since nine o'clock last night? I place my hand on his face, moving his chin up into the light so I can examine the damage he's done to himself.

"I got tangled in your towel . . . I fell . . . hit my stupid face. Does it look like I've been punched? I might pretend I've been punched. I deserve to be punched."

He looks so despondent that all I can think to do is wrap my arms around him, so that's what I do. And there we stay, holding each other, for about ten minutes. I place a kiss on his cheek – his skin is sweaty but cold. Like he's been out jogging in a blizzard.

Max nuzzles into my neck and grabs me tight around my waist, then he sobs into my hair until it's wet and I can feel it sticking to my ear. His sadness brings tears to my own eyes, and I let them fall onto his shoulder. We stay there for a few moments more.

"I'm sorry. I just . . . I can't stop seeing her. I wish you'd have been there. I needed you . . . You would have known what to do."

I move from sitting on my knees to sitting on my bottom and huddle in closer to him. His clammy skin cools my cheek, and I reach for his hand, locking our fingers together tightly. He's definitely having some kind of physical response to this. Shock or post-traumatic something-or-other. I have zero first aid knowledge – anything medical bores the living shit out of me – but my uninformed brain tells me he looks like he's going to pass out at any moment, so I start squeezing his hand tightly in a rhythm to keep him alert.

"There's nothing you could have done, Max. It was an accident."

"It wasn't." His voice cracks as he twists around to look at me, his dull eyes regaining a fraction of their spark. "Don't you see? I gave her the drugs. It's all my fault."

"What?" My mind screams out and I feel pain. Real pain in my chest and my arms and the pit of my stomach.

"She gave me twenty quid, and I gave her the best of what I had."

"What did you give her?" Please, God, don't let him have given her anything Class A.

"Speed. Just two wraps," he replies as he sniffs into his sleeve.

I grip his hand again, making every inch of my touch as reassuring as I can. "That wouldn't have done anything, Max. She hadn't stopped drinking all night, and you don't know what else she'd been taking. Did you spend any time with her? Did you see her take them?"

"No, I didn't speak to her all night. I gave her the wraps when we arrived – an hour before the AdAg Awards started." He tips his head back against my bathroom wall and closes his eyes. He looks like he's searching his memory, but he also looks like he's on the verge of falling asleep. I can see his eyeballs drift in ripples underneath his closed lids.

"Max, you gave her speed at, what? Seven or seven thirty? That was ten hours ago. You can't blame yourself for this. You don't know when, or even if, she took it, and as I said, she was drinking all night."

"What if she dies? She looked really bad – they had to resuscitate her with those electric shock things."

My pulse races with dread and fear, but I keep my rational head on. "Max, none of this is your fault. See, this is how it works. We have some facts here. Carly bought drugs from you, but she also drank all night long. All of these things were her choices, and she knew what she was doing. She passed out, as people do when they party hard, but what happened next was just bad luck. It was an accident. It doesn't make any sense for you to blame yourself."

We sit in silence for a few moments. I wonder about Ethan. He's quiet. I hope he's okay.

"You always say the right things. How do you do that?"

"Because I'm your friend and because I love you."

His nose glistens with tears and mucous. He sniffs then wipes it on his shirt. I watch as he inspects the mess on his sleeve, and all of a sudden he seems as fragile as a six-year-old child. He makes a half-hearted attempt to rub the green stain away with his thumb.

"You need to get some sleep, Max. Why don't you get into my bed for a bit?" His head snaps up and his eyes – his eyes that have been dull all night – are suddenly flashing with life. I do my best not to giggle. "Don't get too excited, I'm not getting in with you." I see a faint impression of a smile and I start to relax a bit. He'll be okay once he sleeps this off. At least, I hope he will.

I stand up and do my best to help him to his feet, but he's almost a foot taller than me, so there's little I can do but hold his hand and lead him through to my bedroom. I lift up the duvet and he flops onto my bed and curls up into a ball. I sit on the edge of the bed and stroke his wild straw-like hair until it's soft against his head. His eyes start to close.

"Sweet dreams, my friend," I whisper before leaving the room.

6

I TAKE A DEEP BREATH as I walk through the door. I anticipate the worst, but I find a scene I don't expect: Ethan is sitting in my armchair wolfing down a plate of toast and fried eggs.

"Make yourself at home," I say with relief as I sit on my sofa opposite him.

Ethan's head snaps up. "I'm sorry, I just needed to eat something. I really wanted bacon, but you don't have any."

"Forgive my kitchen for not being a greasy spoon."

My hungover stomach lurches as he shovels blackened eggs into his mouth whilst crunching on buttery toast. His shirt sleeves are rolled up and there's a streak of melted butter running a shiny golden snail-trail down his arm. I can't remember buying eggs; I don't usually eat them. Oh wait, I bought them for that recipe I wanted to try from Saturday Kitchen. As usual my good intentions to try to actually cook something from scratch never came to fruition. I don't know what I was thinking. Oh, hell, the eggs must have been in my fridge for weeks. He'll be lucky if he's alive by tomorrow morning. Best not tell him. It's too late to save his life – he's only got a few mouthfuls left.

He takes another bite of toast. He isn't making eye contact, and I wonder how long it's going to take before we start talking about what he and Carly did last night. I'm not sure I want to have that conversation with him, because I don't know if I'll be able to hide my feelings. Hell, I don't even know if I can explain my feelings.

Hurt? Disgust? Betrayal? Anger? Those are feelings I don't want to be having. Who Ethan chooses to have sex with in alleys, behind wheelie bins, is none of my business.

And yet, my heart feels like it's breaking in two.

"I'm sorry for waking you. I didn't know what else to do. Max was hysterical."

"He's fine now. He's sleeping."

Ethan nods and finishes his last mouthful of poisonous eggs. "I knew you would know what to say to him. I can handle Max when he's up for a good night out, but when he's like this he freaks me out."

"It's just the way he is. He feels things deeply."

"I'm feeling things pretty deeply right now too," he says with his eyes fixed to his empty plate. "I . . . um . . . you see, me and Carly . . . we . . ." His eyes flit to mine for a brief moment before he looks away again. "Shit."

I decide to help him out. "I know you were with Carly last night," I say softly.

"You know?" he asks, his eyes filled with shame. "How?"

"Um, I just do—"

"I feel terrible, Vi. One minute she's . . . the next, she's just lying there lifeless. I thought she was dead. She still could—"

"Hey, stop." I lean forward and rest my hand on his knee. "Don't think like that. There's no point worrying. It won't change anything."

He smiles and nods his head. "I envy you. You're a machine when it comes to handling a crisis." I stiffen at his phrase, and he immediately backtracks. "I just mean you can switch off and focus on things logically. Max is all emotion, and I'm not much better."

66

"So you think I'm as cold as ice too?" I know that the rest of the creative floor calls me the Snow Queen behind my back. And, no, they're not comparing me to the Disney character with the belting voice. They're thinking of the Hans Christian Andersen original – the evil ice-cold child-abductor.

"No, that's not what I meant," he says sincerely. We sit for a minute in silence, and I spend the time wondering if he knows anything about me at all. Then he turns around to face me. His eyes are beautiful even when they're lost. "I know that whatever chaos life throws my way, I can count on you to get me through it. You're not cold – far from it. You understand things more clearly than anyone I know. As for those idiots who talk about you behind your back, let them talk. They aren't your friends. You understand them, but they don't have a hope in hell of understanding the first thing about you. You're better than all of them, so fuck what they think."

I'm stunned. I know Max depends on me for my logical advice-giving, but I didn't think Ethan did too. "And what about you? Do you understand me?"

His smile lights up the sitting room. "I think I'm getting there . . . almost."

"So, if you understand me – almost – what do you think I'm going to say to you about last night?"

"That's easy. You're going to tell me I wasn't responsible for Carly even though I knew she was drinking herself into a coma. You'll tell me it was an accident and there's nothing I could have done. Then you're going to reassure me that you're not disappointed in me, even though I know you are." His voice trails into a whisper and my heart misses a beat in response. "And when I get a handle on my guilt over

67

what happened, the fact that you're disappointed in me is still going to be there, and that is much harder to live with."

His words take my breath away. "This isn't about me, Ethan. And I hope I'm not that judgemental. Are you disappointed in yourself?"

His body tenses at the question he's probably not ready to answer. He runs his hand through his hair. I love his hair. It's usually so perfectly styled, but I think I love it more right now, when it's ruffled and reflecting how messed up his brain is.

"Yeah, I'm disappointed in myself. I mean, she was just there and she was throwing herself at me and I wish I hadn't. I don't even like her. She's bitchy and shallow and I hate how she speaks to you. Ever since we started working on the Quest campaign she's had it in for you. I knew that, so why did I even go there?" His gaze locks onto mine as he takes a deep but shaky breath. "I'm never doing it again, Vi. You don't shit where you eat, right? That's your law, and I'm going to adopt it too. I've done this way too many times now. You know what I'm like – I get a few drinks inside me and I just want to sleep with somebody. Anybody. I did it with Erin from Sunta Motors, I did it with Kiki the cleaner . . . and I did it with Jenny in HR."

"You didn't? Jenny in HR?" My face twists into an involuntary grimace which he spots immediately. He rolls his eyes at me; he knows I won't be able to let that one pass without a dig. Jenny's antics are legendary. She's slept with two account execs, the guy who couriers our special deliveries, and half the media buying department.

"See? You think I'm disgusting, don't you?"

"I don't think you're disgusting – you haven't done

anything wrong. You and Carly are both single. It's people like Stuart Inman who should be feeling ashamed of themselves—"

"I heard about that. I told you he was a tube, didn't I?"

"After the event, you told me," I remind him, before moving on to the bad news. "I . . . um . . . may have thrown a glass of wine over him in front of half our party guests."

"You didn't?" he says, his eyes bright with mischief.

I start to laugh. "I'll admit it felt pretty amazing, and I'd totally do it again. But – and I'm really sorry about this – he said he's taking the Quest account off me."

Ethan dismisses my apology with a wave of his hand. "We'll face that together. United front, right?"

"Absolutely."

At that moment his phone pings. He moves to pick it up, but then he freezes and I know why.

"Do you want me to get it?" I ask. He nods, his face tense. I reach for his phone, hoping it isn't the bad news he fears, and my stomach dips when I see a text from Stella. "She says that Quentin's heart attack was his fourth, and Carly is in a coma." Ethan sighs deeply and bows his head. "Then she says, '*I'm livid with Violet*' – oh crap, that's not good – '*Couldn't have picked a worse time to*—' wait . . . Assault a client? That's a bit extreme. She ends with, '*If we lose a two-million-pound contract because of her then I'm going to fire both of you.*'" I place the phone back down in front of him, my blood pressure raised to boiling. "She wants to see us first thing on Monday morning."

"Fuck."

"Look, don't worry. This is on me; I'll think of something to get you out of it."

"It isn't just you, Vi, don't you see? We could get past you throwing a drink over Stuart Inman, but if they find out about Max giving Carly drugs and me screwing her, our careers will be over. Why did I do it? It's like . . ." He stands abruptly and starts pacing the floor. "I can't stand this. It feels like I'm losing my mind. Why did I have sex with her? It was like she came from nowhere. She literally leapt into my arms and started whispering filth into my ear – and I fell for all of it. I didn't even like her and I still shagged her. What the hell does that say about me?"

He stops pacing and runs his finger along a patch of bare wood on my windowsill where the paint has chipped away. I walk over to him and rest my hand on his arm. "You're a good person. You have to believe that."

He rests his back against the wall, his gaze fixed to the ceiling. "I'm not a good person, Vi. I didn't give her a second thought. I didn't even realise how wasted she was." The veins in his neck pulse with tension. "She could have died. What if she does die?" His breath rattles in his chest, and tears fall quietly from his eyes. "This is my fault. I'm not a good person . . . Jesus Christ, I'm not . . ."

My own eyes cloud as his anguish washes over me. "I'm not letting you blame yourself for this. It was an accident. Carly is a grown woman who made a series of choices that had a terrible consequence, but none of that is your fault."

He lowers his head and half-smiles at me. "You know I shouldn't have done it, Vi."

"We all make mistakes, Ethan. We've all done things we wish we hadn't."

"Not you. You always do the right thing."

"You couldn't be more wrong," I say, choking on my own regret.

He turns to look at me, his eyes searching my face for answers. "Are you talking about Stuart again?" I shake my head. "Your American guy? That wasn't your fault. He was the married guy with a family."

I don't like talking about Ryan. Ethan and Max both know the bones of what happened in New York, but there are still parts of it I'm not ready to share. I'm not sure I ever will be.

"No, I'm not talking about Ryan either."

"Enlighten me, then." His smile grows wider; I can see he's sceptical. A brief thought ignites in the darkest corner of my mind, and I wonder if revealing the catastrophe I have carried around with me for the past eleven years is a good idea. This is something I've never spoken about to anyone, but all of a sudden my heart is screaming louder than my brain. I know I started this dialogue for a reason. After eleven years, dare I share it to help a friend?

I sit back down on the sofa and he sits next to me. "There's a quote I think is relevant. 'In order for the light to shine so brightly, the darkness must be present.'"

"Nice. Who said that?" he asks.

"Francis Bacon."

"Never heard of him."

"He was a sixteenth-century philosopher. And a scientist and writer."

"How the hell do you know so much about everything? I don't have to Google anything when I have you." He smiles at me and takes hold of my hand, bringing it into his lap. "So, what does it mean?"

"Hmm? Oh, the quote? Well, in this context it means

we all have a dark side, and we all have to accept it as part of who we are. If you run and hide from your past, you're fighting a battle you can't win. Our dark can make us better and stronger people if we embrace it."

I meet his gaze again and his grip on my hand tightens. Suddenly self-conscious, I nervously tuck a stray clump of hair behind my ear. We sit and we wait, and I know we're both wondering where we're going next.

"You don't really share much, Vi. Are you telling me you're running and hiding from something in your past?"

My stomach churns with fear. Am I really doing this? "No, I'm telling you that I prefer to confront my demons in private."

Ethan folds his fingers tightly through mine, intensifying his hold, and I start to shake. "Hey, what is it? You can tell me," he says softly.

I open my mouth but nothing comes out. My throat is dry and my heart is beating so fast I can feel my blood surging through my veins. He notices my knees are trembling and places his other hand on my leg.

"Eleven years ago my life changed forever. There is before and there is after, and nobody in the after knows about the before. It's not that I didn't want to tell you about it, it's just that I haven't told anyone." Silence fills the space between us until all I can hear is the sound of our heartbeats. "I had a sister."

Had. It still pains me to speak in past tense. It still feels like it was yesterday. When she died, I hoped my memories of her would stay with me forever: Christmas mornings, family holidays to the Med, watching Dirty Dancing on repeat, sharing our clothes . . . sharing everything. After she died, I tried so hard to keep all of my memories safe in bottles, sitting on a shelf in my brain. But, as the years go by, too many of them are breaking, their precious contents dissolving with the passage of time. It kills me that I can't remember her smell or her touch or the sound of her laughter anymore.

Ethan blanches. "What happened to her?"

"She drowned. She was eighteen, I was seventeen. We were on a family holiday in Menorca. I knew she wasn't a strong swimmer, but I wanted to go further from the shore. I wasn't thinking about her, it was my fault, and I want to tell you about this because I need you to understand what happens when you allow guilt to consume you."

"Vi, I can't believe this . . ." he says, his eyes cloudy. "Why haven't you told me before? It's like I don't know anything about you at all."

"I don't like talking about her. It hurts . . . still." I withdraw my hand from his so I can hug my arms around my body. "Laurel was so full of life. She was everything I wasn't. Outgoing, sweet, popular . . . She was the sun, whereas I was the moon. My parents used to say they'd named us wrong. Laurel was the flower, and I was the shrub."

"That's a shitty thing to say to your kid," says Ethan, his breath hitching in his throat.

"I did everything I could to make my parents notice me. I excelled at school, I made myself interested in the things they were interested in, but I couldn't come close to being like her. Laurel was their world, and I don't blame them for loving her more than me. I loved her more than me too."

The silence is thick with words waiting to be said. It seems as though hours pass and I will him to speak, but he just sits in silence. A thin, watery veil covers his eyes, and his skin is pale.

"Please say something, Ethan." My voice breaks as I speak.

"I don't know what to say. I always respected that you didn't talk about your family, but I assumed you just didn't get on. I never imagined this . . ." His voice is a whisper, and I can tell he's struggling to process everything I've told him. "What happened after she died?"

"Everyone, except my grandmother, blamed me. We all knew Laurel couldn't swim well. I shouldn't have persuaded her to go further out to sea. She died because of me."

"But you were only a kid." He takes my hand back and holds it tight. And I cry, because after a decade, I'm finally talking to somebody about Laurel, and that someone is him. "You're all they have. Surely they want a relationship with you."

"They don't."

"How do you know?"

"Because I was listening when my father said he wished I'd died instead of her."

His face is crushed with sympathy. I block it out. I don't want him to pity me.

"I don't know what to say, I just . . . Vi, I can't believe this. How do you get over something like that?"

"You don't. I miss her. I miss her every day and I wish I could tell her I'm sorry for what I did, but those feelings don't help. I've had to kill them just so I can function. That is the simple choice I've had to make so I can move forward. It happened and I could easily let it hurt me forever, but instead I've accepted it as part of who I am."

74

His eyes flicker as he lets my story bring meaning to his own. "Thank you." His hold on my hand turns into a gentle rub that makes my skin prick with goosebumps. "I know why you told me this, and . . . thank you." He looks ready to say something else, but instead he reaches his arm around my shoulder and pulls me towards him. He stretches his legs out, lies down, and I'm right there next to him, cuddled in beside him. His arm is still wrapped tightly around me as he jiggles about to get comfortable. I don't know how to respond at first, but as he holds my head close to his chest and starts twirling my long hair around his fingers, I find myself wrapping my arm hesitantly around his middle.

His other arm moves around my waist, and we lie on the sofa together until the early hours turn into mid-morning. He falls asleep, but I don't. I listen to the rhythm that his heart is beating into my eardrum. I enjoy the rise and fall of his chest as he breathes peacefully under me. I inhale his scent and it's different to usual – smoother and richer and tinged with a mix of wine and beer – but the distinction is unique to tonight and I want to remember it.

This doesn't feel like "us", but it feels good. The shift I sensed in our relationship last night has brought us here, and I don't know why or how it happened, but I don't feel scared – I feel safe. We're not "just friends" anymore. We're more than that. But I don't know what *that* is.

7

MAX CRASHES INTO MY SITTING room at ten thirty on Sunday morning, muttering incoherently about turning himself in to the police. Ethan goes home to "get his shit together", and I do my best to calm Max down. After half a day of crying, drinking, freaking out, then crying some more, he finally settles.

By early evening, Max has found a cable channel showing endless reruns of Star Trek and made himself comfortable on my sofa. I join him, but my brain doesn't because it's too busy overthinking every tiny detail of the last two days. I stare up at my ceiling, one part of my brain failing to shut out Captain Kirk's latest foolhardy mission, the other part trying desperately to silence the voices in my head.

I miss him. He only left a few hours ago, but I want to talk to him, hold him again, hear his voice, smell his cologne and feel his breath on my skin. I want to stop replaying and analysing his words, but I can't.

At 10 p.m., I finally manage to send Max home in a taxi with his arms full of Dickens novels I know I'll never see again and a Tesco's tuna pasta bake ready meal for one.

***

I'm at my desk ready for work at precisely 7.43 a.m. on Monday. I am tired and irritable and my eyeballs feel like they've been scraped by a rusty potato peeler.

Normally, the office would be full of chatter at this time, but today the floor is eerily quiet. There are a few members of staff holding subdued, hushed conversations whilst an aura of the macabre clings to the air. Half an hour later, Malcolm Barrett sweeps over to my desk bearing a face that looks like it's been hung out to dry in a thunderstorm.

"Where's your partner in crime?" he asks, his Adam's apple vibrating the crinkly loose skin around his neck. This isn't how he usually speaks to me. He looks stressed to hell, and I feel a swirl of panic twist through my stomach.

I look at my watch to signal that it's still early. "I'm sure he'll be here soon."

"You left the party early on Saturday. Have you heard what happened?" His silvery moustache is damp, and I can smell the aroma of early-morning espresso on it. Moustaches can't be hygienic. They retain taste and they retain smell. I remember a heavy work night out a couple of years ago. I vomited on my hair, and every time the wind blew, I could smell and taste what I'd had for dinner four hours previously. It would be worse with a moustache. It would be right there, under your nose all day long, constantly wafting the aroma of what you've eaten up at you.

"Yes, I heard what happened. I'm sorry about Quentin Hibbard. Had you known him long?"

Malcolm pulls up a chair and wheels himself to the desk next to mine, which I now notice is empty of Mohammed's things. "I met him for the first time at the awards show. Apparently, the stupid old fool had been at death's door for years. He should have retired long ago."

I offer the usual platitudes, but I can tell there's more

on Malcolm's mind than the surprise passing of one of our clients. He wheels his chair closer and I brace myself.

"I want to know two things: what's going on between you and Stuart Inman, and what's going on between Fraser and Carly Hayes?"

I feel my face flush red with embarrassment. No way am I entering into a discussion with Malcolm about Stuart Inman's defective man-parts. "We had a disagreement. Don't worry, I'll apologise for the wine incident."

Malcolm's eyes lock on to mine. "Make sure you do, Violet, because if we lose Quest over this, heads are going to roll, and I want to make sure those heads don't include yours. You don't want to let me in on the deal with Stuart? Fine. Let's talk about Fraser and Carly Hayes instead. A little bird tells me he was sleeping with Carly. Was he? And before you answer, I need the truth. If you lie to me I'll know."

I swivel my chair around and glare at him. "When have I ever lied to you?" I lower my voice even though we're virtually alone in the office. "If you want to know Ethan's business, you'll have to ask him."

"You're lying to me right now. The whole office knows Fraser can't keep it in his pants, but you? I thought you had more class."

I must have raised my eyebrows as high as they'll go because Malcolm responds with an audible gulp that makes his neck skin quiver again.

"What are you accusing me of, Malcolm? Can you actually hear the words coming out of your mouth?"

"No, I can't hear anything because I've had the chairman and partners yelling down the phone at me since six a.m. and I'm stone-cold deaf. This is bad press for us, really bad press. I need to protect the agency."

"Well you can protect it without throwing accusations at me – or Ethan."

"Fine, if that's the way you want to play it. The meeting Stella arranged for nine is now an emergency management meeting. You and Fraser will have to sit in for the creative director. When the hell does Diego get back anyway? He must have been away a month already. Who sanctioned him having that much holiday?"

"Stella did. Diego's mother died. He has family living all over the world and they're having a reunion in Venezuela."

"Did she? Are they? Okay, I didn't know that." Malcolm stands to leave, but swings back. "Get Fraser at that meeting on time. We don't need his usual slack-arsed punctuality on top of everything else."

I send Ethan a text letting him know about the meeting, then my attention shifts back to the floor as Lurch from the Addams Family makes his entrance. I shit you not – Max Wolf has just surpassed himself in the race for the "looking stupid and dressing stupidly" award he previously won for turning up to work wearing odd shoes. I still have no idea how he walked out of his front door – sober – wearing one monochrome checked deck shoe and one red baseball trainer. He stalks over to my desk and I wonder . . . why? Just why? I mean, he isn't renowned for his dress sense. He usually wears a scruffy t-shirt and jeans to work. He keeps a tie in his desk in the rare event a client ever wants to meet him, but as he never comes to work wearing a shirt the gesture is pointless. Well, aside from that one time he put his tie on with a vintage Prodigy t-shirt and Stella threatened to fire him on the spot.

"Max, what's with the suit?" I ask as he walks over to my desk brandishing a luminous green carrier bag.

He stops dead in his tracks and looks down at himself. His left knee bends and I'm sure he's double-checking that he's wearing matching shoes. "I thought it would be respectful. Is it?"

I shake my head. "It's not really necessary to wear black," I say softly. "And why is your jacket too short for your arms?"

"No idea. I don't know where I got it from, but I lost my other jacket at the party, remember? Thankfully I gave a neighbour a spare key, but I lost my iPhone too, so if you need me for anything you'll have to direct tweet my iPad because I don't have a landline."

"Max, you lost a tuxedo jacket on Saturday night. If you hadn't lost it, would you be wearing a rented tuxedo for work today?"

He shrugs. "These are the tuxedo trousers. I didn't have any other black trousers. Do I look stupid?"

"Yeah, a little bit. Sorry. And dare I ask what's in the bag?" I hope with everything I have that it's a change of clothes.

"Oh, I got you this to thank you for looking after me yesterday. I needed you and you were there for me and . . . well, I missed you this morning."

He hands me the carrier bag. I peep inside to find a selection of groceries and a cactus. This is the icing on the cake, and I can't help laughing. Not just because I have told him every day for the last three years that I don't drink either tea or coffee and there's both in the bag. I swear he has a complete mental block on the topic. His brain can't comprehend the existence of a human being who doesn't like hot beverages.

"Thank you, Max. This is very thoughtful of you. I'll pass the teabags and coffee to somebody who actually drinks tea and coffee, but the rest looks lovely. You didn't need to buy me anything though. You're my friend. It's my job to be there for you."

"I just wanted to say thank you. Anyway, it isn't like I pushed out the boat. I went to the mini-market outside Brixton Tube station. They've started stocking Eastern European food as there are a few Poles and Romanians living in my street now. I've told the owner fifty times already that I'm German, not Polish, but she keeps forgetting, so I feel obligated to buy her Polish food. That's why you've got those weird spongy biscuits. Sorry about that."

"Well, I'm sure they'll be lovely, and I'm very grateful."

I turn back to my computer, but Max remains behind me, hovering like a confused hummingbird. I turn back to face him. His eyes are fixed on his shoes. "Max," I say, cocking my head to the side. "What is it?"

"Hmm?" His bright green eyes dim with unease, and I get a flashback to the way he was over the weekend. "I was wondering if you'd heard anything."

"Not yet, but there's an emergency meeting at nine." I stand up and clasp my hands around his forearms. He sinks into me and I swear he drops a few inches in height. "Don't worry. If I hear anything about Carly I'll tell you straight away."

"Do you promise?"

"Of course," I say, reassuring him as sincerely as I can. He turns around and walks in the direction of the art studio. I hope he'll be able to buckle down and get on with work, but I think there's more chance of Malcolm giving Ethan an Employee of the Year trophy.

***

Of course I knew he would be late.

At two minutes to nine, I make my way to the conference room, cursing Ethan under my breath. I curse him even more when I turn the corner and walk headlong into Ridley Gates.

"Ah, Violet, can I have a quick word, please?" Ridley beckons me into a corner behind one of three huge potted palms that line the corridor of the sixteenth floor.

My gut is saying "fuck off", but I take a deep breath and reluctantly join him.

"I just wanted to make sure we're of the same mind on how to handle what happened on Saturday night," he says as a gigantic half-moon grin fills his face. He looks like a demonic incarnation of the Cheshire Cat.

"What particular event are you referring to?" I ask with fake innocence.

Ridley grins again and leans in so close that the overpowering scent of his cologne – Eau de Slimy Shithead – fills my nostrils. "You know what I'm referring to, and nobody else needs to know about it."

Unfortunately for Ridley Gates, my married-cheating-bastard tolerance level is so low even an ant couldn't limbo under it. "Are you asking me not to tell your wife you were screwing around on her?"

Ridley's composure doesn't falter. "I am, and I shouldn't have to remind you that you were screwing around with somebody else's fiancé last week."

What the hell? If I had a glass of wine in my hand right now, Ridley Gates would be wearing it. "Not that

I give a shit what you think about me, Ridley, but I didn't know Adele existed until Carly told me on Saturday night."

"Sure you didn't," he says with a wink. I fight the urge to knee him in the balls.

"As I said, Ridley, I don't care what you think, and I have no reason to lie. You and Stuart have a lot in common. I suppose you're going to steal Stuart's line and insist you and Delfina are having 'relationship problems' too."

Ridley sticks his tongue in the hollow of his cheek as he looks me up and down, his eyes lingering for a moment on the outline of my chest. My skin crawls, but I suck in a breath and square my shoulders.

"Delfina still pleases me in every way a wife should, except for the empty void between her ears. What can I say? I'm attracted to smart women." His eyes wander south once more before he moves away. My stomach lurches as he enters the conference room and I follow behind like a prisoner passing through Traitor's Gate.

We wait for Ethan to arrive, but Malcolm, full of hell and bluster, gives up after ten minutes and starts the meeting. "Okay, first things first," he begins with an air of urgency. "I'm sure it won't surprise any of you to learn that the CEO of Quest, backed by Stuart Inman, is seeking ways to terminate our advertising contract with them. Our legal department has responded with a statement of our intention to hold them to their commitments, but we're on shaky ground. There's a contractual get-out clause if either party – client or agency – brings the other's commercial reputation into disrepute."

"That's fucking bollocks and you know it, Malcolm," says Stella Judd, her voice strong and commanding. "Quentin Hibbard had a heart attack, and the Hayes girl binge-drank herself into a coma. How the hell is any of that our fault?"

"Because it happened on our watch. The awards show party costs the agency six figures to host each year, and this year's event ended up as a cross between a seedy drugs den and an orgy, culminating in a young woman almost choking to death in a pool of her own vomit. I don't blame Quest for wanting to cut ties. Their shares have already nose-dived on the FTSE, so it's basic damage control."

"What happened on Saturday night was tragic," chips in Daniel Noble, his sparkling blue eyes hidden under a serious frown. "But the responsibility for Carly's condition has to be placed with Carly."

"Damn right, it should," Stella says. "They don't have grounds to sue or terminate, so they can fuck off."

"Would you suggest I tell them that?" seethes Malcolm.

"Of course I wouldn't." Stella retrieves a silver cigarette case from her purse. "But Daniel and I have already spoken about this and we're in agreement. We shouldn't accept blame as an agency." She stands and walks towards the door. "If you'll excuse me, I need a cigarette before I blow. I don't know why we're even having this conversation."

Stella swings the door open at the same time as Ethan saunters into the conference room. "Killer timing as usual, Mr Fraser," she says as she leaves.

Ethan takes a seat next to me and makes a roadwork-related apology. Surely he must be aware by now that every single one of us knows he makes up a traffic incident whenever he's late.

Malcolm wraps up the meeting as quickly as he can,

noting that he and Ridley are going to Quest's offices to pay their respects on behalf of the agency. As he leaves, he instructs Daniel to complete the client brief for the Quest Living launch and asks me to work on copy that will "blow Stuart Inman's socks off". He ignores Ethan entirely.

***

I follow Ethan out of the conference room, my shoes sliding over the thin carpeting as I rush to catch up with him. I grab his arm and he spins around. I can see he's pissed off and I assume it's because of Malcolm.

"How are you? I've been thinking about you all weekend." I have so many questions I want to ask him, but I need to know if he's okay first.

He takes my elbow and leads me into one of the smaller meeting rooms to our left. I close the door behind us.

"I just needed to spend yesterday on my own. I didn't see anybody, didn't listen to music, or play guitar . . . I think I'm good though."

"You don't look or sound good." I look into his eyes, seeking for a hint of his usual sparkle, but there's nothing.

Then a faint smile pulls at the corners of his mouth and I feel myself relax a bit. "I'm fine. Honestly. I just needed to get my head in the right place. And I'm sticking to what I said on Sunday morning. I'm turning over a new leaf, just like you. From now on, I don't shit where I eat. I'm adopting your law."

"Great, welcome to the town of Celibacy, population two."

He smiles at me and my heart melts. God, I love his smile. "I'm totally onboard with this, Vi. I'm tired of having one-night hook-ups with never-see-you-again nobodies."

"I believe you," I say, although I don't think for one second he's going to be able to stick to it. "So why were you late this morning? You didn't reply to my text."

"I had to pick something up." He dips his hand into the inside pocket of his jacket and pulls out a small black box. "It's for you. I wanted to thank you for telling me about your sister. I know it was hard and I know you did it to help me. By the time I got home yesterday I'd already made peace with my guilt over Carly, but I couldn't stop thinking about you."

My breath gets caught in my throat. I don't know what to say. He hands me the box, and my stomach flips. I can't open it. I just hold it in my hands, my fingers digging into the cushioned fabric. It's as if I'm holding his heart but I'm afraid to unlock it. Shit, is that what's happening here?

"Aren't you going to open it?"

I clear my throat and feel my eyes water as I open the box. Tears are the last things I need. I summon some resolve.

"Hey, it's okay." He pulls me into him, resting his chin on the top of my head. I take the delicate silver pendant out of the box and grip the disc, which is engraved with a laurel branch. My Laurel. A huge lump forms in my throat. Nobody has ever done anything like this for me before. He helps me put on the necklace, and for a split second I wish I could kiss him. But then my brain takes up arms against my ridiculous heart again and forces the thought away. Whatever this feels like, it's friendship – and it can never be anything more.

"Thank you. I have the best friend in the world."

He shoots me a wink. "No, you don't. I do."

8

THE NEXT DAY ARRIVES WITH a bang. Literally.

I wake to the sound of my mobile ringing, reach over to my nightstand to pick it up, stretch too far, lose my balance and whack my head on my bedpost. I'm still wincing in agony as I scramble, blinded with pain, to answer the call.

"What? . . . What time is it? . . . Urgh . . . what do you want?"

"Sorry, did I wake you?" Ethan asks as I groan some more. "What's up? Do you have a bloke staying over?"

"What? No! I've just banged my stupid head on my stupid bedpost. And I've sworn off men, remember?"

He laughs. "Sorry. It was just the noise you made . . ."

"I was groaning in agony. If that resembles the sex noises you elicit from women, you might want to work on your technique."

"I've never had any complaints in that department. In fact, there was this one time I was with this girl, and I was under the sheets giving her—"

"Oh my god, shut up now! Please. My head feels like I've been drinking all night. The last thing I want to hear about is you fumbling around some poor woman's chuff like an unqualified gynaecologist."

"Ew!" he says, laughing even harder. "You've spoiled my happy memory now. Why did you have to do that?"

"Just tell me why you called and make it quick. My forehead is in desperate need of an ice pack."

"Jeez, you're as soft as shite, Vi. It can't be that bad."

"Says the man who cried for a day when his mum's puppy nipped his scrotum."

"I'd give you that, except Angus isn't a puppy; he's a fully grown dog." he says, protesting a little too hard.

"He's a Highland terrier – the smallest and most puppy-like of dogs."

"He's a fucking bastard is what he is. I hate that dog. And I hated him long before he morphed into a heat-seeking missile and attached himself to my family jewels. The evil bloody thing nipped clean through my jeans and my pants. I had to prise his jaws off my balls."

"I know, it was terrible," I say with mock sympathy. "But why are we talking so early?"

"I have good news and bad news. What do you want first?"

My stomach dips. "How bad is the bad?"

"Not as bad as a dog biting your bollocks, but worse than a bump on the head."

"Okay . . . give me the good," I say as I stumble out of bed and head for the bathroom.

"Quest's legal team have spoken with ours, and they concede there's no concrete grounds for termination. So we get to complete the TV commercial for their new winter range, but after that, we're done. No Quest Living brand launch."

"Despite our big win at the AdAg Awards?"

"Yup. And despite the hours of work the Strategy department has done in preparation for the campaign. They won't even view our planning or market research. They want to hand the contract to another agency."

"Shit." I hover over the sink, inspecting the red mark

on my forehead in the mirror. If I get a bruise I won't be pleased. "Okay, let me get into the office and we'll get to work on Daniel's brief."

"You don't want to hear the bad news?"

"Quest ditching us isn't the bad news?"

"Erm . . . not exactly. There's no easy way of saying this, but Stuart Inman has sacked us. Well, not us – you. He's demanding Stella appoint another creative team immediately."

"Oh my god, seriously?"

"Yes, seriously. Sorry. Stella wants to see us at eight thirty."

"How mad is she?"

"Volcanic eruption imminent, so strap on your lava boots."

***

I make it to work on time and head straight for the executive offices on the fourteenth floor. I wish I could say I'm feeling cool, calm and collected, but I'd rather eat a hedgehog smeared in Tabasco sauce than face Stella Judd this morning. I'm also starving. I didn't stop by Juicy Lucy's for my usual morning smoothie because my stomach is whirling with dread.

Surprisingly, given his rubbish timekeeping, Ethan is already seated when I wade through the cigarette smoke and sit down next to him, my throat rasping at the stale air in the room. The 1970s have called numerous times to demand their Marlboro Man back, but Stella firmly believes Britain's smoking ban doesn't apply to her if she smokes outside the hours of nine to five and opens the windows twice a day.

As if reading my mind, she stubs out her cigarette and opens the window. The cool spring air rushes in, mixes with the cigarette smoke and scratches the back of my throat, making me cough.

"Sorry, terribly bad habit," Stella says in her upper-crust English accent. She reminds me of a younger version of Helen Mirren, but with a Dior power suit and a potty mouth. "So, I'll cut to the chase – Stuart Inman. Why won't he work with you?"

"Did he not give you a reason?" I ask apprehensively.

"Lack of talent and a bad attitude. Apparently Quest's marketing team are in agreement that Ethan is BMG's shining star and you feed off his success."

I feel my jaw drop in shock as a pang of insecurity settles into my gut.

"That isn't true at all, Stella," Ethan says firmly. "We're a team and I couldn't do what I do without Violet."

Stella waves her hand dismissively in Ethan's direction. "I know, I know. I wasn't born yesterday. I've been head of this department for ten years. How many copywriters and art directors do you think I've managed? I know this job, I know my team, I know Violet and I don't buy Stuart Inman's bullshit for one second. So I ask again, what's the story?"

I squirm in my seat, my rage against Stuart building. "We went on a date that didn't work out."

Stella inhales a sharp breath and rolls her eyes. "I fucking knew it," she declares, thumping her fist down on her desk and making my heart jump into my throat. "This is why I have zero tolerance for personal relationships in my department. I heard the rumours and I heard about the wine-throwing. What did he do? Is this all on him?"

"In my opinion it is," I say with as much conviction as I can muster.

"Mine too," says Ethan.

"I don't recall asking what you thought," Stella barks. "And what on earth have you done to your hair? Are you trying to look like Hugh Grant?"

Ethan adjusts his tie, his eyes retreating under a bewildered frown. "Erm, no. I'm not trying to look like Hugh Grant."

"Good, because you'll never pull it off." She folds her hands together on the desk in front of her. "Now, Violet. You're a good-looking girl –, smart, funny, talented . . . and I have eyes, so I can see that Stuart Inman is a six foot stack of ripped and toned muscle. But he's also a human-sized bollock. What were you thinking?"

"Well, in retrospect, it wasn't my finest moment," I admit sheepishly.

"You're damn right it wasn't. How old are you?"

"Twenty-eight."

"Twenty-eight . . ." She stands up and closes the window, giving the metal handle an almighty tug. Unfortunately the cold shiver down my spine seems to still be there. "You know what I was doing when I was twenty-eight?"

"Erm . . . no."

"I was going through my second of four divorces. Phillip Lovett, have you heard of him? He's the son of Lovett Ives's co-founder. Ah, Phillip . . ." she mutters pensively, her blue eyes sparkling with nostalgia. "He used to be so much fun, until career competitiveness turned him into a jealous prat. We were on secondment to New York. It was horrific. Never, ever fall in love with someone you work with. Phillip has turned into a stuffed-shirt and I'm still bitter. We were true bohemians back in the day."

Stella, a bohemian? The woman who lives in Chelsea, buys her groceries from Harrods and wears Chanel cocktail dresses to put the bins out? Have I stepped into the Twilight Zone? "I'm sorry to hear that, Stella, but I was never in love with Stuart Inman."

She looks at me in surprise. "So what's the problem?"

My brain is screaming at me to flee the interrogation and try to forget any of this ever happened. I glance briefly at Ethan just as he shifts nervously in his seat. Stella notices him too.

"Fake Hugh Grant, why are *you* being so twitchy?"

"For the last time, I'm not trying to look like Hugh Grant. This isn't 1995 and he's old enough to be my father. Nobody wants to look like Hugh Grant."

"Tell that to your hair," says Stella, and I have to suck in a breath before I collapse into laughter. Funnily enough, Ethan doesn't look anything like Hugh Grant – not even the hot-for-Julia-Roberts Hugh Grant of twenty years ago. "Now back to you, Violet. I'm still waiting for information. Don't make me wait any longer."

"We went out, had a nice time, one thing led to another . . . but it didn't go too well . . ." I take a deep breath. "Um, okay, he couldn't perform, and he blamed me for it."

"He blamed you for what?"

"For his poor performance."

Stella's body stiffens and the angles of her face harden. "Violet, I'm still bitter about the plot holes in Lost. When I only get half a story I tend to get really pissed off."

"Stuart dropped his bombs before the mission completed," interjects Ethan, and my mouth falls open. I fire a glare at him. He responds with a shrug.

"You're kidding me. Stuart Inman? Really?" Stella says, her eyes creased with laughter.

"Technically, the bombs were dropped before the mission even got started," I add for clarity.

"Oh, Jesus Christ," she cries, holding her sides. "Well, who'd have thought that? Stuart Inman, one of the most arrogant piss-ants I've ever met, is a flop in the sack."

"That's not all," says Ethan with a hint of mischief. "He's hung like a field mouse and he couldn't find a clitoris if it painted itself purple and danced the tango on top of Tower Hill."

"Ethan, do you mind?" I snap. "I don't want the most intimate regions of my anatomy discussed with our head of department."

"I'm sorry, Vi," he says. "But this isn't right. You're not taking the blame for this."

"So, let me get this straight," Stella says after regaining her composure. "Stuart Inman was rubbish in bed, blamed you for it and now he's trying to get you fired?"

"Yes, and he also has a fiancée he didn't tell me about."

Stella's eyebrows arch to the heavens. Without a word to either of us she picks up her phone. "Gabriel, get me Stuart Inman," she barks at her executive assistant.

Moments later, Stuart's voice erupts through the phone's speaker. "What can I do for you, Ms Judd?"

"I just wanted to let you know that I've spoken with

both Ethan and Violet and under no circumstances am I removing them from your campaign. As head of the city's most prestigious advertising creative department, it would be professional suicide following our win at the AdAg Awards, so it isn't happening. Have I made myself clear, Stuart?"

"I'm afraid not, Stella. I made it clear to you that we don't want Violet Archer on our campaign."

"Is that a 'we' as in your board of directors, or a 'we' as in just you?"

"I'm the marketing director, Stella. I have the authority to make this decision."

Stella rises from her chair and rests her balled-up fists on the desk in front of her. "Okay, listen to me, you conniving little shitgibbon. Violet Archer is my best copywriter, she's a valuable member of my team, and an attack on her is an attack on me. If you insist on bumping her because you flopped in the bedroom, then I'm going to fight you with everything I have, starting with a lawsuit. Now, is *that* clear?"

Silence. Except for the rumbles of my half-starved stomach. Jesus Christ, I wish I'd eaten some breakfast.

"What did you just say to me?" comes the crackly voice of a broken man.

"You heard me. And if you ever mention removing Violet from your campaign again, I'll take your lying, cheating arse straight to your CEO. Now, if you'll excuse me, I have work to do. I'll get Gabriel to set up a meeting once Daniel Noble signs off on our creative work."

She ends the call before Stuart has a chance to respond.

Ethan starts to clap. "That was awesome. Absolutely awesome." I have to admit, I feel the same way. I don't want to be Stella when I grow up any more – I want to be Stella right now.

She sits back down at her desk, but she isn't smiling. Her demeanour has returned to stone-cold serious. "Consider both of your arses covered, but a warning – when workplace relationships jeopardise the reputation of my department, I always take a very dim view. Some discretion from now on, please."

We agree. I'm pretty confident workplace relationships won't be an issue for either of us ever again.

***

I head to the break room and grab one of Max's Polish cereal bars from a box marked "*Finger weg!*". I don't know German, but it's either a warning or the name of the food I'm stealing. I eagerly rip open the pink wrapper and stare down at a grainy, rectangular dog turd.

"Ew, that looks gross." Ethan appears over my left shoulder. He opens the fridge and takes out a bottle of mineral water, also labelled "*Finger weg*". He doesn't think twice about snapping the plastic tab, unscrewing the top and taking a gigantic swig. Maybe "*Finger weg*" means "help yourself" in German.

"So, what did you make of Stella back there?" I take a tentative bite of the cereal bar. Urgh! It tastes like a dog turd too. I rip a square of kitchen roll off the stand and empty the contents of my mouth into it.

"I think she's amazing," says Ethan, like a schoolboy with a crush on his headmistress.

"And her parting shot?"

He hesitates for a moment, then takes another swig of water. "She made a fair point. We've both fucked up, Vi. You with Stuart. Me with Carly—"

"And Zoe, and Kiki, and Jenny in HR, and Erin from Sunta Motors, and the emaciated receptionist with the unfeasibly large chest."

"Her name is Pamela, and she has a very lovely chest."

"I don't know how she paid for it. BMG must pay their receptionists well above average."

"She saved for years, but Pamela's chest is irrelevant. Don't lay this all on me. Stuart Inman can't be your only workplace dalliance."

"Aside from Ryan when I worked in New York, he is. Eugene is up for debate due to him knocking himself out a couple of hours into our one and only date."

"I don't believe that's it."

"You've known me for three years. All my dates have happened off-site. And now, I'm committed to obeying my law. In fact, I've already turned down a very interested party."

The expression on his face changes to one I don't expect. It's as though the air has been knocked out of him. He awkwardly lowers his eyes to the carpet-tiled floor.

"Oh," he says, and even though my brain has already prepped a witty retort, I swallow it back down. His skin reddens and I don't understand why.

"Yes . . . um . . . Daniel Noble asked me to have dinner with him, but I explained my law. *I* have self-control. You, on the other hand . . ."

I meant it as a joke, but as I watch him swallow hard, his Adam's apple locking against the collar of his shirt, I regret saying it. He forces a smile onto his face.

"Hey, I've had an idea. Why don't we have a little wager? Spice things up a bit? You think you're going to see this out longer than me, so we need a bet... I know, I'll buy you one of those 'Patron of the Royal Opera House' things you're always talking about."

Oh my god, he's an idiot. "A patronage at the Royal Opera?" I raise my eyebrows. "I think you should check out how much they cost before you start making those kinds of wagers."

"Doesn't matter. I'm not going to lose."

"Fine then. You're on."

"Okay," he says with a smile that slowly fades as his curiosity sets in. "Erm . . . so how much are they?"

"Almost six."

"Hundred?" he asks hopefully.

"Thousand."

"Fuck."

"Yep, and that's something you're not going to be doing for a while."

"What if I win?"

"I'll buy you a pint." I laugh as he screws up his face. "Don't look at me like that. You only gamble what you can afford to lose, and I had to invest in a new tumble dryer last month."

He snatches up the remnants of the discarded Polish cereal bar and takes a bite. I wait for him to spit it out, but he finishes his mouthful and takes another bite instead. "How about you buy me a pint and clean my apartment every Saturday for a month?"

"Not fair. I hate cleaning."

"So don't lose," he says with a wink, extending his hand.

I consider the repercussions of the bet for a moment. Given that Ethan is a virtual man-slut, it's a hundred times more likely that he'll fail than I will. "You're on," I say, "but one last thing before we shake. Why don't we spice things up a little bit?"

One of his eyebrows heads skywards and he retracts his hand. "What do you mean?" he asks suspiciously.

"How about we're both allowed to indulge in ways to get the other party to fail?"

A glint of mischief twinkles in his eye, and he extends his hand for a second time. "Deal."

We shake, smiling. But deep down I'm wondering whether I want him to fail.

9

FINISHING THE COPY OF QUEST'S winter catalogue TV commercial is proving as difficult as getting front-row tickets at the latest West End show on opening night. I came up with nothing useful yesterday due to being boiling mad at Stuart, and I'm sure my brain no longer works. I run my fingers over the silver pendant Ethan gave me, and my mind throws up question after question. When did he get so thoughtful? When did I start to notice how beautiful he was, not to mention kind, funny and smart? He's *the* most perfect best friend.

I'm still holding on to my necklace when Ethan arrives at his desk.

"Can you believe Malcolm Barrett has just cornered me outside the loos demanding I have twenty different ideas to fit the Quest campaign by four thirty?" He throws our newest client brief down on his desk. "We need a week to work on something as important as this. I don't suppose you've got anywhere yet?"

I rummage through my notebook and rip out a page of scribble. "This is all I have. It's mostly crap, but it's a start."

He takes the piece of paper and scans through it. "Well the first one is out. They don't want to give off a 'value brand' vibe. Number two is out for the same reason. Number three is bollocks. Number four . . . I'll do my best to un-see that one. Number five . . . eh? Were you high when you came up with this?"

"No, but I was tired of doing your job as well as

mine. You're the ideas person; I'm words, remember?" I snatch my paper back off him, scrunch it into a ball and launch it towards the bin, but I can't even do that right. I miss and it rolls across the floor, landing at his feet.

"Okay, calm down. I'm sorry."

Fucking "calm down". Seriously? Does he have a death wish? He retrieves the paper ball and tries to iron it out with the palms of his hands. "I didn't read number six." He tries to stifle a grin. "Nope, that's shit too. Seven we could work on, though."

"You think so?"

"Possibly, but there's just one thing wrong."

"What?"

"All of the words."

"Are you kidding me?" Remember what I was saying about Ethan being a perfect best friend? Well, he's perfect except for the countless times per day when he's being an infuriating arse. "This isn't funny. We need to do our magic."

"Do you think I don't know that?" He flops down in his chair, takes off his jacket, rolls up his shirt sleeves and adjusts his tie. "Right, prepare yourself. I'm about to magic up some awesome."

I laugh. "Is there anything I can do to help speed up the magic? Get you a cold beer? A club sandwich from Pret? A shoulder massage?"

"Yeah, shoulder massage would be good, thanks. Can you do it here, or do I have to be naked and covered in oil?"

"You mean you're not going to strip off at your desk?"

"Hmm . . . maybe after hours."

I imagine him naked. I imagine rubbing oil over the

taut muscles of his chest . . . Oh my god, why? What the hell is my brain doing to me? I need to change the topic of conversation fast, so I flick onto Quest's homepage. "Christ almighty, who wears this stuff?" I ask as I scroll through the womenswear section.

He rolls his eyes. "Tell me about it. I wouldn't even buy a pair of socks from Quest. It's for boring middle-aged dads who take backpacks full of sensible healthy snacks on trips to museums with the kids."

"Nothing wrong with visiting museums."

"Not if you're over sixty-five, or boring," he says.

"Hey, *I* like museums," I say, faking outrage.

"Proving my point," he says with a laugh. I love his laugh, even when he's being a pain in the arse.

"You must be able to find something to inspire you."

"Trust me, I can't. Not even their website promo for a pair of khaki corduroy trousers is doing it for me. Shoot me if I ever wear anything made from corduroy, will you?"

"Okay," I say, half listening as I sign into my email.

He peers over our cubicle wall. "What are you doing now?"

"Hmm? Oh, I'm just writing an email to IT. I want a new keyboard."

"Are you blaming your tools for that crap you wrote earlier? A new keyboard won't make you come up with better copy, you know."

I shoot him a glare, but I can't stop a smile from creeping up on me. He's beating me hands down on insults today. I'll have to up my game. "No, it's just that Jack Shipley spent hours using it to recover that corrupt file last week. Did you see what he was doing on the dance floor on Saturday night? I don't want my nice clean fingers to go where his disgusting dirty ones have been."

"You're crazy," he replies, his eyes glued to his screen. He scoots backwards in his chair and picks up the client brief. "Okay, I need an hour or two to think. I'm going to grab a cup of coffee and head over to the break room."

***

I work through lunch, and when Ethan returns from inspiring himself, we both get our heads down. My stomach growls as I search in the bottom of my desk drawer for anything worth eating. I produce a week-old apple with crinkly skin and take a reluctant bite.

"Do you have any more apples?"

I peer over the top of our cubicle divide and see the back of Ethan's head. He's hunched over a pile of handwritten notes and drawings. "No, sorry."

His head snaps up and I'm confronted by a pathetic pet lip. "I'm starving. I can't believe we rushed to get this work to Malcolm for four thirty and then he phoned to tell us he'll be away for the rest of the day. I swear to god, Vi, if that man doesn't give me a break I'm going to end up clocking him."

"He's a dick to everybody. Don't let him bother you."

"Not to you, he isn't. He thinks the sun shines out of your arse."

I smirk and take another bite of my apple. "He knows I'm awesome. What can I say?"

Ethan watches me; he's practically drooling. I toss him the apple and my stomach roars angrily in response.

"He doesn't love you for your awesome. He's got an old-man crush on you."

"Oh, fuck off. Seriously, Ethan, don't even go there. That's the last thing I want embedded in my mind."

"Just telling you how it is." He crunches a mouthful of apple as he talks, and the sound gnaws at the back of my hungry brain.

"You're not. You're trying to gross me out, and it's not working."

His eyes dart around the room to check we're alone, then he leans over the divide, his eyes creasing as he smiles. "You must have noticed him eyeing your holy grails."

"My what?"

"You know . . . Bert and Ernie, the Siamese twins, your speed bumps, your devil's dumplings . . ." He laughs as his favourite boob-words tumble out.

I shake my head. "Firstly, are you twelve years old? Secondly, his eyes never head south. I'd notice."

"They totally do. I reckon he thinks he's found a new home for Basil Brush between your hills."

I feel my eyes pop. "Basil . . . who?"

"Basil Brush – his moustache."

"Oh my god, no. Just no! He's like a father to me. That's . . . um . . ." I lose my train of thought as I catch the change in Ethan's expression when I say the word "father". It's a mixture of sympathy, regret and anger . . . something I've never seen in his face before, because I've never talked about my family before. I subconsciously run my fingers over the silver pendant he gave me as I mourn this sudden change in our dynamic.

"I'm glad you're wearing it," he says, giving me a smile which lights up his eyes and does something funny to my stomach.

"I love it, and I'm glad I told you about Laurel. I kept her memory inside me for so long because I didn't want to share her. I wanted to keep her all to myself. She belonged to me, but talking about her . . . well, it wasn't so bad."

"What you told me about your family upset me, but what hit me harder is you keeping it buried for so long. Hiding how you feel isn't good for you. I think you're amazing and I care about you too much to not say this. You need to open up more. Promise me you won't keep anything serious from me again."

My mouth goes dry because I know I can't make that promise. I don't share, I don't like discussing my feelings and I don't like showing weakness. "I'll try," I say unconvincingly.

He smiles at me and it's as if even his smile has changed recently. I've only seen this new smile on his face when he looks at me. It's wide, making his cheeks dimple and the blue of his eyes glisten. I look away because I feel that strange feeling again. A warmth inside my body that makes my heart rate quicken.

"I think I might be onto something," Ethan proclaims suddenly, passing his notepad over our cubicle wall. I flip through his pages of sketches and notes. "What do you think?"

"You want to shoot in a mountain location?"

"Yeah, we have the budget. We need to inject more 'quest' into Quest. The original *questforlife* campaign was urban, but a bit static. If we're doing a winter catalogue and new clothing range, then mountains would work."

"There's only one problem with doing a winter catalogue shoot on location: it's almost summer."

"Doesn't matter," he says. "This is Britain. What's the weather going to be like up north at the end of spring?"

"You make a fair point."

"Yeah, the more I think about it . . . mountains, green hills, rolling valleys, icy streams, lots of wind, rustling trees – the great British outdoors. Run the *questforlife* hashtag through it, and slam in a sense of adventure."

"Okay, I got it." I stand, snap the notebook shut and pick up my handbag. "I need sustenance before I do any more work. I'm going to Juicy Lucy's for a smoothie, you want anything?"

"No, no, I'm fine. That apple you gave me has given me indigestion."

***

I cross the street, turn the corner and make my way to Juicy Lucy's, a bright and breezy organic drink shop famous with the office workers of the City. I open the white-painted door and I'm bombarded by an orchard of citrusy smells. My mouth starts to water as I order my favourite smoothie: almond milk, banana, kale and cinnamon. The server takes my payment and hands me my bright green drink just as a familiar face enters the shop.

Zoe Callaghan, Malcolm Barrett's executive assistant, is one of those girls nobody tries to compete with because everything about her is flawless, from her infectious laughter and sweet naivety to her glossy dark hair, which is always elegantly styled in a pleat with romantic wisps framing her heart-shaped face. Last year, she and Ethan dated for six months, but despite her loveliness, she always seemed to find fault with him.

"Hi, Violet. How's everything going with the new Quest brief?" She manages to sound genuinely interested, even though I'm sure she's just being her impeccably good-mannered self and making small talk.

"It's going great. I'm just grabbing some vitamin C to charge my batteries in case I have to work into the night," I reply, pointing to my drink.

"You guys work so hard." She looks up at me, her blue eyes sparkling with a kind-hearted smile. "You shouldn't work so late. Nobody can function with less than a solid eight hours' sleep."

"We'll be fine – we're used to it."

Zoe's smile fades and her Cupid's-bow lips thin. I'm not great at bonding with other women, but I can sense she's unhappy. A thought dawns on me – maybe I can set her up with Ethan and get him to lose the bet . . .

"How have you been, Zoe?" I ask as she places an order for an iced mocha latte. I don't know why I'm heading down this road. The words are tumbling out of my mouth, but while my competitive brain wants to win that bet, my heart is screaming "no". I tell it to shut up.

"Oh, I'm fine," she replies unconvincingly, tucking a stray tendril of shiny dark hair behind her ear. "Except for that awful business at the weekend, of course. I missed the party, but I'm pretty shaken up about Quentin and poor Carly. She's such a lovely girl – so warm and generous."

I manage to put a sympathetic smile on my face despite wondering if Zoe is certifiably insane. "Carly Hayes" and "lovely" aren't words I'd put in the same sentence – unless "is anything but" was squeezed in the middle.

"Things are pretty tense on our floor," Zoe continues as she pays for a sludgy brown drink packed with ice and chocolate chunks. "Malcolm has been battling all week to get our PR back on track, and Stella has been on his case constantly. His stress levels are through the roof. I don't know how you cope working under Stella – she terrifies me. Malcolm is a sweetie in comparison."

Malcolm Barrett is a "sweetie"? Again, Zoe Callaghan, are you certifiably insane?

"Sounds rough," I say with all the empathy of a lump of coal, before changing the subject so unskilfully I make myself cringe. "I was sad when you and Ethan broke up. I thought you two were great together."

She raises her eyebrows. "Were you sad?"

I'm confused by the unfriendliness in her tone and the way she's scrutinising my expression. I scan my memory to try to think of anything I've done in the past few weeks to upset her and draw a blank. "Well, yes, of course I was sad."

Her eyes narrow and I shift uncomfortably under her gaze. "I've been fine, thank you." she says, but a flame has been lit now, and I can't let it burn unchallenged. She leaves the shop with her drink, and I follow her into the street.

"You don't look or sound fine. What's up?"

She stops walking and ushers me towards the wall of a stone building housing an investment bank. "If you must know, Violet, my split from Ethan hit me hard, and I guess ... well, my feelings for him are unresolved. One minute my relationship was going well, the next minute I felt like the third wheel in his

108

relationship with you."

"What?" I say with a gasp of horror. This isn't the line Ethan spun me after their break-up. How didn't I pick up on any of this bad feeling? I know there were times Ethan cancelled dates because we were working late at the office together, but I always apologised to her when *our* time encroached on *their* time. "Zoe, I thought you were okay with our long hours. Why didn't you say something?"

"Oh, I did say something, to Ethan . . . often." A flash of guilt sweeps over her face. "I shouldn't have said anything to you, I'm sorry. It isn't your fault and it's all water under the bridge now."

"I didn't know. Ethan told me you were tired of his late-night jamming sessions with the lads, and he said his brother had urged him to end it . . ."

"I ended the relationship, not him," she says firmly. "It took me six months to work out that another woman would always come first with him."

I exhale heavily into the crisp spring air, as a busload of tourists hops off a sightseeing tour and heads into the Stock Exchange. "Okay . . . I don't know why, but Ethan didn't tell me any of this. If he had I would have—"

"You would have what?" she interrupts, her vowels clipped like a governess scolding her charge. Shit, she's Mary Poppins – yet probably more perfect. "You would have left BMG and found a job somewhere else? Because that's the only way we could have survived."

I feel my cheeks burn and my temper flare. "Zoe, what exactly are you accusing me of?"

She sucks in a breath. God, is this going to be the first time ever that Zoe Callaghan loses her cool? "I guess Ethan and I weren't meant to be. He didn't follow me when I walked away, and that told me to keep walking. Look, I don't work on the creative floor and I don't understand why you and Ethan are so tied to each other. I admit I was jealous. I wanted him to be tied to me."

Jealous? How was the prettiest, most popular girl at the agency jealous of me? I feel like shit. I can't think of anything to say to her, so I apologise again and start to walk back to the office.

"Are you in love with him?"

Her question stops me dead in my tracks, and I feel like I've been caught injecting poison into a basket of apples.

"No, I'm not."

But as I walk away, I can't help but wonder if I am.

10

WHEN I RETURN TO MY desk, still reeling from my conversation with Zoe, I see I have a new neighbour. Ethan and I sit opposite each other in a quiet corner of the fifteenth floor, facing out over Old Broad Street in the heart of the City. Will Thornton, Ethan's art director rival, sits next to him, but in the seat opposite Will, recently vacated by Mohammed, is a new figure. If Paul "Pinkie" Pinkerton has been installed as Will's new partner, this could either be a stroke of genius or the worst move since a bunch of turkeys voted for Christmas.

Pinkie is a walking, talking, living, breathing human incarnation of the Oxford English Dictionary combined with the Encyclopaedia Britannica. He is the only person at BMG who owns more books than I do. I've admired Pinkie ever since his extraordinary vocabulary placed him in the winner's seat on *Countdown*, but his social awkwardness makes him a sitting duck for practical jokes.

I give him two weeks.

"Wow, have you been promoted, Pinkie?" I pull out my chair and plonk my smoothie down on my desk.

Pinkie rises with difficulty, his ample bottom moulded to his seat, while his round belly strains against the buttons on his shirt. "Aye, thank you Violet, I have," he says, sticking out his hand for me to shake. Like me, Pinkie hails from Yorkshire, but his Leeds accent is much thicker.

"Congratulations, that's great news." I shake his

hand. His palms are hot and slippery, and the unnecessary handshake lasts far too long.

"Thank you. I'm technically experiencing a period of probation, but it is a fact that I am no longer a junior of the profession." We both sit down and he swivels his chair around to face me, his smile dimpling his round, rosy cheeks. "I know this could place us in competition over any headline campaigns Barrett McAllen Gray procures, but I want you to know that, as far as I'm concerned, you're the best copywriter in the agency. I'm looking forward to learning from you."

"Aw, thanks, Pinkie. That's really sweet," I say, smiling at his kindness. Pinkie definitely walks the oddball high-wire, but I've always found him to be a caring, decent guy. "I hope to learn from you too."

"He won't be staying!" Will barks.

Ethan starts to snigger.

"Now, William, it's only been half an hour," chirps Pinkie. "Wait until you read the copy I've written for Sunta Motors' Busan car launch. I have sixty-seven possible straplines for the print ad and I've already started drafting a script for the TV commercial."

"Doesn't matter. You're not staying. And don't call me fucking 'William', okay?" Will says in his chesty East London accent. "You're a nice guy, but you'd be better off with someone your own age. How the hell old are you anyway? Have you even started shaving yet?"

"Erm . . . I was late to puberty, but I'm twenty-five years old," Pinkie replies innocently. "I assure you I'm fully qualified for my new position."

"Your probationary position," corrects Will as Ethan sniggers again.

"Don't worry, Pinkie. Will is just bitter because he wanted to partner with Ruby Sloan." My comment

112

produces a smirk from Will.

Pinkie's dark eyebrows meet in a frown. "But Ruby is still on the graduate programme. She's three years younger than me."

"Ruby is qualified in *different* ways," Ethan says in a tone everyone but Pinkie picks up on. His frowning eyebrows have now merged into one spectacularly confused uni-brow.

"I don't understand. Ruby has a 2:1 in business marketing from Newcastle, which is an okay university, but I have a first class bachelor's degree in modern world history and a masters' distinction in business communications from Oxford. I think a case can easily be made that I am more qualified."

"Ethan's talking about tits," says Will wearily. Will is one of the most open-minded, opinionated and creative people I know, but he's saddled with the patience of a toddler and a persecution complex so big it could choke a horse.

"Oh, I see." Pinkie's round cheeks flush with embarrassment.

"Pinkie, it's early days, but you'll soon learn that Ethan and Will may look like grown men, but their brains stopped developing when they were fourteen. Sadly, they're far more interested in the contents of a woman's bra than they are in her personality or mind."

"On balance, I'm more interested in the contents of a woman's knickers," says Will, who remains the most impossible man on the planet to guilt-trip.

"That's gross, Will," I snap. There's a fine line between office banter and being a sexist pig. Will walks that fine line like a tightrope walker without a safety net.

"You know I'm gross," he says, completely

undeterred. "And don't worry, Pinkie. This isn't your fault. I knew the agency would be showering a pile of shit onto my shoulders the second Mohammed resigned. Stella has had it in for me ever since she stumbled upon my Twitter account on the day I retweeted that Jim Davidson joke."

"You deserved the roasting you got for that," I say, recalling Stella's threat to send Will on equality awareness training for a week unless he ceased being a misogynistic prick. "And I already told you that after the knickers incident there was no way in hell I was letting you have Ruby."

Will twists his face into a sulky pout, before changing the subject entirely. "Hey, speaking of the knickers incident, have you seen the state of Max this morning? He looks like he hasn't slept for a year, and I wouldn't be surprised if he's high."

Ethan's head shoots up and we share a worried glance. "No, I haven't seen him," I say, but my stomach is already churning with worry.

Will stands and starts bundling a pile of papers into a folder. "I'll go check on him. We need to visit the design studio anyway. Are you coming with me, hotshot?" he asks his new partner.

Pinkie springs to his feet so quickly that his plump stomach bangs against his keyboard. "Does this mean you like my copy?"

"How could it? I haven't seen it yet." Will rolls his eyes. "Run your fifty-nine awesome straplines by me in the studio. We can ask Max what he thinks too."

"It was sixty-seven, but now it's seventy-three," replies Pinkie eagerly. "And just one more thing, what was the knickers incident?"

"Shut up and never mention it again," Will barks as

he leads the way to the design studio. Pinkie trots behind him like a portly spring lamb.

"Oh my god, this is going to be hilarious." I finish the last of my smoothie, the peppery green liquid cooling my throat and tingling my tongue.

"Sure is," Ethan replies, but I sense there's something up. He would usually have a lot more to say about a scenario with this much comedic value.

"You're quiet."

"Hmm? Oh, I've just got a surprise text from Zoe and now my head's in a bit of a strange place."

I feel a rush of panic in my gut. "What does she say?"

"She wants to meet up tonight. She says she wants "resolution". What the hell is that supposed to mean?"

I clear my throat nervously. I know this is down to me and the stupid conversation I struck up with her. I wish I hadn't meddled now. When we added the betting element to our no-shag pact yesterday, I didn't think I'd feel so strange about the possibility of a win that could only occur if Ethan slept with one of our colleagues or clients.

I also didn't think Zoe would be so quick off the starting blocks.

"What are you going to do?" I ask him.

"I'm going to meet her. I mean, I can't really say no, can I?" he asks, his brain clearly ticking away as he reads and re-reads the message on his iPhone. I chew on my lip just as Ethan looks up at me. "Wait a minute, is this down to you?"

I shrug. "I bumped into Zoe at Juicy Lucy's earlier. We had a bit of a chat."

He groans, then he gets up and walks over to me, perching on the end of my desk. "I applaud your

115

Machiavellian skills of manipulation, but you're not going to beat me this early in the game. Zoe's a nice girl, but I never pray at the same temple twice."

"Temple? Really?"

"Yes, and don't question my adjectives."

"Metaphors."

"Whatever. How did you get her to do this?"

I stop flicking through the open windows on my screen and turn to face him. "As much as I'd love to take full credit, we just started talking and—"

"About me?" His smile begins to fade. "What did she say?"

Where do I start? Probably best to totally skip the part where she admitted being jealous of me and then asked me if I was in love with him. "I know you didn't tell me the truth about your break-up."

His eyebrows dip and he turns to gaze out of the office window. "She told you how we broke up?"

"She told me why she ended things with you, yes. Why didn't you tell me how she felt about us?"

Ethan nods his head in resignation, but he doesn't look at me. His eyes turn their attention from the city skyline to his shoes. "Zoe didn't understand us. Our closeness hurt her."

His regretful tone makes me draw in a shaky breath. He turns to face me and our eyes lock for a moment. Instinctively, I reach for my silver pendant and twirl it between my fingers.

"I'd never let anyone come between us," he says, and my entire body cries out in response, a warm heat surging into my belly. "We're best mates, right?"

He gives me a friendly bump to my shoulder before sitting back down at his desk. I dip behind our cubicle wall to hide as my mind starts to race. What the fuck just happened there? He managed to turn it around at the last minute with the "best mates" comment, but I'm not an idiot. I know that conversation was layered with meaning. What was he trying to tell me? Could it be . . . ?

No.

No, it couldn't.

Jesus, Violet don't even go there.

***

The four of us work at our desks until 7 p.m., when Ethan leaves for his get-together with Zoe. Will heads off for his weekly pool game at the same time. That leaves me and my new neighbour, Pinkie, who spends the next hour and a half bombarding me with information I have never had any reason to Google in my twenty-eight years of life. By eight thirty, I know all about the gestation of an orca, the French Salic law of royal heredity, and how many characters in Harry Potter have alliterative names. Useful, eh?

Pinkie finally heads home to feed his cat, and when I power down my computer at 9 p.m. I'm very much aware of how late it is, how famished I am and that I'm the last person on the floor. I gather up my scarf and cardigan and head for the lifts. I'm still straightening the folds of my scarf when I hear a familiar ping followed by the swish of the lift doors opening. I put one foot in front of the other and almost walk straight into Ridley Gates.

"Excuse me," I say as I move to one side. He looks at me like I'm dog shit, and a rush of annoyance surges through me. "What the hell's your problem?" I blurt out, then instantly wish I hadn't. Ridley might be a slimy dickhead, but he's also an executive director and head of department.

He spins around to face me, his heels clicking on the tiled floor. His hair is slicked back into its normal greasy style. He shoots me one of those up-and-down, who-do-you-think-you're-talking-to looks, but says nothing.

I walk into the lift, muttering "Fucking wanker" under my breath, but as soon as the doors close I realise I've forgotten my bag. Shit and bollocks. I press the button to reopen the doors and I make my way back to my desk.

On my return journey I'm drawn towards raised voices inside Diego's vacant office. I hover outside the door for a moment.

Have you ever heard the saying that nothing good was ever learned from eavesdropping? Yeah, well I've always disputed that. I know it's wrong and I know I'm nosy, but I can't help myself if there's a chance of overhearing something juicy.

"Don't you dare bring that into this. I've known you since you were a kid, Ridley, but this? This is a step too far and you know it," says Malcolm Barrett's authoritative, yet weasel-like, voice.

Ridley bites back. "You owe me, Malcolm. I've kept quiet for you, so now I need you to do this for me. I'm calling in my chit."

"I've already paid you your dues more than once," Malcolm says.

"Yeah, yeah, you have my undying gratitude."

"All I ever asked from you was loyalty, Ridley. But this isn't loyalty. Blackmailing me every time you want something – that's not loyalty. Carly was your bit on the side. You were with her when she almost died, and you did nothing. I'm not giving you a fake alibi while that girl's lying in a hospital bed fighting for her life. Have you thought about what happens if she doesn't wake up?"

"Yeah, that's why I need the alibi."

"I'm not lying to the police for you, Ridley. I'm not living like this anymore."

I'm so shocked that I stagger backwards, hitting the outside of the office wall. My heart bangs inside my chest when the heel of my left shoe clatters against the skirting board. Why? Why did I have to be so nosy? And why the hell do I have to be so bloody noisy?

I move my feet as quietly as I can over the thin carpet, walking over the softer edge and avoiding the grey-blue centre, which is thin and well worn through years of footfall. I look over my shoulder as I pick up pace. What should I do? If I were braver I'd turn back and confront them both. I open the door to the lobby and look behind me one last time.

And then the bottom falls out of my world.

Ridley Gates is standing in the middle of the corridor. His arms are folded and he's staring straight at me. I shudder as I feel the walls close in around me, and I can't move. I stare back at him until he walks away.

11

I WATCH RIDLEY WALK OFF, but for some stupid reason my feet are carrying me back to the scene.

I guess I'll decide to ask myself why I'm doing this after I've done it.

I duck my head around the open doorway to Diego's office. Malcolm is sitting at the desk with his head resting on his hand, flicking through a bundle of files. I knock lightly, then enter.

"What did you hear?" he says without lifting his head.

I stare at him for a few moments, my stomach flipping over until I need to inhale sharply to settle it back down into position. "I heard everything. What has Ridley got on you?"

He runs his tongue along the edge of his moustache and then looks up into my eyes. "You know, Violet, I saw something special in you right from the start. For three years I've championed you. I like you – you're switched on, you're talented and you've got great potential." He looks away again and starts clearing up the desk. "Just tell me what you want."

"What I want? What do you mean?"

He raises his eyebrows. "Don't tell me you don't want something? I would distrust you if you said you didn't. So name it? Money, a promotion, my firstborn child?"

"No, what . . . ? Malcolm, what do you take me for?" I take a step back. I wonder what on earth is running through his mind. Is he so used to being blackmailed?

"And your firstborn child is older than I am, for Christ's sake."

A faint smile tweaks the edges of his silver moustache, but his eyes remain filled with sadness.

"Why is he doing this to you, Malcolm? Just tell me." I take a seat opposite him.

He closes the files and stretches an elastic band around them. "It's about money. I took some money."

"You took money?" My heart sinks. Do I want to know any more? "Who from?"

"From the agency." He looks at his hands, then locks his fingers together and bows his head. "Emily's cancer returned. I needed money fast for experimental treatment. All my funds were tied up in property, and the investments I've made over the years haven't worked out. Neither the NHS nor my private insurance would fund what we needed. I wanted the best for her." He raises his head and looks me straight in the eye. "None of us thought she'd beat it a second time, but she did, so I'm not sorry. I'm halfway clear to paying the money back."

I flop backwards in the chair, my heart breaking. Malcolm and Emily have been married for over forty years. I don't blame him for doing everything he could to save her, but stealing? "Why don't you just come clean, Malcolm? Surely it would be better than this."

"Because I don't want to go to prison, and I don't want Emily to find out," he says quietly.

I nod my head, trying to imagine myself faced with the prospect of losing someone I loved. "I won't say a word."

"Thank you Violet," he says sincerely. "I trust you, and whatever you want in your career, just tell me and I'll make sure—"

121

"No! Malcolm, seriously . . ." I lean forward on the desk and take a moment to gather my thoughts. "I don't want anything from you, and I promise I won't say a word about the money, but . . . okay . . . Ridley and Carly – that's a whole different ball game."

Malcolm's skin greys. "No, you can't say anything about that either. If Ridley's wife found out about him and Carly, he'd turn on me even harder. Please, Violet. You can't."

My heart feels like it's being torn in two. Malcolm is clearly desperate, but Ethan and Max need to know the truth and I want to tell them. My thoughts fight against each other, but the fear in Malcolm's eyes chills me to the bone and seals the deal. "Okay, I promise I won't say a word about any of it. Not to anybody."

He thanks me and I stumble out of the office in a daze.

I have always hated Ridley Gates, but now I know what he's been doing to Malcolm, I have an overwhelming urge to ram his head through a brick wall and make him eat a wasp sandwich.

***

The streets are dark and empty when I leave the building and head for Bank Tube station. As I change to the Bakerloo line at Oxford Circus, on autopilot, the sound of trains rattling through the tunnels jangles inside my head. I decide I need my friend.

I pull out my phone to call Ethan, but then I remember he's meeting Zoe tonight. This makes me feel even worse. Are they technically on a date? Will I turn up to work tomorrow and find out they're back together? My stomach twists itself into a knot, making it clear that these feelings I've been having for the past few days aren't going to go away unless I confront them . . . head-on.

I put my phone back in my bag and go home.

***

I glance at my clock for the twentieth time and see that the number three is flanked by a hideously menacing forty-four. Shit, this is bad. It's nearly 4 a.m. – the point of no return, the time when I may as well give up, get up and go to work early. I'm still wide awake. I tell myself my body will survive if I miss one night of sleep, as long as I catch up tomorrow.

Why did I have to do it? Just fucking why? I always do shit like this. I'm a chaos-and-crap magnet. Just look at the last few days: despite my brilliance with words, I couldn't produce a plausible excuse to miss the AdAg Awards and I had the worst night of my entire life as a result. And now? Now my gigantic nose has landed me in a pile of steaming shit so colossal that I'm going to need a bulldozer and an industrial excavator to get myself out of it.

Why couldn't I have just got my bag and gone home? My heart is telling me to ring Ethan at stupid o'clock and tell him everything I know, but I can't. Aside from the fact he's probably sharing his bed with Zoe Callaghan, I need to speak to Malcolm again first. I want to help him get out of this. Maybe if we put our heads together we can think of a way to fix it. I wish I could think of something . . . anything . . . but as my brain whirrs and my stomach churns, I can't forget my promise to Ethan. I told him I wouldn't keep anything from him ever again, so why aren't I picking up my blasted phone and telling him everything I know?

I want to kill myself.

Not violently kill myself.

I couldn't throw myself off a bridge onto a motorway, but if someone offered to suffocate me in my sleep, I might be tempted.

I turn over, close my eyes for the five hundredth time and start counting wildebeest. It's so much easier than counting sheep because they move faster, but occasionally you have to let a lion catch one for reasons of authenticity. It may be bloody, but I swear it totally works.

***

I hit the snooze button on my alarm clock fourteen times, from 5 a.m. to 6.10 a.m. I've had two hours of sleep and an hour of dozing. I feel like shit. My head is begging for more sleep, my eyes feel like they've been forced open by a medieval instrument of torture, and my common sense has disconnected from my brain, meaning I'm thinking of calling in sick. I drag my zombified carcass into the shower instead. A blast of hot water and some minty shower gel might bring me back to life.

It's 8.35 a.m. when I arrive at work, step into the lift and get a Facebook message from Daniel Noble.

Glad you came around. I'll pick you up at your place at 7.30. Looking forward to it.

Shit. What the actual hell have I done and when did I do it? Did I sleep-mail Daniel Noble? I scroll upwards and find another message apparently from me, except it isn't:

Hi Daniel, I've been thinking about your proposition. All of this business with Quest is really taking its toll and I need to let my hair down. What do you say to dinner tonight?

Two things:

I really need to change my Facebook password.

I really need to kick Ethan Fraser's head in.

I take a deep breath as the lift takes me to the executive floor. The soft hum of the cold metal box sets my teeth on edge. I make the exact same journey every day, yet today is different because my stomach has climbed so far into my mouth it's threatening to get wedged in my throat.

When the lift doors open, my whole body is shaking. The noise from the offices is louder than normal. Hushed conversations sound like yelling; footsteps against the soft carpet sound like galloping horses' hooves at the Grand National.

My heart pounds as I approach Malcolm's office and see Zoe sitting at her desk outside. I don't know whether it's pounding because I'm worried about Malcolm or because I don't want to see evidence that Zoe got laid last night. I check her over as I approach: make-up immaculate, clothing different to yesterday, and no post-sex bed hair. Phew!

"Wow, Violet, you look wrecked. Are you okay?"

I rub at my cheeks to wake my face up. "I didn't get much sleep last night – worked late."

"Here, drink this." She passes me a bottle of mineral water.

I thank her and take a drink. The cool liquid does little to soothe my nerves, but at least it eases my stomach back into position and I no longer feel like I'm going to choke.

"What can I do for you? Is it Quest-related? I'm not sure if Malcolm can take any more bad news."

"I need a private word with him. Is he in?"

Zoe shakes her head, and I'm instantly relieved. "He's in a meeting with the board right now, then he has a meeting scheduled at Quest's head office at ten thirty, then he has a finance meeting pencilled in with Karen Mark, but he'll probably rearrange that. He hates finance meetings and you know what Karen is like."

I nod in recognition. Karen Mark, our always-serious head of finance, protects her budgets like a fire-breathing dragon. I don't think I've ever heard her laugh.

"Okay, can you let me know the second he's back in the office? It's quite important."

"Of course," replies Zoe with a smile. "Hey, have you heard the good news? Carly is out of danger. They say she's going to make a full recovery."

"Oh, that's brilliant news," I say, and then immediately ask myself if I mean it. Yeah ... I do mean it! Hoorah, I'm not a sociopath.

"Ruby and I bought a get-well-soon card for her on behalf of everyone. Will you sign it?"

Jesus, no. Carly hates me. And yet the rules of etiquette and not being a sociopath compel me to write "*Glad you're on the mend, V x*" inside the card. Genius! My greeting could be attributed to Victor in CGI, Vinnie in payroll or Vanessa in accounts.

I'm just about to make my way to the stairwell when Ridley Gates's secretary, Lucille, calls me over.

Lucille's eyes slowly rise above her glasses as I approach her desk opposite her boss's corner office.

126

"Mr Gates says he wants to see you." Despite living in London for most of her life, Lucille still has an unmistakeable Caribbean accent which evokes happy images of rum cocktails and calypso music. Her voice is like sunshine and I love talking to her. "He's been in a foul mood since he got in this morning, so don't be expecting no manners from him."

I feel sick. I don't usually give a damn about confronting people – particularly when I'm in the right – but what can I do? I'd rather drink bleach than have to speak to him. "Do you know what he wants?" I ask, forcing my voice to stay strong.

Lucille looks at me with eyes that don't miss a thing. She pushes her glasses up onto her nose and cocks her head towards her boss's door. "Best get yourself inside and find out, but word of advice: watch how you go."

I hesitate for a moment. I look back at Lucille, but she's picked up the phone to make a call. I consider turning back, but why should I? The moral high ground belongs to me. I take a deep breath, and into the lion's den I go.

Ridley is at his desk when I enter his office and close the door behind me. He looks up from his computer briefly, then returns his gaze to the screen, an insincere smile tugging at his mouth. "Miss Archer, I'm assuming you know why I want a quiet word."

I don't reply. I don't know what to say. Damn, I needed to see Malcolm again first. How much does Ridley know that I know?

He leans casually back in his chair. He isn't worried. There is no anxiousness in his expression at all. He grins, and I notice how white his teeth are. He looks like a poster boy for a toothpaste ad. "I can see you're hesitating, so let me help you out. Obviously you know my relationship with Carly was more than what you walked in on at the party. If you want the gory details, here they are. Yeah, I was seeing her; no, it wasn't serious; and no, my wife doesn't know. Being married to Delfina is like owning a beautiful vase – she's great to look at, but sadly she's hollow inside. I told you before that I like smart women. Trying to have an intelligent conversation with Delfina is as futile as polishing a turd."

Urgh, he's vile. *The only turd in this room is you*, I think but don't dare say out loud.

Ridley gets up from his chair and walks towards me. I instinctively take a step backwards. He has always made my flesh crawl, but feeling like I want to flay my skin from my body is a whole new reaction. I discreetly scratch my arm. "I'm not worried that you know I was with Carly when she got into trouble. I know you won't say anything. Do you want to know how I know?"

I force out a short laugh, but my insides are churning. "I'm sure you're going to tell me."

"If you open your mouth to anybody, I promise I'll take Malcolm and his entire family down with me. And then I'll come after you."

The cold determination in his tone sends a shiver down my spine, but I force myself to look unconcerned. "What makes you think I care what happens to Malcolm?"

He shrugs, and his grin widens. Ridley's eyes are the same shade of light blue as Ethan's. I wonder what it is that makes Ridley's gaze so much colder. "I know you care. Despite what everyone around here says, you're not a cold, heartless bitch."

His words cut into me. People really say that about me? "You're right. I'm not heartless or cold, but you are."

"Yes, I am, but what can I say? They're both attributes that serve me well."

"Don't you care about Carly? You were seeing her and—"

"Correction, I was fucking her." I swallow my revulsion as a wave of nausea hits me. He laughs again. "Look, there was nothing I could have done. It was just bad luck. We had a heavy night – sex, drugs, drink . . . more sex. We both know what Carly is. I've seen the way you look down on her. You think she's a cheap slut and I'm not disagreeing with you on that assessment. I know she screwed Fraser that night too."

"This has nothing to do with me or Ethan," I say in disgust, recoiling at the way he's looking at me – his eyes scanning my body as I stand before him trying to keep it together. "But as for Malcolm, you have something on him. He has something on you. So, it's time to call it a day."

"Malcolm?" Ridley's sunbed-tanned skin creases as a frown creeps across his face. Ridley must be approaching fifty and the cracks are beginning to show. "Ah, I see what's happening. He's told you everything, hasn't he? He's told you about our arrangement."

"He told me you're blackmailing him."

For the first time I see Ridley's demeanour falter, but his composure quickly returns. He dips his head and grins as if this is the best fun he's had in years. "So Malcolm told you he stole thousands of pounds from the agency and you're fine with that? What the hell is this? Love a crook day?"

"It wasn't like that. His wife was seriously ill." I think about Ridley's wife and I don't know how he can't empathise. "Haven't you ever loved someone that much?"

His leathery brow crinkles as he raises his eyebrows, his slicked-back hair gleaming under the office lights. "Aside from myself? No, probably not," he says with a sneer. He moves closer and I step backwards until my back hits a filing cabinet and I can go no further. "Look, I don't want you thinking I'm a complete bastard, so I'll cut you a deal. I can think of a compelling incentive for me to back off Malcolm Barrett."

"An incentive?" He's standing so close to me I can feel his breath on my face. My nausea intensifies. "What do you mean?"

"Well, now that Carly is incapacitated, I have an opening. How do you feel about filling her position?"

My stomach turns over. *Focus, Violet. Do not let him get to you.* "I say go to hell."

He raises his hand and caresses my face. I shove him backwards, but he just laughs at me. "Now, now. Play nicely and hear me out. I'll be honest here – I like you. I've always liked you. You've got balls, you've got class, and you look pretty good too."

He runs his hand over my arm until I jerk it away. "Keep your hands off me."

"Sleep with me."

"What?" My pulse is ringing in my ears and I want to bolt for the door. Is he for real, or is he just trying to break me? "Why the hell would I do that?"

"Just think about it . . . Malcolm's worries gone forever, just for one amazing fuck. I'll even make sure you enjoy it. In fact, once you've had me, you'll probably want to make it a regular thing – just like Carly."

Bile rises into my throat and burns as I swallow it

back down. I take a deep, if shaky, breath and look him square in the eye. "I'd rather set myself on fire."

He laughs coldly. I have no idea if he's being serious, or if this is just a sick, twisted game, but I'm not sticking around to find out. I make my bid for freedom, shoving him out of the way and scrambling for the door. I all but run out of his office. Lucille calls after me, but I can't decipher her words. All I can hear is the rich tone of her voice as it rises above the noise of blood pounding in my ears.

And god, I feel sick. Not drunk-sick, or ill-sick, but a horrible mix of fear-disgust-rage-sick.

I clatter through the doors of the nearest toilets, where I find a cubicle, fall to my knees and throw up.

12

I HATE VOMITING.

Thankfully, it doesn't happen too often. I haven't had a stomach bug for years and I try to go easy on the drink, so spewing my guts up is a rare event.

I must have been in the executive-floor toilets for ages, and I don't feel like leaving any time soon. I tried to front it out with Ridley earlier, but right now I'm anything but the badass I thought I was. I wanted him to see I wasn't afraid of him. I told myself his threats meant nothing. So why does my stomach feel like it's going to hurl itself out of my mouth every time I think about him? Why does my skin crawl when I see his slimy-slimeball face in my mind?

And I know I still need to face Malcolm.

And I'm still pissed off that I can't tell Ethan.

And I still feel like shit.

And my arse has gone to sleep.

I carefully get up off the hard toilet seat and go to the sinks, splashing lukewarm water into my mouth to try and wash away the taste of puke. It doesn't work. I still have the coarse aftertaste from my semi-digested bran flakes in my mouth. I don't even know how long I've been in here. It seems like hours, but my watch says it's only 10 a.m. so it's probably been closer to twenty minutes. Is it too early for Häagen-Dazs? The Tesco Express around the corner stocks strawberry cheesecake, and I feel like I could eat a whole tub in one sitting.

When I arrive at my desk I see Ethan has made it

into the office, dragging with him an exhausted face which mirrors my own.

"You look like hell," I say.

"So says an extra from *The Walking Dead*," he replies, rubbing his eyes and letting out a gigantic yawn.

I sit down and switch on my computer. Will and Pinkie aren't at their desks, which is good. The last thing I need this morning is those two bickering away like a budget reboot of a Laurel and Hardy movie. "Before the day begins, I need to remind you how lucky you are that my knee hasn't made contact with the collection of objects in your pants yet."

He breaks out into laughter. "Whatever do you mean?"

"Daniel is what I mean. It appears he's taking me to dinner tonight."

"Just getting you back."

He yawns again and I brace myself for news I don't want to hear. "Good night, then?"

He shoots me a glare. "Don't get too excited. You haven't won your bet. Zoe and I talked and we had a nice evening, but I was done by ten."

"Really?" I ask with genuine disbelief. "Ten o'clock? I don't believe you."

"Would I lie to you?"

"Based exclusively on the three years I've known you? Yes, you absolutely would."

"Look, I'm sorry I lied about why I broke up with Zoe." He scans the room, making sure we're still alone before continuing. "I didn't want you to know that she made our break-up all about you because it was unfair of her. You did nothing wrong."

A wave of relief washes over me. I'm not entirely

sure why, but I sense it would be harder to navigate my newfound terrifyingly confusing feelings for Ethan if he and Zoe had become an item again. He winces and rubs his forehead. "After I left Zoe last night, I called Max. We went out and . . . well, we had a bit of a mad night."

"Oh no. How mad?"

"Well Max hasn't turned up for work yet, and I have the worst hangover of my life."

"Oh shit, I'm worried about Max. He isn't coping. Does he have a new phone yet? Zoe told me this morning that Carly is on the mend. We need to let him know."

"She's out of the coma?" Ethan asks, his eyes bright with hope. I nod. "Thank heavens for that. No, Max doesn't have a replacement phone. I'll DM him on Twitter."

I'm relieved for a moment. Then I see Ridley Gates's face in my mind. I hear his threats, smell his breath, feel him touching me . . . I grab a plastic cup that's half full of warm water from yesterday and take a sip.

"Shit, Vi, you look like death warmed up," Ethan says.

"I'm just tired. I'll be fine once I wake up." I swallow another mouthful of water, willing myself not to be sick again, although I'm sure I've nothing left in my stomach to bring up. "So, did you enjoy your night with Max?"

"Suffice it to say, going clubbing with him is comparable to hell on earth. I can't get my head around that scene, Vi. The music is horrendous. It goes right through you and every track sounds the bloody same – thud, thud, thud, thud, thud, thud. Jesus Christ, if I ever have to listen to that shit Euro dance-y trance-y music

134

again I'll drive a chainsaw through my skull. It's absolute torture. And that's before we start on the drugs. Every single person there was high as a kite."

I'm only half listening to him. I'm exhausted, grossed out, worried sick and suffering from post-vomiting dehydration. All I can hear is noise that I can't tune out – including the "thud, thud, thud" he's put in my mind. I flop down into my chair and rest my head on my desk.

"Are you okay?"

I don't look up. "Yeah. I wish I was dead, but other than that I'm okay."

"Right, well you don't have time to kill yourself now. We have a meeting with Stuart Inman at ten fifteen."

"What? No, we don't. No way in hell am I having a meeting with him this morning."

Ethan stares briefly at me as if I've lost my mind, then he shrugs. "Daniel signed off on our Quest TV commercial, but we need to present it to Stuart first. I know you're still pissed with him, but I've got your back. You'll be fine."

"I don't want to see him. Why do I have to?"

"Because he's the client and it's his money we're spending? What do you suggest I tell him?"

"Tell him I don't want to see him. Tell him to fuck off!"

Ethan's eyes pop. "Vi, this isn't like you. You can handle Stuart Inman. Your balls are ten times as big as his."

I raise my eyebrows. The last thing I want to be reminded about is the size of Stuart's man-parts.

"Sorry, I misjudged that," he says quickly. "Come on, this is work. Stella's put him back in his box

135

already."

"It isn't just him . . ." I open my mouth and almost spill the Ridley-beans, but as if from nowhere my brain-to-mouth filter springs into life and stops me. "He's just a dick," I say instead.

"Yeah, I know he's a dick, but he's also just walked onto the floor so shush."

I turn around just in time to see Stuart stride across the room like a man who doesn't want the world to know he has an infinitesimally small penis. Ethan beckons him into Diego's vacant office.

I follow them and take a seat. Ethan hands both of us a spiral-bound copy of his TV commercial pitch and talks us through it with much exuberance. Stuart listens intently, but I feel his eyes watching me the whole time. My skin boils. I blow a breath onto my face out of the corner of my mouth, cooling the beads of anger-sweat on my forehead. My arms, my eyes, my shoulders are on fire, and I wonder if I'd be forgiven for taking my Ridley-rage out on Stuart by stapling his head to the desk.

"Okay, great, I'm sure this will work. How many models will you need? What agency are you using?" Stuart asks as he thumbs through the costings in Ethan's proposal.

"We'd only need to hire two or three for a couple of days. I'll give Lucinda at Siren a call and see who she can get for us. Obviously, we have our own TV production team – one producer and a crew of four," says Ethan.

"Great. Our CEO will have to rubber-stamp it, but I don't see any issues. We're looking for something more adventurous this season – something that sets us apart from our competitors – I think the Lake District location will be ideal. The USP on this is originality, so stay away from cost and quality in the copy, Violet. Focus on the unique. I think it could be a good time to change the 'Quest for Life' hashtag to maybe . . . 'Quest for Adventure' or 'Quest for Freedom' across all media. 'Quest for Life' has had its day."

I feel like he's just killed one of my children.

"I can't believe you're suggesting we modify a hashtag that already has consumer presence and is almost a brand itself. Quest for Life features on every single one of your current ads, not to mention social media outlets, your website, a clothing range and even a pair of bloody bendy buses!" Stuart scowls at me and I can see he's biting his tongue. Ethan clears his throat nervously, and I wonder if I've gone too far. But, Jesus, do I care? In my war against all men, this guy is the idiot who started the ball rolling. He shot Franz Ferdinand and invaded Poland all in one weekend, so I'm not scared to tell him what I think of his shitty idea.

"Okay, let's just see what you both come up with," Stuart replies, a smug smirk plastered across his lying, cheating piece-of-shit face.

"Well, I can tell you right now we won't be coming up with that," I bite back.

"Um . . . we'll look at all the possibilities," says Ethan, clearly in appeaser mode.

Stuart rises from the chair, straightens his suit and bundles up his paperwork. His gaze flits to me as he chews the inside of his cheek. My narrowed eyes and clenched teeth challenge him to dare open his mouth.

"I'm truly sorry about our misunderstanding, Violet," he says.

"Which misunderstanding was that? Blaming me for your lacklustre bedroom skills, using me to cheat on your fiancée, or trying to get me fired?"

A nerve at the base of Stuart's chiselled cheekbones starts to pulse and an angry red vein bulges in his neck. "The bedroom skills are debatable," he says in a hushed, embarrassed tone.

"Debatable or not, none of it was *my* fault, and pulling me off your campaign was a dick move."

"I did that because you threw a drink over me. It was unprofessional."

"You deserved more than a drink on your head, Stuart."

"I'm trying to apologise, Violet. Adele and I have broken up for good. We were all but over last week, so I wasn't really cheating. I like you. I . . . um . . . I'd like to make things up to you . . . Maybe we could talk later?" He glances over at Ethan, who clears his throat and makes a should-I-leave-the-room hand signal. I shoot him a don't-you-even-fucking-think-about-it glare.

"We have nothing to talk about, Stuart. Don't kid yourself that you weren't cheating on your fiancée last week, because you were. How low would my self-esteem have to get, and how desperate would I have to be, to get into a relationship with a known cheater? If you were the last man on earth I'd demand a recount. Oh, and one last thing, your marketing plan for Quest Living is crap. You're going to destroy your brand if you go to another agency."

Stuart stares at me for a moment. My heart thuds in my chest as I wait for him to speak, but a deathly silence fills the office. His face is fully charged with tension, but he says nothing, gathers up his things and walks out of the room.

The second he's gone, Ethan spins around and lets

me have it. "What the hell was that?"

"What was what? Are you serious?"

"Yes, I'm serious," he says, his eyes wide. "Look, I know you're pissed at Stuart, but you've just blown any chance we had of keeping Quest, and I'd really like it if you considered my career once in a while."

A pang of betrayal settles into my gut. "You said you'd have my back," I say, my voice breaking.

"I do have your back, I'll always have your back, but when you're out of line I'm going to tell you. This isn't how we work. How many clueless clients have we had over the years? How many rubbish briefs have account directors passed us? You know what we do – we listen, we nod our heads, then we do our magic and convince everyone we know best." He stands and starts pacing the room. He's furious, and my stomach sinks. Deep down, I know I've overstepped the mark, but my head is in a mess and all I want is to close my eyes and have it all go away.

"It's like you said. I was just trying to convince Stuart that changing the hashtag was a bad idea," I say, trying in vain to defend myself.

"No you bloody weren't," he yells. "You more or less told him he was a fucking idiot!"

"Well, he is a fucking idiot!" I scream back.

"Alright, his idea was shit, but so what? Anyone can have a stupid idea from time to time – well, everyone except you, that is."

My hands go to my hips. "What the hell is that supposed to mean?"

"It means this isn't the first time you've done this and we're gaining a reputation for it. Remember Edward Asquith's client brief for that garden centre chain?"

"I remember Edward Asquith taking it upon himself to pitch a TV character called Harry Cox, if that's what you're referring to." I groan as I recall the innuendo. "You know as well as I do that all anyone watching that ad would have heard was 'hairy cock'. It was worse than offensive."

"Edward still won't work with us, Vi. We've lost some great opportunities because of your outburst over that. Why couldn't you have just let it go with Stuart?"

"I just . . . don't like him . . . He . . ." Tears well in my eyes and I hope with everything I have that Ethan doesn't notice, but I see panic of the *shit, a woman is crying, what do I do?* variety sweep across his face.

"Is this about Ryan?"

"What . . . why? How could you even ask me that?"

He gulps audibly. "Um . . . Never mind—"

"No, don't you dare backtrack. You said that for a reason. Why?"

His angry-face melts away. "Okay, I'm saying this because I'm your friend and I care about you. I only know what you've told me about Ryan, which isn't very much, but all those years ago you had a relationship with a married man . . ."

I give up all hope of stopping my tears from falling. "I can't believe you're bringing this up. You think I've got no right to complain about what Stuart did because of Ryan?"

"No, that's not what I'm saying at all. I'm just wondering if that experience has made you more sensitive about this one."

I sniff back what's left of my tears. "I hadn't even thought about Ryan, but thanks for dredging up my past and using it against me. You're a great friend."

"Vi, that's bullshit and you know it." His eyes fix on

mine and I know he's being honest. "I'm just trying to understand what's made you throw a hand grenade at the bridge we've spent all week trying to rebuild."

"I guess some of us would rather swim across the river than cross a bridge owned by a total bastard!"

"Can you two keep the noise down?" Will thunders into the room. "The entire floor can hear you hollering at each other." He stops dead and looks at me before scowling at Ethan. "Has he upset you?"

"Just a difference of opinion, Will," I say as I wipe the wetness from my cheeks. I curse myself for crumbling. I never cry.

"Okay, well let me know if you're looking for a new partner, because Pinkie-Winkie has just insulted the living shit out of Jae-kwang from Sunta. He straight up asked him if he missed eating dog now he lives in London."

"Oh my god, he didn't."

"He bloody did," says Will. "Jae-kwang has lived here for seventeen years. What did I do to earn getting saddled with that Yorkshire pudding? He has the social awareness of a fucking potato. Anyway, that's not why I'm here. Max hasn't turned up for work and nobody can trace him. Ethan, I've called your brother, and I've called his idiot friend Marek. Nobody has seen him and Stella is on the warpath."

"Has anybody been to his flat?" asks Ethan.

"Your Rory said he was going to head over now, but he has to be at work by six."

"Okay, I'll chase Rory up, see if he's had any luck." Ethan gives me a friendly smile as he leaves the office. I try to return it, but I'm not sure I manage.

***

We spend the afternoon and into the early evening making arrangements for next week's shoot. At 6 p.m. Ethan's brother phones to say he's had to give up his search for Max and go to work at the bar.

"Did you message Max earlier about Carly?" I ask.

"Yes, but he hasn't responded." Ethan picks up his iPhone and flicks through to his notifications. Then he stands up so quickly he sends his desk chair flying backwards on its wheels.

"What is it?" My pulse starts to race and I hope with everything I have it isn't bad news.

"I contacted a couple of Max's bonkers Euro mates. Remember that dickhead Dieter who bummed a stay on his sofa for weeks on end last year? He's just texted to say he saw Max heading into Tanzen."

"Oh, thank god."

Ethan stands over his desk and starts to gather his things. "Looks like I'm going to spend yet another evening in that hellhole of a nightclub." He shuts down his system and turns to face me. His smile is encouraging, but I can sense he's anxious. "Don't worry. I'll find him."

"I'm coming with you."

"No, it's fine."

"Are you still angry with me?"

He pauses, tipping his head to one side and giving me a lopsided smile. "I shouldn't have said what I said about Ryan, and I'm sorry. Just go out on your date with Daniel. Try to enjoy yourself."

"I'm not sure I can . . . or if I even want to. I'm too worried. I'm not in the mood for a night out."

"I'll text you updates, I promise."

13

"THAT MUST BE THE TWENTIETH time you've checked your phone tonight," Daniel says. He's being generous. It's probably closer to the fiftieth.

"I'm really sorry. I'm not being good company, am I? I just have something on my mind."

"Oh? Is there anything I can help with?"

I shake my head as I twist the stem of my wine glass between my thumb and forefinger. Daniel Noble must be Barrett McAllan Gray's most eligible bachelor. At forty years old, he has somehow avoided marriage, but he has a reputation for dating beautiful, successful women. I feel more than honoured to be sitting opposite him in the Michelin-starred Club Gascon, looking into his dark blue eyes that perfectly match the navy of his Tom Ford suit.

But I'm not feeling it. Daniel is lovely – charming, successful, good-looking and great conversation – but even if my law wasn't in place, I don't think I'd be interested in him romantically. It's just not there. I'm also worried sick about Max.

A waiter clears our plates and pours more wine into our glasses. "Could I bring you the dessert menu, sir, madam?" he says. We both decline.

"How did you get a table here at such short notice?" I ask. Club Gascon must have a lengthy waiting list.

"The maître d' owes me a favour. Plus it's a Thursday." Daniel smiles, and I notice how strong and defined his features are – just like a Renaissance statue of a Roman emperor. I imagine him in golden armour for a moment and smile.

I have a sip of wine, then my fingers subconsciously move to tap my phone for an update. I catch Daniel's knowing glance. *Busted.* I guiltily withdraw my hand and apologise again.

"It's okay, Violet. If you need to check your phone, go ahead."

I sigh. He's being so sweet, and I'm being an ungrateful cow. "It's Max. He didn't show up for work today and we can't contact him. Ethan is out searching the nightclubs of south London, where he was last seen. He said he'd update me."

"Oh, I see. Well, out of all our artists, he has always struck me as having the most 'artistic' temperament. Does he disappear often?"

"Not really, but he's definitely high maintenance. I love him to death, but sometimes I could throttle him."

"My accounts team call him 'the nutty professor'."

I start to laugh. "Given what they call me, that's quite complimentary."

"Ah, the Snow Queen, right?" asks Daniel, his Home Counties accent as smooth as the expensive wine we're drinking. "I do believe one of my account managers could have started that. She may have had a thing for your partner."

"Really?" I raise my eyebrows. "Who was it? And why would having a thing for Ethan make her call me names?"

Daniel clears his throat and takes another drink of wine. "I couldn't possibly say."

"Yes, you could. You don't have to tell me who she is, just why?"

I fix my eyes on him until he acquiesces. "Okay, there's a longstanding rumour you two are an item. I know you're just friends, but . . . well . . ."

"Well, what?"

He forces a smile. "I shouldn't have said anything, but . . . I have noticed how Ethan looks at you, and it does seem to be more than mere friendship sometimes."

Oh my god, not again. Just when I manage to get thoughts about Ethan's recent odd behaviour under control, somebody else insinuates there's something between us.

"Ethan and I are best friends. It is possible for two people of the opposite sex to be great friends and work together without falling in love, you know."

"Forgive me, I shouldn't have commented. I just wanted to know where I stood."

"What do you mean?"

Daniel's gaze is fixed to his wine glass. The crisp white tablecloth in front of him is clean, aside from a small daub of sauce from his main course. He moves his thumb over it in a futile attempt to remove it. "I know you're not here because you changed your mind."

I shift nervously in my seat. No, forget that – I *squirm* in my seat. "Why do you say that?"

"Because you have live location sharing on your Facebook and the message you sent at two a.m. came from Soho, not Kilburn. Of course, you could very well have been staying at Ethan's place last night, but I figured it's more likely he knows your login."

Double, triple shit. Busted again. "So why did you . . ."

"Why did I play along?" he says with the confidence of a man who has the upper hand. "I've had a lovely evening with you, so it was no hardship. I am intrigued to learn the truth, however."

I feel terrible. I imagine accidentally spilling wine on

my dress, or accidentally stabbing myself in the eye with a fork – anything – to avoid giving him the confession I'm about to give him. "Okay, I didn't know Ethan was going to do this, but remember I told you about my law?" He nods and I continue. "Well, he decided to adopt it too, and we're in competition to see who can keep going the longest. He wants to win, so he . . . well, that's why he messaged you."

Daniel downs the dregs of his wine and dabs his napkin to the corners of his mouth. "I've got to tell you, that's the last thing I expected to hear."

He looks around the restaurant and catches the eye of our waiter, giving me time to think about how horrible I am. I should never have done this. What on earth was I thinking? I take my credit card out of my purse. "I'm paying for dinner," I say decisively.

"Don't be silly," he says with kindness I don't deserve. "I told you I already knew you hadn't changed your mind. I've had a lovely evening, but I think we should cut it short so you can help Ethan find Max." He stands and picks my credit card up off the table, offering it back to me.

"I really think I should pay, Daniel. It would make me feel better. I should have told you the truth straight away."

He takes hold of my hand, places the credit card in it and closes his fingers around mine. He smiles as he holds me for a moment. "You haven't done anything wrong. I reserve the right to give Fraser a solid kicking in the Lakes next week though."

Crap, I forgot he's coming on the shoot too. Awkward much?

I text Ethan for his location while Daniel pays the bill and asks the maître d' to call me a taxi. I wish

Daniel goodnight, and he offers a neutral "You too" in return.

Great. Yet another person I have to work with who hates me.

***

The charmingly named Dance Sewer is located underground on Brixton Road, not far from Max's flat. Two ten-foot-tall bouncers guard the door of the hidden-away nightclub, which is sandwiched between Bob's Burger Bar and a pawnbrokers. A group of six teenagers barge their way through the doors in front of me wearing clothes last seen on a beach in Ibiza. I, on the other hand, am wearing clothes last seen in a Michelin-starred restaurant. For the first time in my life I curse my favourite Donna Karan cocktail dress and wish I were ten years younger.

I enter the club to the sound of *thud, thud, thud, thud, thud, thud*. Ethan was right – the music goes right through you. The dry ice catches the back of my throat as I descend a metal staircase and almost get carried into the crowd of people who aren't so much dancing as jumping. Some have whistles, others have luminous glow sticks, and the guy in front of me has come dressed as a horse. I kid you not – he's wearing a horse's head and he has a tail sewn onto his cycling shorts. I can't imagine why he thought purple Lycra resembled a horse's arse, but there you go. Maybe he doesn't own any brown trousers.

More dry ice is pumped through the air as I trudge over the moist, sticky carpet on my hunt for Ethan . . . and hopefully, Max. A cocktail of aromas lingers on the air: sweaty bodies, weed and cheap alcopops. I conclude there is no better name for this nightclub than Dance Sewer.

The DJ shouts into his mic. There are cheers, but he's as coherent as Charlie Brown's schoolteacher, so I don't have a clue what he's saying. The music changes to a slower-tempo track. Arms are raised in the air, the horse-guy neighs to a round of applause, and then the music ramps back up to a different, yet exactly the same, version of the previous song.

Absolute torture.

I pull my phone from my bag, and I'm about to send Ethan a "where the hell are you?" text when it's knocked out of my hand by a tall black guy wearing knee-socks and a tutu. He apologises; at least I think he does – I can't hear a bloody thing. I bend down to rescue my phone and finally locate Ethan. He's standing at the bar, yelling at Max's friend Marek.

"You're a moron, Marek! I told you to keep him here," yells Ethan, acknowledging me with a nod as I approach.

"Max has gone home, he's good . . . let him work it out . . . peace, man," Marek blabbers. His light-brown eyes look like they've just made a return trip from Mars. In fact, calling Marek spaced out would be an understatement. He's dressed in jeans that are three sizes too tight, with a rope belt clinging to his waist. His frayed shirt is opened to his chest, displaying a medallion made out of seashells. Is this what the kids are wearing these days? I have no idea. Max is three years older than Ethan and I, but Marek is barely in his twenties. He shares a flat with three other Eastern Europeans and works in an Oxford Street sports shop.

"I said very clearly that you were to keep him here,

you dipshit!" Oh no, Ethan's accent is getting more Scottish – therefore more angry.

"He's home, he's good . . ." repeats Marek, and I have to take Ethan to one side before he starts laying into him.

Marek meanders into the crowd, half dancing and half jogging. "Fucking idiot," Ethan mutters as he goes.

"Why don't we go to Max's flat?" I yell into Ethan's ear.

He turns to answer, but just then a guy with luminous white skin and dreadlocks that look like they've been spun from the pubic hair of a camel comes up to us, shoves his face into mine and shouts "Rrrrooooaaarrrrr!"

Before I know what's happening, Ethan has dreadlocks-guy by the shoulders and is screaming in his face. "What the hell was that? What's wrong with you?"

Dreadlocks-guy does his best to escape from Ethan's hold whilst shouting "Do you know who I am?" and "I'll have you barred for this." Is he a DJ? Or a barman? He doesn't look like he'd own the place, but you never know.

I can't get near Ethan to pull him off the guy. A sea of people rush forward shouting "Fight!" as bottles and glasses fly off the bar. I try to squeeze through an opening, but I'm shoved backwards against a steel pillar. I fall to the floor, and a searing pain flashes across my head as it lands on broken glass.

I manage to pick myself up with help from three people I don't know, only to see Ethan being hauled away by one of the huge bouncers. I follow after them, hearing my own pulse mix with the *thud, thud, thud, thud, thud* of the techno music.

When I get outside, I follow the sound of Ethan's yelling to a taxi rank, where three bouncers are trying to persuade him to get into a taxi and go home. "My friend is still in there! Get off me! I need to go back for her!"

"No way are you going back in there, mate. Now get yourself home or we'll call the police."

"Ethan!" I shout as loud as I can, but my head is hurting so much it feels like a family of woodpeckers have taken up residence inside it. Do I have concussion? No, I'm conscious, I can't have it. Wait . . . you don't have to be unconscious, do you? Does this mean I could just fall unconscious at any moment? No. That's narcolepsy. *Don't be stupid, Violet.*

When Ethan sees me, he pulls out of the bouncer's hold and runs up to me. "Are you okay?" he asks, his eyes frantically searching mine.

"I hit my head and I got knocked over. I'll be fine. I just want to go home."

"I'll take you. Get in the taxi."

Ethan takes my arm and guides me to the waiting black cab. "But what about Max?" I say.

"Marek said he'd gone home, so fuck him. All of this is his fault anyway."

***

It takes just over half an hour for us to get from Brixton to my flat. I spend most of the ride with my eyes shut, trying to block out the pain in my skull. When we get inside, the first thing Ethan does is go to my bathroom to get a pack of paracetamol. He also gets a tumbler of cold water, a bottle of wine and two glasses. The

150

absolute last thing I want right now is alcohol, but apparently the wine is for him. He fills a glass and downs it in one.

"Jesus, what a night." He refills his glass and sits down next to me on the sofa, rolling up his shirt sleeves to inspect his arms for bruises. "I should sue that shithole of a club."

I take the medicine then instinctively rub my head, moving my hand through my tangled hair until I stop at a clump of wetness. "Shit," I say as I pull my hand away to see blood coating my fingertips.

Ethan instantly moves closer as I fight the panic that always comes with the sight of blood.

"Let me see." He parts my hair and gently separates a handful at a time, looking for the source of the blood. "Where does it hurt?"

"Everywhere. I got knocked into a metal beam and then I fell. I hit my head on glass. Shit . . . do I have glass in my head? Please tell me I don't have glass in my head. I hate hospitals. Whatever happens, I'm not going to A&E! Not even if I'm bleeding to death."

"Calm down, Joan of Arc," he says with a laugh. "After this, you will *never* tease me over Angus savaging my bollocks, by the way." He slowly detangles the bloodied clump of hair with his fingers. "Aha," he says finally, letting my hair fall back over my shoulders.

"What?" I ask nervously. "Do I need stitches? I don't need my head shaved for it, do I? It would take at least five years for my hair to grow back this long."

"I don't think so, but you've cut just behind your ear. Back in a minute." He disappears into my bathroom again, emerging minutes later with a pack of plasters, a bag of cotton wool and a cup of water.

"You're shit at shopping, Vi. I have a proper first aid kit – they're only ten quid or so on Amazon. You don't have any antiseptic cream, so don't blame me if your ear turns black and drops off."

A few minutes later, I have a clean ear sporting a modified plaster and Ethan is back on the wine. He rests his arm against the back of the sofa, then he moves his leg to get comfortable and suddenly it's resting against mine. Heat rises inside me, settling low down in a soft ache. I think back to the last time we were this close, our bodies pressed against each other's as I watched him sleep, and my skin begins to warm.

"Three years we've been friends, and I don't think I know you half as well as I thought I did." His voice is quiet. A fleck of silver in his blue eyes sparkles as it catches the light from the chandelier in my sitting room.

"Are you talking about Laurel?"

"Yes and no. I was shocked when you told me about your family. Then all of a sudden I realised how much you meant to me. It hit me that night . . . in that moment . . . and, well, you're my best friend. I know you think I have tons of friends, but none of them mean as much to me as you do. I know what real friendship is and I only have it with you. I trust you completely. If my life became a living hell overnight, I know you'd be there in the middle of it all, propping me up and trying to fix everything for me."

I reach for the other empty glass, fill it with wine and take a long drink. My hands shake as I place the glass back on the table. "That's because you're all I have."

He nods sadly, and I have no idea why my heart is hammering in my chest. "I'm sorry about Carly," he says softly. "It was thoughtless and stupid and I betrayed you. I knew how you felt about her."

Whoa, where did that come from? "It doesn't matter," I lie. I wonder if he notices that I'm gnawing on my bottom lip to stop it from trembling.

"It does matter. I shouldn't have done it, and I know how I'd feel if it was you with someone I hated."

"I admit that it did hurt, a little, but we're just friends, Ethan, and . . ." My voice drops to a whisper and crawls away when his expression changes from sheepish apology to deep regret.

"You're more than just a friend . . ."

We're both breathing in gasps and I don't know which breaths are mine and which are his. He opens his mouth to talk, but nothing happens. He turns his face away from me, so I place my hand on his knee to bring him back. He flinches in surprise before covering my hand with his and giving it a squeeze.

I shiver as he holds my hand. I feel his touch in every part of my body, on every inch of my skin. It feels like he is buried deep inside me, and I wonder if he's as scared as I am. Does he know this is me, or have I become the "anybody" he told me he seeks out when he's emotional and drinking?

Ethan moves even closer and rests his forehead on mine. I can smell the scent of his cologne mixed with red wine and a coarse sweat. He moves his hands to the nape of my neck and caresses light waves onto my skin that tingle and pulse through my body. I drop my hand to the hard curve of his chest and I feel his heart thud under his shirt.

I feel myself falling . . . I feel myself wanting . . . but then reality kicks in. He's seeking comfort, reassurance, pleasure . . . and I don't want to be his anybody.

Becoming that, even just once, could ruin everything. How would we move on? What would we become?

"Ethan, don't do this . . ." I whisper desperately as my desire is slowly beaten back by my fear.

He brushes his thumb against my cheek. "Shh." His skin is damp with sweat against my forehead. Neither of us moves. It's as if we're stuck together, scared to go forward but refusing to go back.

I let out a shaky breath. "I think you should go."

"I don't think I want to go."

"This isn't us."

"Why not? It could be . . ."

"Ethan, no," I say as his mouth starts to seek out mine. "No."

He breaks free and I catch my breath. I search his eyes and all I see is confusion. He turns away from me, bends forward and holds his head in his hands. "I'm sorry . . . I think I've had too much wine. I need to stop doing this. Fucking hell. I'm sorry. I could have destroyed everything."

Tears prick my eyes as I realise I was right. He was performing to type – seeking out comfort through sex, just like he did with Carly and Erin and Jenny and god knows who else. But none of those women were his best friend; it didn't matter if they walked out of his life afterwards. I'm different, and the fear in his eyes tells me he knows he's gone too far.

He picks up his jacket, puts it on and downs the last remnants of his drink. He turns around and cocks his head to one side, his mouth lifting into an apologetic smile. "I'm sorry. I'll see you tomorrow," he says, and leaves.

I watch him go. It feels unreal. I wonder why my legs aren't carrying me after him, and I wonder why

I'm not hearing my voice calling him back.

I return to bed and attempt to count wildebeests, but my brain has placed the events of the evening on a vicious cycle of repeat in my mind and I can't fall back to sleep.

It feels like my world has changed forever, and I don't know how to get it back.

14

I CAN'T REMEMBER THE LAST time I overslept and was late for work. The gigantic clock which hangs on the back wall of our lobby over a bronze silhouette relief of the London skyline is telling me it's almost ten o'clock. I can remember snoozing my alarm. I can also remember switching it off, thinking I'd get up in a minute.

Well, that minute somehow turned into two hours.

I walk out onto the fifteenth floor and head straight to my desk, my pulse racing. I hold my breath, expecting to see him. But he isn't there. Then I see something else . . . a Post-it note stuck to my computer screen: *Fuck it.*

Fuck it? Fuck what?

I recognise the handwriting as Max's barely legible scrawl. It looks like a cockroach has dipped its bottom in ink and scuttled over the note, but there's nothing unusual in that. *Thank god he's alive* is my first thought. *Thank god he's in work* is my second.

I peel the note off the screen and switch on my computer. I'm just about to call Ethan to find out where he is and ask him if he's seen Max when I notice an email in my inbox.

Max wasted – taken him home.

Oh god, not again. My stomach churns as I remember our search for Max yesterday, the search that ended with a nightclub brawl, a bloodied ear and the realisation that I came close to smooching the face off my best friend. I lay awake for hours last night,

156

overthinking what happened in my flat. I can't deny that part of me wanted Ethan to kiss me last night. My heart was already being carried away, but I'm thankful my brain kicked in. Would our friendship survive? Would our working relationship survive? I couldn't stop the images invading my mind, imagining what his kisses would be like, wondering what sex with him would be like . . . The early hours of this morning became a guilty, erotic adventure as thoughts that had only ever been idle and fleeting became all-consuming.

We'll have to talk about what happened at some point, and I find that positively terrifying. I don't enjoy discussing my feelings. I much prefer pretending I don't have any. I'm sure it will be easier if I push it out of my mind and forget it happened, yet I don't know if I can. I want to know what he's thinking.

I take out my phone and send Ethan a text: *How is he? Are you at his place or yours? – Vi xx*

A minute later, my stomach leaps into my mouth when my phone pings with his reply: *His place. He's totally lost the plot. Need help please. PLEASE.*

I'm shocked that Ethan has given up and engaged the Bat-signal so soon, but I know he finds Max's moods difficult. I text him back to say I'm on my way and email Gabriel, Stella's assistant, to tell him I have a family emergency. We need to prep for the Lakes shoot today, so I hope I can fix this quickly.

***

Max's flat is on the main street in Brixton, above a fried chicken takeaway separated from a slightly differently named fried chicken takeaway by a bookies,

157

a greengrocers and one of those awful payday loans shops. He could afford a better flat. I'm not being snobbish (much), but this area of London is shit. I have absolutely no idea what Max does with his money, aside from pissing it up the wall. But still, he has two bedrooms and his place is twice as big as Ethan's pretentious Soho penthouse. Ethan calls it a penthouse; I call it a cupboard. But at least his place doesn't smell like Colonel Sanders' final resting place.

I press the doorbell and wait for the familiar buzzing noise which allows me to enter the building. I walk up the back stairs and my stomach growls hungrily in response to the aroma of fried poultry that Captain Cluck declares has been "spiced to ten different secret recipes". I knock on the door. Ethan answers, his face bearing a frown that could crack rocks.

"What the hell took you so long?"

I have spent the last twelve hours wondering what Ethan would say to me the morning after last night happened, and not once did that greeting feature. "I literally came straight over."

"Sorry. I . . . um . . . couldn't sleep last night, so I got into work early. Max arrived at eight thirty and he was up the wall. I had to get him out of the office before Malcolm clocked the state of him."

I walk into Max's sitting room. I'm pleased to see it's still paying homage to the Tate Modern. Max is a graphic designer, but he dabbles in fine art in his spare time. His flat is like a cool, bohemian art gallery – every surface is painted white, and every wall is decorated with breathtaking canvasses and framed photographic art. And sitting on a yellow plastic Ikea armchair in the middle of it all is Max.

I go straight to him and crouch down in front of him.

He's staring intently at his feet and it takes him a few seconds to register my presence. "Violet, what are you doing here?" The skin around his eyes is dark, his pupils are dilated, and his thinning hair is wet with sweat. He's wearing torn jeans and a greyed t-shirt which looks like it's been over-washed from black over the course of a decade.

"I'm here to see how you are. And I must say you've looked better, my friend."

"Before you tell me to go to bed, I don't want to go to bed. He's been telling me to go to bed since he dragged me home, threatening to kick the shit out of me if I didn't." He scowls at Ethan. "You're such a fucking shithead."

I look between the pair of them. Ethan shrugs. I can imagine the scene and I can imagine the threat of physical violence was the absolute last resort. Max huddles into his squeaky plastic chair, his body jerking unnaturally as his long limbs sway with the effects of whatever he's been pumping into his body.

"Max, what have you done to yourself?"

"What do you mean?"

My heart is breaking for him. I raise my hands to his jaw and cup his face. He responds by closing his eyes and gently rubbing his cheek on my palm in a silent plea for comfort. "Just tell me what you've taken, sweetheart."

He sniffs and opens his eyes, which are dead to the world, his gaze struggling to focus on mine. "Pills and stuff. It's the only way to block it out."

I feel like crying. I didn't know he was still suffering. How didn't I know?

He climbs down onto the floor to sit next to me and places his head on my shoulder. I wrap my arms around

159

him and feel his hand move up my arm, holding on to me desperately as he starts to sob. "Shush, it's okay," I whisper into his ear as my own eyes fill with tears.

"I keep seeing her in my brain." He crosses his arms around my shoulders and I have to reposition myself to cope with the weight of his body resting on mine. "And I know she's not in a coma anymore, but that doesn't make me feel better. I didn't even like her. I thought she was a bitch, so if she'd died they'd have put me in prison for murder."

"Oh, Max, you have this so wrong. That makes no sense at all. Carly is a grown woman; you weren't responsible for her. Can't you remember what I said to you over the weekend?"

"Yes, and I believed you, but when I was on my own I started thinking you were just saying nice things to make me feel better."

"Max, you know me. You know I always say what I think. I'd never lie to you."

He raises his chin and looks at me. "Tell me how to stop thinking about her."

"If I knew how to stop thinking about things you don't want to think about, I'd own the world. But, look . . . Carly is going to get better. She's going to be fine. You don't need to worry anymore, and getting high isn't helping. In fact, it's making things worse. Ethan's right. You need to sleep all of this off. Do you think you can do that for me?"

"Only if you stay. Don't leave me."

"Max, we have a ton of work to do today for our shoot next week." He looks like he's about to cry. "Okay, I'll stay a little while – until I can find someone else to sit with you."

He nods his head. "Thank you, Violet, thank you. I

really mean it. You're a true friend, and I know I'm a disgrace right now, but I promise when all of this is over, you and me are going to do something exciting together. I know! I've been planning a weekend trip to Bruges – why don't you come with me? There's a meat-curing festival on in September and it's supposed to be awesome. What do you say?"

I can't help but look at him as if he's just invited me to my own funeral. "Cured meat? Hmm . . . I'll think about it."

Somehow I help him to his feet and walk him to his bedroom. He goes inside, flops face down onto the bed and sighs as his body relaxes onto his navy-blue denim duvet. For a brief moment I consider tucking the duvet around him, but he seems peaceful enough, so I wish him sweet dreams and close the door.

As I walk back into the sitting room, relieved that Max is safe, my guilt escalates. I could have prevented this. For days, my friend has pumped himself with drugs to block out a pain I could have made vanish if I'd shared what I know about Ridley and Carly. This is all my fault.

"You deserve a medal for that." Ethan is sitting on Max's striped armless sofa. He looks on edge, as if he's ready to charge for the door and make a bid for freedom.

"A medal for what?"

"For getting him to go to bed. He took a swing at me three times before you got here. I thought I'd have to knock him out to get him to calm down."

"Oh, that bad? He didn't seem too bad just now."

"That's because you can handle him better than I can. I told you before that he freaks me out when he's like this. He's had these episodes ever since we were at

161

uni together." He offers me a half smile and a glance so fleeting that I know he's afraid to look at me directly. Is this us now? Is this the way things are going to be from now on? Is our friendship going to be awkward and uncomfortable and embarrassing? My eyes fill up at the prospect of having lost the one thing that means more to me than anything else in the world. And then I think about Max and how I could have helped him, and I can't stop the onslaught. The regret is so intense that it almost takes my feet from under me.

"What's the matter?" His tone is off. He sounds more terrified than concerned.

"It's nothing." Yes, I know I just said "nothing" was the matter, and yes, I realise that's lame, and yes, I'd punch myself in my own stupid face if I could.

He shifts nervously in his seat, pulling one leg up over his knee then placing it straight back on the floor again. He glances at me and quickly looks away. I bite my bottom lip to stop my tears from falling, but one sneaks out. I hope with everything I have that he didn't notice.

"Look, I'm sorry about last night," he says tentatively.

"Let's just forget about it."

He stares blankly at me, no doubt wondering what's running through my mind. I'm wondering myself. I don't know what I want or expect him to say, but I know I can't bear this. This isn't us. None of this is right. We seem broken. Are we broken?

"Violet, please. I've said I was sorry, I thought . . ."

I walk further into the room and sit down on the yellow plastic armchair. My legs are trembling and my stomach feels like it's about to hurl my breakfast across the room. Words I don't want to say appear in my brain, and before I know it they've leapt out of my mouth. "I need to tell you something. I've fucked up and I don't know what to do. This thing with Max is all my fault."

"What are you talking about? You did great with him – at the weekend and now."

"No, you don't understand. I don't mean that."

"Then what?"

I don't look at him. I can hear the worry in his voice and that alone is breaking my heart, so god knows what looking into his eyes would do to me.

"Violet, please. You're never like this. Whatever it is, just tell me."

I rock forward in the squeaky chair, wrapping my arms protectively around my body. I inhale a lungful of air to help me force out the words I need to say. "It happened on Wednesday night. I stayed late to finish some work. I was almost at the lifts to go home when I realised I'd forgotten my bag, and I went back . . ." I bite on my lip again as another tear makes its escape. I quickly bat it off my face. "Ridley and Malcolm were in Diego's office. I didn't know why and I could hear them fighting, so I listened at the door."

Ethan's eyes widen. "What did you hear?"

"I'm sorry, Ethan . . . I couldn't tell you . . . I . . ."

"Violet. What did they say?" His voice is loud and firm.

"Ridley was having an affair with Carly. He was with her when she got into trouble."

"What?" he gasps into the room, and for what seems like hours I think that's all he's going to say. The silence is heavy, weighed down by words needing to be spoken, but nothing is said.

"Say something, Ethan. Please."

163

"I don't know what to say. Ridley was screwing around with Carly when I was . . . fuck's sake! He was with her when she passed out and he didn't call for help? He didn't do anything? He was with her when she choked? We found her, Vi. Max and me. What if we hadn't found her? She almost died."

"I don't know why he didn't help her. Maybe he panicked . . ."

I finally look at him. He flops back on the sofa. "And Malcolm knows this?"

"Yes, Ridley is blackmailing him. He said he needed an alibi. You have to believe me . . . I wanted to tell you so much. For two days this has been killing me, but Malcolm begged me not to say anything."

He gets up from the sofa so quickly that he scatters three cushions to the ground. "Jesus Christ, this is huge!" He runs his hand through his hair and starts pacing the floor, backwards and forwards, as if the repetitive movements will help him order his thoughts. "What kind of an animal is he?"

I consider telling him about the encounter I had with Ridley in his office yesterday, but given that Ethan physically attacked a space cadet for roaring in my face last night, I decide to keep it to myself. "Maybe he'd gone to find help . . . I don't know."

"What do you mean, you don't know?" He's yelling at me now. I hope Max is able to sleep through all of this.

"I don't know how or why or what they were doing when she passed out, and will you stop shouting at me?"

"You don't like me shouting at you? Jesus, Violet, I could kill you, never mind shout at you. You kept this from me and Max – the two people in the entire world

164

who most needed to know about it. Have you any idea what I've been going through? I mean, you know about Max lying in his bed trying to sleep off the shit he's taken to block out his guilt, don't you?" I can't bear the disappointment in his face as he slowly looks away from me and shakes his head in exasperation. "You knew how much having sex with Carly that night was playing on my mind. How could you do this?"

"Don't you think I wanted to tell you?"

"Then why the fuck didn't you? It isn't difficult. 'Oh hey, Ethan, you'll never guess what I just overheard. Ridley Gates was screwing around with Carly when she almost died.' What's so bloody hard about that? You've just told me now and it took, what, thirty seconds? Why would you keep something like this from me? Is this all you're keeping from me?"

I can think of one huge thing I'm keeping from him, but a grandiose I'm-terrified-by-these-weird-feelings-I'm-suddenly-having-for-you revelation might send our current shitfest into the murky depths of unrecoverable disaster, so I come clean with the other thing. In for a penny, in for a pound, right? "I already knew Ridley and Carly were an item. I saw them together at the awards show party and they both warned me off. That's when Carly told me about Stuart's fiancée."

The utter desolation which flashes across his face makes me want to sink to my knees, curl up into a ball and hibernate for infinity. "You knew that when we arrived at your flat after the party? You knew? Does Ridley know about me and Carly?"

"Yes, but he doesn't care." Ethan's eyes narrow and he shakes his head as if physically trying to shrug off the news I've given him. "This has been eating me up for days, Ethan, and I didn't know what to do. Just tell me what I can do now."

"Don't keep secrets from me – ever. Like you promised. That would be a good start."

I whisper another apology, but he isn't won over. We've argued many times before, but it's always been about silly work stuff and it's never ever been as bad as this.

"What's Ridley got on Malcolm?"

I open my mouth but then think twice and close it again. He notices and my stomach dives when I see the frustration embedded in his eyes.

"Oh for Christ's sake, you're kidding me. Seriously?"

"I'm sorry. I can't. I promised him I wouldn't tell anybody."

"And what about the promise you made to me?" He picks up his suit jacket from the back of the sofa and walks towards the door.

"Where are you going?"

He spins around, puts on his jacket and straightens his tie. "Back to the office. One of us needs to work." His eyes are glassy, his face flushed red. He's furious with me, and I hate it.

"You can't go like this. We haven't finished talking yet."

"We're finished for now. I need to go and you need to watch Max." He walks away and I can't breathe. I don't know how to make him stay and listen to me. He opens the door, but before he walks through it he turns around to face me. "I said the other night that I didn't think I knew you half as well as I thought, but now I don't think I know you at all."

And then he's gone.

And I collapse onto the sofa and replay everything

he said to me until my head aches.

15

MAX SLEEPS FOR THE REST of the morning. I try to work, but I've taken several trips to Facebook, Amazon and a fan page for Robert Downey Jr. instead. What can I say? When I'm on a downer, I seek solace in Iron Man.

Today my brain decides, for the first time in its life, that Ethan bears a passing resemblance to Tony Stark, so I flick over to my YouTube playlist to take my mind off him. But this makes everything worse. First up on my playlist is Coldplay's "The Scientist" . . . or rather the cover version Ethan and Rory did a couple of years ago. My insides spin as his strong voice draws me in and I imagine he's singing about me. Oh my god, why? I've listened to their songs on YouTube dozens of times, but I've never felt like this before.

I switch it off and decide to punish myself with Candy Crush, but I'm rewarded at precisely 12.54 p.m. when I finally achieve the unachievable – the completion of Level 374. This means I'm king of the world and I need to celebrate with food.

I take a trip to Max's fridge, which is in much better shape than mine. Fruit, vegetables, raw ingredients to make stuff. Wow, I'm in awe. I consider cooking something for all of ten seconds, before immersing myself in the creation of a celebratory sandwich instead. Bread, spread, Polish cold meats and some suspicious-looking smoked cheese with black skin. Clearly Max is still convenience-shopping at the Happy Shopper next to Brixton Tube.

After lunch, a text message from the office brings good news.

Zoe visited Carly in hospital yesterday. Carly said she was taking coke with "a mystery man" at the party, and her parents have booked her into rehab. Carly didn't mention Ridley at all. Rory has the night off so he can watch Max from three. See you back at the office."

***

Rory Fraser's timekeeping is as bad as his brother's, so I'm still here when Max wakes up at three thirty and stumbles into the sitting room like a zombie searching for a limb to chew on. He grabs some cold meat from his fridge and eats it straight from the packet.

"I have some good news to tell you," I say when he takes a seat next to me on his stripy Kermit-green sofa. "Zoe says Carly is on the mend. Apparently, she was with a guy when she passed out. They were drinking and taking cocaine. Carly's parents have sent her off to rehab. See, I told you this wasn't your fault. None of it was your fault."

I watch with pleasure as the relief slowly washes over him – ripples at first, then his muscles relax, and finally I see his spark return. I put my arm around him and give him a peck on the cheek. He responds with a smile so big it overtakes his face in a gigantic crescent moon. "Oh, shit. You're serious, aren't you?" He laughs and pulls me into a hug. And just like that, I have my happy Max back again.

Rory arrives at four thirty with food sent up from Captain Cluck – secret recipe number three of ten

(Cajun Hot). I leave them to it and hail a taxi to take me straight to the office.

***

"Ah, there you are," says a voice from behind me, two seconds after I sit down at my desk. I turn around and my stomach falls flat. It's Malcolm, accompanied by his twitching, pissed-off moustache. "Good of you to grace us with your presence. Now, would you mind telling me where you've been all day?"

"I messaged Gabriel to say I had a family emergency and I'd take the day as annual leave."

"Not good enough!" he snaps. Will and Pinkie look up from their desks in surprise. "We have a major account to save and you're integral to us doing that. I've been fire-fighting since the weekend, and everyone had their noses to the grindstone yesterday. Fraser has been in a meeting with TV Production all afternoon – without you. We needed you, you weren't there, and I want the truth – not something plucked from Fraser's book of top fifty pathetic excuses."

I can't believe he's pushing this. Just a week ago I would have felt sick to my stomach at the thought of being disrespectful to Malcolm, but everything has changed now. I'm not apologising for needing most of the day off to deal with the car crash he created. "I've already said it was a family thing."

"My office. Now."

And suddenly I'm no longer so sure of myself.

I follow him to his office on the floor below, my skirt swishing and the pencil pleats flicking at the back of my knees. He closes the door behind us and slowly turns around. I fully expect him to attack with teeth bared, but instead his face is drawn and anxious. "Do you know what your disappearing act did to me today?" he asks pitifully.

I shift awkwardly on my heels, wondering if I should continue my lie or brave it out. As usual, I go for the easier option. "I'm sorry. Something came up."

"You're lying to me." His moustache twitches angrily again. "What's going on?"

"I tried to see you yesterday, but this morning, like I told you, something came up."

"Rubbish. No it didn't." He picks up a pen and starts banging it on the desk in front of him, one end then the other, making a see-saw between his fingers. "You're lying to me. Where were you? Who did you see and who did you talk to?"

"Look, Malcolm, you're making me feel very uncomfortable here. I already told you it was a personal matter which has nothing to do with you."

"I don't believe you."

"I don't care."

"Yeah well, time to start caring!" He stands up sharply and his chair slams into the wall behind him, making my heart leap into my throat. "Tell me where you were, or so help me god, I'll fire you."

"You're going to fire me?" I ask in amazement. I put my hands on my hips, infuriated by his ridiculous behaviour. "After the conversation we had on Wednesday night?" For the first time in my life I start to wonder about employment rights and what the agency's bullying policy looks like, but then I try to put myself in Malcolm's position. He's stressed and he's scared. I let my arms drop to my sides. "Okay, if you must know, I was with Max this morning."

"Max? You mean Max Wolf? He rang in sick yesterday. Is he sick?"

"He was having a hard time, but I can't give you too many details. He blamed himself for what happened to Carly Hayes."

Malcolm's eyebrows shoot upwards. "Was Wolf screwing her too?"

I know I should not be giving Malcolm this information, but I don't know how to get around it. "Let's just say Max may have acquainted Carly with some Class B substances, but we learned today that she is already familiar with the Class A variety."

"Yeah, she's a cokehead. How did you find out?"

Oh shit, was I not supposed to know about that? "Um . . . a friend of Carly's told me."

"The only person who knows, aside from me and Ridley Gates, is Zoe. Did she tell you?" His face turns ashen, and I know the penny has dropped. "Damn, Fraser's the missing link in this, isn't he?"

I sigh and slowly nod my head. Malcolm thuds his fists on his desk, clenching his jaw tight. "Have you told him about me? How much does he know?"

"I only told him about Ridley and Carly. I didn't tell him about the money. He won't say anything, he—"

"Don't be stupid. The man hates me!"

"What do you want me to say, Malcolm? You're in the wrong here, not me."

"I want you to say you'll keep quiet like you promised and you won't tell anyone else. If Ridley Gates follows through with his threats, it won't be just my life and Emily's . . . I have children and grandchildren. All their lives will be ruined."

I look away. I feel guilty, but at the same time I'm pissed off that he's making me feel guilty. "I had to tell

Ethan. For the same reason I had to tell Max. They were both blaming themselves and it wasn't fair. I wanted to see you yesterday because I think you should call Ridley's bluff. He has something on you, and you have something on him. You're even now."

He looks at me as if I were an idiot. "You think it's that easy? Have you any idea what Ridley Gates is capable of?"

I think back to yesterday. I remember how he threatened me, his lewd behaviour and the disgusting things he said . . . Was that him at his worst? I hope so, because I convinced myself I could handle him. "You can't let him get away with this, Malcolm."

He shakes his head wearily. "Thank you, Violet, that'll be all."

I don't have the energy or the inclination to try to reason with him, so I leave his office and head back to my desk, but I have to pass Ridley Gates's office on the way. My stomach sinks when I see him at the water cooler outside.

"Ah, Miss Archer, are you coming to see me?" he asks, his face fixed in a nauseating grin. I glance at Lucille, who shoots me an uneasy smile.

"No, why would I?"

"No reason," he says with a wink as he slithers towards me. "There *is* something I wanted to see you about. It'll only take a moment."

He beckons me into his lair, and I have two possible courses of action. The easiest would be to make up a lie and excuse myself. The hardest would be to pull myself together, walk into his office like I own it and refuse to let him beat me.

I surprise myself by choosing the most difficult one.

As soon as the door closes behind me, I set the tone.

"So I hear Carly's out of the coma. Does she know you left her to die yet?"

Ridley's expression is unreadable. There's no anger, no anxiety, and his trademark slimy smirk hasn't been summoned. "Take a seat." He walks around me to sit in his black leather desk chair.

"I'm fine standing."

Ridley's smirk returns. "Fine. Stand then."

I try not to let him get to me, but I can feel my pulse start to race. "If you've called me in here for a repeat performance of yesterday, then I *will* make a complaint about you."

He lounges back in his chair like a Bond villain, his hands folded in his lap. "Who would you complain to? Malcolm?" He starts to laugh. Oh my god, how much do I hate this man? I briefly contemplate smacking him in the face, but then I remember I've never hit anybody in my life and I have no way of knowing how good my aim is.

"No, I'll speak to Human Resources."

"Human Resources? Oh, now I'm scared. Please, Violet, anything but that." He laughs harder and I ball my left hand into a fist, just in case I need it.

"Ridley, I have a lot of work to get through. Can we speed this up?" He says nothing. All he does is recline in his chair and swivel it from side to side. If "shitweasels" were actual creatures, he'd have one as his spirit animal. "Okay, you've had your fun. I'm going back to my desk." I turn around, walk to the door and take hold of the metal door handle . . .

"What happened to Laurel?"

I stop dead. My hold on the door handle tightens, but I can't move and I can't speak. The only sounds I can hear are my own breaths.

"I don't know if you've given my proposal any more thought, Violet, but I did some research on you just in case. I wanted to get to know you better, but none of the staff could help me out. It seems you're quite the enigma. I find that intriguing."

I'm still facing the door when I hear him get up from his desk and walk over to me. My breathing gets louder and my skin crawls with rage and disgust . . . *No!* I tell myself. No, I'm not going to let him win. I won't. I inhale deeply and hold my breath for a moment, forcing some calm into my body.

I turn to face him. "Laurel was my sister. But judging by the look on your face, you already know that."

He grins, and his pearly white teeth glow against his leathery skin. "I do."

My hand loosens slightly on the door handle as I stare into his cold, dead eyes. "So, there's nothing more to talk about." I turn and grip the handle again to pull it towards me.

But Ridley is quicker. He slams the door shut with both hands, his arms braced at either side of my body. I try to move, but my back is pressing against his chest and my legs are straddled by his. I recoil as I feel his breath on my neck. "You're not talking about me to anybody. If you do, I will destroy Malcolm, and you won't be able to take a step in this industry without everyone knowing you got your sister killed." He removes one of his hands from the door and grips my upper arm tight. I push back and try to break free, but I'm trapped, his body pinning me in place.

"Get off me now," I say as firmly as I can.

He presses even harder against me, his fingers digging painfully into my flesh. I fight the urge to scream. "You know what I want," he hisses into my ear, then he nestles his face against my cheek. "I'm bored with Malcolm. Give me what I want, or I'll destroy him."

I tell myself this isn't happening . . . it can't be. His other hand moves over my hips and across my thigh. I feel like I'm drowning as the weight of his body crushes me against the door. But I'm not underwater. I'm at work and there are people – friends – on the other side. "Get your hands off me and move out of my way, or so help me god, I'm going to start screaming."

For the first time, I sense his sleazy-evil-bastard resolve wavering. He releases my arm, but his body is still slammed up against mine. I'm not going to give in and I'm not going to cry. I take a deep breath, and I'm just about to tell him to get off me again when I hear a knock, followed by a creak as the door handle slowly turns ninety degrees.

Ridley lets go immediately, and I step back just in time for Lucille to enter the office. Her arms are full of files.

"Sorry to interrupt Mr Gates, but I have three proposals for you to look through, and Avery Hill needs you to sign off her brief before she sends it to Creative."

There's silence in the room as he takes the papers from his secretary, his eyes fixed on me the whole time. Lucille's eyes are trained on me too and, heart pounding, I take the opportunity to escape.

***

I need to see Ethan, but he's already gone home,

leaving me a Post-it note message: *All sorted. We're driving on Monday. Pick you up around ten.*

I slump forward in my chair, ducking my head behind my cubicle wall so nobody can see me. I brush a tear off my cheek and bite down on my lip. I will not cry. I refuse to crack. I adjust my shirt and gag as the smell of Ridley's cologne floats from the black chiffon. I can still feel him on me, my arm burning from where he held me. I roll my shirt sleeve and my stomach heaves when I see his angry red fingerprints marking my skin. I try to order my thoughts, but my brain is whirring with revulsion. Then I hear footsteps behind me and Lucille appears holding a blue plastic folder, which she places on Pinkie's desk before sitting down.

Lucille smiles and tilts her head sympathetically. "I'm so sorry," she says in her sing-song accent. The string of pearls draped around her neck bounces off her ample chest as she talks. "I should have barged in there sooner. I know what he did. This is sexual harassment, plain and simple. Did he hurt you?"

My breath catches in my throat as I exhale with relief. If I'm forced to act against Ridley in the future, at least I have a witness. "He didn't hurt me . . ." I rub my sore arm, wondering why the hell I'm denying the fact that he obviously did hurt me. "He held me too tight, that's all."

Lucille scoots her chair closer to mine and lowers her voice to a gentle hush. "Sweetheart, if he laid his hands on you, then you need to take things further. That man is the dictionary definition of a dirty dog, and he needs putting down."

I wrap my arms around myself as the horrific reality sinks in. This really happened. He said all that to me and he did hurt me . . . he did. But I don't want to acknowledge it. I hate all kinds of attention, but the kind that gets dished up with a side-serving of pity makes me want to puke. I refuse to be a victim. *His* victim.

"You can't let him get away with this. I heard what he said to you and I'll back you. You're not alone."

My eyes water at Lucille's kindness. "You'd do that?"

She quirks an eyebrow. "You're damn right I would. I've been that man's secretary for five years. I know what he is. Now, how about we find you some support from high up? Malcolm Barrett is about as useful as a zip on a hat, Diego Vega is still away . . . what about Stella?"

"Stella? Oh god, no," I say. "She already thinks I'm emotionally unstable for dousing Stuart Inman with a glass of wine. Stella is my last resort."

"*Our* last resort," Lucille corrects. "You're not alone, remember?"

I smile at her gesture of solidarity. She picks up the blue folder she left on Pinkie's desk and hands it to me. "What's this?" I ask as I flick through the folder, which appears to be full of photocopies of emails, photographs, spreadsheets, bank records and . . . oh my god, is it a file on Ridley?

"It's yours, and you can do whatever you need with it." She stands up and rests her hand on my shoulder. "I told you, sweetheart, I know what Ridley Gates is . . . and I've been waiting years to give this to the right person – someone I trust."

I'm stunned. "Are you sure? I mean, what if he finds out you gave it to me?"

"Then he finds out." Lucille smiles at me again, her eyes sparkling like black opals.

"I don't know what to say. Thank you."

She gives me a hug as she leaves. On the Tube ride home I start reading through Lucille's collection of documents. Given the risks, I can't help being impressed that a secretary in her sixties has bigger balls than most of the men I know.

16

I'VE BEEN WAITING OUTSIDE MY apartment, accompanied by my overnight bag, handbag and laptop bag, for the past ten minutes. Ethan's never on time for anything, so I should have expected I'd be standing in my street like an idiot for half an hour.

I can't say I've put the time to good use. I've been wondering and worrying about how I'm going to handle the next couple of days away with him. We need to talk, but the thought of talking about him almost kissing me . . . I'll admit I'm afraid. I'm afraid of what I'm feeling, afraid of losing control and afraid of having to expose emotions I want to keep hidden.

And then there's Ridley. I made sure I wore a top with sleeves to hide the bruises he gave me yesterday. I keep telling myself he didn't mean to mark me, but I feel like a battered wife making up excuses so I don't have to deal with the truth. He did a very bad thing and I have to act. The folder Lucille gave me last night contains the most explosive information known to mankind since the Watergate tapes. I kid you not. I need to think long and hard about how – or if – I'm going to use the information, because one wrong step and . . . BOOM. I could be responsible for destroying more than just the life of BMG's very own Richard Nixon.

As the minutes tick by, I decide the best course of action maybe to think about Ridley later, but tackle the near-kiss issue head-on. No pussyfooting around, no procrastination, no wishing it away . . . just steamroll straight in. But promises are easy to make to yourself when it's early in the morning, the sun is shining, the birds are singing and you haven't quite overthought every single possible consequence of steamrolling yet. What if he thinks the near-kiss was the worst mistake of his life? How will I feel if he blames the wine? How will I feel if he suggests round two . . . And why the hell is the thought of round two so enticing that I made a conscious decision to pack sexier-than-normal underwear in my overnight bag?

Seriously? What the hell is wrong with me? I can't even think about why I'm thinking about this. Even if Ethan were to confess his undying love for me, it wouldn't work. I'm totally wrong for him. He dates models, actresses and "perfect" secretaries. He doesn't date women like me.

I hate feeling like this. Violet Archer does not worry about what people think of her. She's chilled and confident and courageous, remember? Although I usually despise my frosty nickname, I'd much rather be Violet, the aloof office Snow Queen, than Violet, the fragile office drama queen.

My worries are interrupted by a screech of titanium alloy wheels as Ethan pulls up in his vintage navy Jaguar XK8. I was expecting the BMG "vomit van" – so named because Will threw up in it three times on the way to a shoot for Chez Marie jam in northern France – and I expected our full team, not just him.

He grins at me through the tinted windows as the car roof retracts. His designer shades and black Henley t-shirt are giving off a bad-boy vibe that destroys my vow to not think about ripping his clothes off and doing rude things with him.

"Oh, no. No, no, no. I am not travelling up to

Cumbria al fresco."

"What? Why not?" Ethan pops the boot open so I can put my bags inside.

"Wind, dirt, cold and flies. And why is it just us? I was expecting the vomit van."

"No room. Daniel's driving up with Wendy, Stuart, three film techs, two models and a make-up artist." The car roof makes a vroom noise as it closes shut again. Ethan removes his shades and pops them in the glove compartment. "If the sun is shining like a bastard the whole way up the M6, the roof is coming back down. You know the score – we usually only get five days of summer in between the rain, and Nessie is lucky if she gets her top down once a year."

"Nessie?" I climb into the car and get comfortable on the ivory leather seats. Ethan loves this car and takes great care of it, but living in central London makes driving about as enjoyable as taking a bath in a bucket of ice.

"Yeah, I named her. Do you think it suits?" he says as we pull away.

"You named her Nessie, as in . . . ?"

"Ferocious-*Ness*," he replies, a tiny twitch of embarrassment dimpling his left cheek.

I laugh. "Nothing to do with the Loch Ness monster, then?"

"Yeah, totally the Loch Ness monster! Don't say you haven't heard of *The Family-Ness* cartoons? Ferocious-Ness was the main character and he rocked."

I think I vaguely remember an animated kids' TV show featuring a group of monsters that looked like yellow dinosaurs with fat noses and googly eyes. "So, that was your favourite show when you were a kid?"

"I loved it. I had a teddy called Nessie. He was green

and threadbare and my gran had to knit him some trousers just so his legs wouldn't fall off and—" He stops suddenly and looks at me out of the corner of his eye. "I don't trust you with any more details. This is highly sensitive material."

"I think it's sweet," I say with a smile as I start checking through the messages on my phone. This would normally be a good time to launch into a merciless piss-take session, but I seem to have lost my teasing mojo. The only thing that's running through my brain is a heart-melting image of Ethan as an adorable little Scottish boy.

We hit traffic and it takes us ages to get out of the city. We're heading for the Midlands by the time I finally pluck up the courage to speak to him about last Thursday.

"Okay, so I guess now's a good a time as any to talk about the kiss that almost happened last week?"

Ethan freezes, and so do his hands – which wouldn't be so bad except he's driving a car that's heading around a bend. He swerves to avoid hitting an articulated lorry to the sound of a gigantic, roaring *beeeeeeeeeeeeeep!* "Jesus Christ, Vi!" he exclaims, straightening up the steering wheel. He clutches his chest, his breathing shallow and rapid. "Are you trying to kill us?"

My heart is racing as I grip the door handle for dear life. "That wasn't my plan."

His breathing calms, but the colour of his face doesn't. A flush of pink spreads from his neck to his cheeks and then up through to his forehead, bringing tiny beads of sweat bubbling to the boil. I stare at him because I'm finding the physical reaction fascinating for purely scientific reasons.

He turns and meets my gaze briefly before returning his attention to the road. "Why are you staring at me?"

"I'm just waiting for you to speak."

"Well, I'm not talking about *that* now."

"Why? Because you can't run away and hide?"

"No," he says sharply, meeting my gaze for another millisecond. "Okay . . . yes. And because of reasons."

"Such as?"

He shakes his head in despair. "Such as I'm driving and I don't want to be distracted."

"Okay, how about I drive so you can talk."

"Are you insane? No way are you driving Nessie."

"Why not?"

"Because you drive like an old lady with cataracts."

I summon some mock outrage. "How dare you? I'm cautious, that's all."

"Yeah, well I want us to get to Cumbria by teatime, not next week."

His colour slowly fades down a level from beetroot to tomato. It's funny – he's always been far more willing to talk about his feelings than I am. He's an open book. It's usually him who can't settle until we thrash through our differences and it's always me who resists. But he definitely doesn't want to talk about this, so the next few hours of the drive are spent in awkward silence. A stop at a noisy service station for a sandwich is crippled with awkwardness too. Ethan spends the whole half hour faffing with his phone, his body language screaming "leave me the fuck alone".

The traffic slows down as we approach Manchester. The radio gives a warning about a serious car accident on the M6 – police and ambulances are apparently in attendance, but they're reporting a five-mile tailback. It's two thirty in the afternoon and we're still an hour and a half away from our hotel in the Lake District.

"This is all we need," says Ethan, checking his watch. "I wanted to have plenty of time to talk through the shoot with Wendy before tomorrow."

"It'll be fine. And at least we're fine. There'll be people up ahead having a much worse day than we are."

"You think I don't know that?" he snaps.

I fall silent, hurt that he's shouting at me again and wondering how – or if – we'll ever be able to get our friendship back on track. I stare out of the window and I'm greeted by three bored kids in the back of a beige Ford Focus. I smile at them, and in return one sticks his tongue out, another sticks a pen up his own nose, and the biggest one . . . ugh, is the horrible little sod mooning us? He is! Gross.

A few minutes later, I can't bear the silence any longer. "Ethan, I get you don't want to talk about what happened last week, and that's fine. I'm sure I'll be able to push it out of my mind and forget about it, but right now you're being a dick and I'm sick of you yelling at me."

He sighs as the car rolls from one mile an hour to a complete stop. For the tenth time. "I'm sorry."

"Are you sorry?"

"What? Yes, of course I am."

"You apologised for yelling at me on Friday, and now you're yelling at me again. Over nothing."

"Friday wasn't nothing," he says reaching for his shades as the sun beats down through the windscreen. "I was just disappointed that you didn't trust me."

My stomach dips. I can't bear disappointing people – Ethan most of all. "I do trust you. I just made a promise. One which I did eventually break, by the way.

185

For you."

"I realise that now," he says softly, his eyes hidden by dark glass so I can't see if his expression matches his tone. "That's why I apologised. I just expected you to do what I would have done. If our roles were reversed and I had information like that, I'd have put you first."

"I guess you must be a better friend than I am, then."

"Oh, Vi, don't be like that, for Christ's sake. That's not what I meant."

"It was exactly what you meant. I come up short in the friend department – got it."

He sighs and drives the car a further few feet, his jaw tensing the second he's forced to stop again. "You didn't come up short. You were just 'you'."

"What the hell is that supposed to mean? Are you calling me cold or unfeeling or like a bloody machine again?"

His hands brace tight around the steering wheel. I wish I hadn't started this. "Again, that's not what I meant," he says as a gap in the traffic opens up in front of us. I wait for him to continue, but he says nothing. He shifts into first and crawls forward another few metres. Then he goes back to neutral, pulls the handbrake on and turns away from me, staring out at the speeding traffic on the other side of the motorway.

I have an impulse to get out of the car, stand in the middle of the road, scream in frustration and start walking. Nessie is a metal prison on wheels – a twenty-first-century instrument of torture from which there's no escape. I gaze out of my window again. One of the kids in the Focus makes a snout by pushing his nose flat against his window.

"I meant you're always trying to fix other people's

186

problems. That's all you seem to care about."

What was the question again? I think back to ten minutes ago. *You were just you.* "So, me fixing other people's problems makes you angry?"

He winds down his window and rolls up the sleeves of his dark t-shirt. My eyes fix onto his bronzed, defined lower arms and I imagine being held by him. I realise that not only are these fantasies becoming more frequent, but I'm no longer forcing them out of my head. I'm even starting to enjoy the places my debauched brain is taking me – a guilty pleasure.

"Other people don't need to be fixed as much, Vi," he says with forced casualness, one arm resting on the opened window frame. "Me, Max, Malcolm – we're all big enough and ugly enough to sort out our own problems . . . or we should be."

I have literally no idea what he's talking about. "Max needed me last week. And I think I can help Malcolm. At least I'm trying to. But I can assure you the last thing I want is to be involved with any of this—"

"No, that's not it. Listen, you're great at fixing stuff. I don't know what I'd have done without you through all the stuff with Carly and I know Max feels the same. But Malcolm? You don't have to clean up after him. It's like you're putting so much effort into fixing other people's problems to avoid having to fix your own."

I'm still confused. Shit, has he found out about Ridley? No, he can't have. Lucille wouldn't have told him. "Ethan, I don't have any problems."

"The hell you don't."

"What? Is this about Stuart, again? I've told you that chapter of my life is closed. I have my law. I know where I am."

"Screw your law and screw our stupid bet!" He removes his sunglasses, and his icy blue gaze makes me shiver. "You're running. You were running the first day I met you and you've been running ever since. That's all you ever do – run and hide and build walls around yourself to shut people out. Why does nobody else know about your sister? I only know fragments of information about Ryan – the guy who broke your heart so badly you left the job of your dreams in New York. Why? I don't even know your parents' names. I don't know who your best friend was growing up. I don't know if you had a pet dog or a pony or a fluorescent-pink unicorn. I don't know anything about you, yet I care for you so fucking much I . . . I just . . ." His voice breaks up, and I feel my heart break with it. "I wish you would stop thinking about other people and concentrate on yourself."

I swallow hard as I let his words drip into my brain like honey. This is him caring about me. I always knew he cared – we're best friends, of course he cares – but this is more than that. Is he telling me he wants to know me in a way no one ever has before? No one except Laurel? I take a deep breath as I think about what to say next, but my train of thought is interrupted by the screech of a car horn.

"Wanker," says Ethan, his eyes fixed on his rear-view mirror. I look forwards to see a huge gap has built up in the traffic, and we get Nessie to drive at a whopping seven miles per hour for a good thirty seconds. "Yeah yeah, mate, tooting your horn like a geriatric Mr Toad will get you to your destination all of ten seconds quicker. Well done for being a prize bellend."

I peek in the mirror at the guy behind us. The silver-haired Volvo driver does look rather amphibian, in a bloated, warty, wide-mouthed kind of way.

"So, do you accept you need to fix your own life first?" Ethan says.

"When I told you about Laurel I said I was dealing with what happened all by myself. I'm already fixing that." He sighs and shakes his head, which is infuriating because I'm telling him the truth. "There's no rule to say I have to share my secrets with the world, Ethan. Talking about my feelings doesn't come easily."

"Why not?"

I can't think of a decent answer. Which is crap considering my livelihood revolves around my ability to arrange beautiful words into meaningful, coherent sentences. I shrug and pull my left knee up, resting my chin on it. "You're viewing me through your own lens. You share and talk and have a huge support network of friends to lean on, but I don't. I prefer to sort my own messes out. By myself. In private."

"You don't sort them out though. You just bury them and pretend they don't exist."

"Maybe. But you're the one who doesn't want to talk about last week."

His jaw stiffens and the interrogation ends. He pops his sunglasses back on, puts the car back into gear and travels another inch down the road. This time the inch turns into yards, and the seconds turn into hours, but we're no further forwards. At least the Ford Focus pissed off towards Blackpool at the last junction, saving me from having to get out of the car and give the mooning, piggy-snouted kid a piece of my mind.

"Are you finished with that bottle of water you bought at the service station?" asks Ethan as we come to another dead stop.

189

"Yeah, sorry. Are you thirsty?"

"No, I just want the bottle. I really need to pee. I've been holding it for over an hour."

"Ew, you want to pee in the bottle?"

"Yes. Can I have it, please?"

"No! That's gross. Plus, as soon as you stick your . . . erm . . . knob in it, you'll create a vacuum and there'll be pee everywhere. Do it outside."

"What? I'm not peeing outside. Everyone will see."

He looks out over the central reservation and I can't help but laugh. "I'm not recommending you pee onto oncoming traffic, Ethan. There's bushes and trees our side."

"People will still see me. And know what I'm doing."

"I'll see you if you do it in here, and believe me, the last thing I want – and Nessie wants – is to be covered in urine splashback."

"That's disgusting."

"You're disgusting. Can you not keep it in?"

"No, I've got a pain now." He opens the car door and gets out. "Right, I'm going for it. If the traffic starts moving and Mr Toad starts beeping his horn again, just beep back at him."

I look in the wing mirror and watch him dodge through the cars and choose the bushiest hedge at the side of the road to relieve himself into.

And then the traffic starts moving.

Shit. Typical.

Beeeeeeeeeeeeep!

I look frantically behind me as Ethan stands, open legged, at the side of the road. How much pee does he have in there?

Beeeeeeeeeeeeep! Beeeeeeeeeeeeep!

Jesus Christ, Mr Toad has instigated a riot! Three or four angry drivers are beeping behind us now, which is ridiculous. After two hours of deadlock, the cars in front are only moving down the motorway marginally faster than I can walk. Idiots.

I check back in my mirror; Ethan is still peeing. What the hell did he drink today? Half a reservoir?

Beeeeeeeeeeeeeeep!   Beeeeeeeeeeeeeeep! Beeeeeeeeeeeeeeep! Beeeeeeeeeeeeeeep!

Oh, for crying out loud.

I glance in my mirror again. Finally! Ethan zips up his trousers, and thirty seconds later he's back in the driver's seat.

"About time," I say. "Do you feel better?"

A smirk appears on his face. "Yep. There's nothing like an al-fresco piss. Now, adventure awaits, so let's get up to the Lakes before nightfall."

"Ooh, 'adventure awaits'? 'I love to sail forbidden seas and land on barbarous coasts.'"

"Eh?"

"Moby-Dick . . . you know . . . adventure awaits and all that."

His expression is blank. "Never read it."

"Just drive on."

17

THE HAYFIELD HOTEL IS SITUATED on the banks of Lake Windermere, offering spectacular views of rolling green hills, mossy banks and woodlands. There are sailing boats moored in a tiny harbour, and a small wooden pier where a family with young children wearing brightly coloured wellington boots have congregated with fishing nets.

I had just enough time to change into a figure-hugging turquoise floral dress before dinner. I head down to the bar but nobody is there. Terrific.

I order a Pimm's with lime, fresh strawberries and a sprig of mint from a good-looking, dark-haired barman dressed in a striped waistcoat and bowtie.

"Oh my goodness, Vee-o-let! You're here, finally."

My heart sinks as I recognise the throaty Brazilian accent. It couldn't be, could it? I turn around and . . . Oh my god, it is. "Delfina, how lovely to see you again. Um . . . have we hired you?"

"Yes, you have. I was working on a photoshoot for Stella McCartney in Milan when Lucinda gave me the call. My Ridley couldn't believe it. Of all the models in London, what is the chance you pick me for one of his TV adverts?"

Delfina's jet-black hair, olive skin and striking Amerindian features are certainly going to be perfect for our shoot tomorrow. But having to work all day up a mountain with a girl whose husband tried to blackmail me into having sex with him? Not the nicest coincidence I've ever experienced.

"How perfect," I say as she glides over and gives me a kiss on the cheek. "You have the exact look we need."

"You're so kind, but I've been feeling horrible recently. I put on five pounds over the last two weeks. Ridley says I eat too much rice and potatoes. I hope I still look okay for you."

Oh god, the woman occupies a whole different universe, doesn't she? Five bloody pounds? I feel like telling her she has far more important things to worry about than that – like the fact her husband is a lying, cheating, creepy sexual predator – but then I look at Delfina's innocent dark eyes, her perfectly sculpted eyebrows arched over natural long lashes that Bambi would envy, and I can't summon any dislike for her, only pity.

"Don't worry. You look absolutely stunning, as always," I assure her, and her face lights up.

"You're so kind, Vee-o-let. And so pretty too." I thank her, just as Stuart appears at the bar. "Stuart, Stuart, come over here for a minute," she calls out. My stomach groans – and not just through hunger. "I was just saying to Vee-o-let how pretty she is. Don't you agree?" She turns back to me. "Poor Stuart has just broken up with his girlfriend. Why don't you two sit together at dinner and get to know one another personally?"

"We're already acquainted, um, personally, thank you," I say.

"Yeah, I'm just in here to get another beer, Daphne," adds Stuart.

Delfina tuts and tosses her mane of shiny black hair over her shoulder. Her skin is bronzed, with light golden freckles, and she's wearing a white backless top with dark skinny jeans that ruffle at the ankle. "My

193

name is Delfina. *Del-fee-na* – it means 'dolphin' in Portuguese."

Stuart makes a brusque apology, grabs his beer and heads outside.

"What is the matter with him?" asks Delfina, her voice filled with genuine hurt.

If I were the type of girl who has friends who are girls and has experience of talking about girl stuff, then I would be telling her all about Stuart right now. But as I can't be bothered to indulge in any sort of female bonding, I don't.

"He was so lovely on the drive up here. He told me how sad he was about breaking up with his beautiful girlfriend. Did you ever meet Adele? He showed me a photo. She looks just like Gigi Hadid – simply gorgeous – and Stuart's so adorable."

I have no idea who Gigi Hadid is, but I have a vision of puking up my still-beating heart at the thought of anyone describing Stuart Inman as adorable.

"Come on, Vee-o-let. Everyone is outside enjoying the warm evening."

Delfina takes my arm and leads me out to a garden which backs straight onto the lake. Daniel is sitting next to Stuart, looking the epitome of cool sophistication in a crisp white shirt and dark jeans. He meets my gaze and smiles warmly as I approach. For the hundredth time I wonder why I didn't try to make a go of dating him.

The three film crew members finish their beers and say they're foregoing dinner in favour of heading out to search the area for a great shoot location. I don't know the guys well, but one of them is called Dave Handcock, which I don't think I'll ever stop finding hilarious.

Wendy Smith, our TV producer, is dressed in her usual casual trousers, vest and open shirt with a trio of brightly coloured bead necklaces draped around her neck. The bangles, woven fabric bracelets and politically charged rubber slogan bands around her wrists complete her look, as does her cropped grey hair, which is wispy and feathered around her face. Wendy is too young to be grey, but she's a vegan, a Green Party activist and the single mother of twins, so I guess her hair perfectly complements her whole "peace and love" hippie-mum persona.

Wendy introduces another model, Alyssa, who is married to an actor called Richie Robbins. I pretend to know who Richie is, but I don't have a clue. The very mention of his name makes make-up artist Chip, a girl with a dyed-pink pixie cut, swoon like a teenager. As I listen to them gush about Richie's recent stint in a daytime soap I've never heard of, I feel a tap on my shoulder. It's Stuart.

"Hi. I wanted to talk to you about last week. I have no excuse for my behaviour, but things have been really rough for me, and you know Adele and I have broken up for good. I hope . . . I mean . . . I want to make it up to you."

"I'm not going out with you again, Stuart."

"No, I know that," he says. I catch Daniel glancing my way protectively. He's trying his best not to look like he's listening, but he has no choice given he's sitting right next to us. Stuart leans in closer and lowers his voice. "I know I've blown it with you, and I know I'm a total prick—"

"Are you just going to tell me things I already know?"

He leans back in his chair and gulps another

mouthful of beer. His strong jaw is clenched and I can tell he's annoyed. Maybe I should ease up on him.

"I just want us to get on. We still have a couple of months left until our contract ends. And I'm truly sorry for what I did."

I glance back over at Daniel, who gives me a friendly wink, before returning my attention to Stuart. "Okay, you're forgiven. And I'm sorry for throwing wine over your head. Well . . . on balance, you did deserve the wine, so I'm only a tiny bit sorry."

"That's good enough for me. Can I buy you another drink?"

"Don't push it."

"Okay. Erm . . . we'll talk later then."

I look up as Ethan descends the few small steps from the hotel bar to the garden area. He's wearing a fitted grey t-shirt with pale jeans, and as he sits down between me and Stuart, I inhale his cologne; sea breeze mixed with peppermint – perfect. He starts up a conversation with Stuart about Carly, and I overhear that she's staying with her parents in Southampton while she's in rehab. She was discharged from hospital yesterday and Stuart says she's taking a six-month sabbatical from work.

This may not be great news. I was hoping she'd be around in case I needed her to help me with Ridley. Which, in hindsight, was stupid considering she hates me, but the option was at least there. Except now it isn't.

We're called to the hotel restaurant at nine. I sit next to Wendy at dinner and she shows me photos of her adorable kids – a boy dressed in a Motörhead t-shirt with the same woven bracelets around his wrists that Wendy wears, and a girl in pigtails wearing a bright-pink bicycle helmet and braces on her teeth.

"They're gorgeous, Wendy. I don't know how you manage a family on your own *and* do your job so well. Who's looking after them now?"

"My parents live close by. They've been great with the twins. Carl has always been so close to his Grandma, while Isla only has eyes for Gramps."

Wendy smiles with pride as she talks about her family. I try to remember what happened to their dad. I'm sure he was a wrong'un, but I can't remember the details. I don't mention him just in case there's a tragedy I've forgotten lurking in the background. "You're so lucky to have them."

"I know," she says with a beaming smile. "I'm truly blessed. But what about you? Is there anyone special in your life at the moment?"

Oh god, here we go. Cue everyone around the table telling me I should be out dating and enjoying myself. "Actually, I've sworn off men for the foreseeable future."

Delfina overhears and shrieks so loud her voice echoes through the hills. "You can't! You're too beautiful to be on your own! It's such a waste. You're so talented and clever and funny . . . and you have an amazing figure. Tell her, Ethan."

Okay. Awkward on a scale of fucking infinity . . .

"Nobody can tell Violet anything," Ethan replies. His tone is firm and his expression is serious.

What? What the hell does that mean? I'm just about to question him further when Delfina says something stupid again. "My Ridley is such a gentleman. He is handsome and successful, and he treats me like a princess. You need to find your own Ridley, Vee-o-let."

Don't tell her to fuck off. Don't tell her to fuck off.

197

Don't tell her to fuck off.

"There's only one Ridley Gates in this world, Delfina. You won the jackpot."

Ethan shoots me a warning look that could make sugar turn sour. It wasn't so much what I said, but the way I said it. I hope my sarcasm gets lost in translation.

"What is a jackpot?" she asks in her breathy accent.

"A prize," I say.

"Oh," she replies, sadness and confusion in her voice. I'll have to watch my mouth. Using sarcasm on Delfina is like pulling the wings off a butterfly – it's very easy to do, yet heartbreakingly cruel.

Stuart finishes his drink, stands up and smooths down the crumples in his shirt. "If you'll excuse me, I think I'll turn in for the night."

"Oh no, why are you leaving so soon, Stuart?" Delfina asks. She still sounds sad and confused.

"Busy day tomorrow."

"Have you got a date with Mrs Palm and her five daughters?" asks Ethan, grinning mischievously. But Stuart isn't laughing.

"What do you mean?" Delfina says as Ethan chuckles away at his own childishness. "Who is this Mrs Palm? Have you met a new lady already, Stuart?"

"You'll have to forgive Ethan. All he thinks about is sex and he's probably been wondering if he'll get any tonight." Touché, Stuart, touché. Ethan smirks and takes the retort on the chin, but unfortunately Stuart doesn't leave the matter alone. "It's just a shame he tends to wait until women are smashed out of their skulls before he screws them."

Oh my god, why? Talk about fighting a lit match with a nuclear bomb.

Ethan is on his feet before I have time to calm him

down. "What the hell did you just say to me?" he yells, squaring up to Stuart. "Repeat it!"

"You heard what I said the first time," Stuart says flippantly. Ethan moves towards him.

My insides twist themselves into a knot and fear forces me to my feet. "Ethan, leave it!"

To my great relief Daniel places his body between them. "Both of you need to calm down, right now. Remember we're here on business and you're both representing your companies."

Stuart fixes his gaze on Ethan, refusing to be the first to back down.

Ethan throws his arms up in the air and takes a step back.

Delfina starts to cry.

"As I said – time for me to turn in." Stuart takes a final swig of beer and swiftly leaves the hotel restaurant. Ethan mutters "Wanker" under his breath as he watches him leave, his jaw clenching tight.

"Is this my fault? I don't even understand what this is about . . ." bawls Delfina. Wendy leaves her seat to throw motherly arms around her while Alyssa and Chip make soothing "there, there" noises.

Ethan retakes his seat. "I'm sorry," he says to the table. I should be angry with him, but his sorrowful expression, coupled with his refusal to make eye contact, makes my heart ache.

"Why did you have to be so rude, Ethan?" Delfina says. "Stuart has been so sad about breaking up with Adele, and who is this Mrs Palm?"

"Just leave it, Delfina. I've said I'm sorry," says Ethan.

I interject quickly, hoping to move the conversation on. "We've all had a bit of a rough time recently.

There's still some friction between us and the client."

"I know what's going on, I'm not stupid. Ridley told me all about you and poor Carly," says Delfina. Would now be the right time to tell her she actually is stupid? Anybody who chooses to marry pervy philanderer Ridley Gates has clearly parked their head then forgotten where they've left it.

"Look, this is none of your business," Ethan snaps.

"Stuart was talking about you when he said you wait until 'women are smashed out of their skulls', wasn't he?" Delfina says. "You should have looked after Carly better."

Don't tell her Carly was screwing her husband. Don't tell her Carly was screwing her husband. I think the irony is burning my brain even more than the anger.

"You don't know the full story, Delfina," says Ethan. "Can we talk about something else, please?"

Delfina wipes the tears from her face, and Wendy passes her a tissue from her purse. "I do not understand men in this country. Brazilian men have much more respect for women. If it wasn't for my Ridley, I would have no faith in British men—"

"Oh please, save us. Your Ridley is a vile pig, and the only person who can't see it is you. Are you blind as well as shallow?"

Shit. The words are out of my mouth before I can stop them. I know I shouldn't have said that, but at least I didn't tell her about the cheating. The entire table falls silent, waiting for the apocalyptic event we all know will follow. If using sarcasm on Delfina is like pulling the wings off a butterfly, then criticising her beloved husband is like ripping off its legs and decorating a cupcake with them.

Delfina pulls out of Wendy's hold, stands up and

throws me a glare filled with pure hate. My body tenses. But instead of sniping back at me, she runs off. Wendy chases after her, leaving Alyssa and Chip to scowl at me with all the intensity of a pair of velociraptors.

And I feel like shit. Although calling Ridley Gates a vile pig is insulting to every pig in the world, none of this is Delfina's fault.

"What's the deal with Ridley?" asks Daniel, his voice steady and direct. Ethan's eyes grow wide, urging me not to let the kittens, catnip, kitty litter, tins of tuna and pint of milk out of the bag with the cat. As if I would.

"I just don't like him," I say in a whisper.

"Nobody does. But there's obviously more to it than that," Daniel says.

I stand, forcing a smile. "It's been a long day." I want to say more, but I'm too upset with myself. Instead, I leave the restaurant and head for my room, pretending I don't notice Wendy and a sobbing Delfina huddled in a stairwell on my way.

I'm rummaging in my purse for my door key – just metres away from my room – when Ethan catches up with me. "Hey, Violet. Wait up."

My body sighs. I put the key back in my purse and stop walking.

"Are you okay?" he asks, his head bent to the side and his eyes filled with concern.

"Aside from devastating Delfina for no good reason, you mean?"

He shrugs. "She's an idiot."

"She didn't deserve that." I suck on my bottom lip to stop my tears from falling.

"Apologise to her tomorrow. It'll be fine."

My eyes glass over, and his face blurs. I take a deep breath. "I feel terrible," I say with a shaky sob.

He swings his arm around me and pulls me into his chest. "It's not your fault." The delicious smell of his cologne and the feel of his hard body makes me cry even more. "If anything, it's my fault. I know you were trying to defend me."

He strokes my hair gently and my grip tightens around his waist. Our bodies mould together, and his hand moves to cup my cheek, his thumb brushing softly against my warm skin.

I can't move. And I don't think I want to move.

His fingers slide under my chin, and he lifts my face to his. I feel his breath float across my body, softly tickling my chest, as his eyes search out mine. What is he searching for? He's been drinking all night. Is he seeking out comfort again?

I let my arm fall from his waist and I take a step back, my back pressing against the wall. I expect him to apologise, but he doesn't. I expect him to walk away, but he comes towards me instead. His breathing is fast. My heart rate speeds up and synchronises with it.

"I should go," I say.

"I . . . just wanted to make sure you were okay . . ." He repeats his earlier words, but this time his voice gets lost in his throat. He moves closer again. We're inches apart, and even though we're not touching, I can feel him all over me. He rests one of his hands on the wall behind my head, bracketing me against it. His body is hard and strong and he's close enough that I can smell his skin. He touches my hair and my knees wobble.

"I'm not okay . . ." I say softly.

"Neither am I."

"What are we doing?"

"This."

He brings his lips to mine. His tongue sweeps into my mouth as his hand moves from my hair to my neck, pulling me even closer in to him. My purse drops to the floor as I move both my hands to cup his face. A swell of desire forms in my belly, urging my lips to part wider and taste even more of him.

But then he pulls away.

"I'm sorry," he gasps, rubbing at the back of his neck. "I . . . I . . . we can't . . ."

My eyes frantically search his, but he looks away. What on earth is he thinking? Why is he doing this to me? He takes a step back. Then another. And another.

"I'm so sorry. You have your law, and . . ." He backs away again, but then he stops and turns to face me. "We have everything already."

"You think we have *everything*?" I ask, wondering what on earth he means.

"Yes, our friendship is everything."

He turns away again, and this time he leaves. I watch him walk away, my body groaning with loss as he leaves my sight. These feelings I've been so determined to ignore are real and I'm certain he's feeling it too.

I pick my purse up off the floor, find my key and retreat to my room, wondering if that kiss means I've lost my best friend.

18

AS YOU'D EXPECT, I DIDN'T sleep well last night. There's just something about my best friend kissing me – with tongue – that frazzles my brain.

And when I say frazzle, I mean *frazzle*.

I hoped that getting out of the city for a few days would be a wonderful opportunity to order my thoughts. I wanted to use the time away to come up with a plan to help Malcolm. I also wanted to work out how to silence Ridley – for good.

Most of all, I hoped to find a way to navigate my relationship with Ethan. But I'm no further forward.

In fact, I feel like I'm stuck in a huge pit of thick, paralysing mud and every move I make is sinking me further towards the bottom. I'm losing control – the thing I hate most – and, because I'm always firmly in the driving seat of my life, it's impossible to stop freaking out . . .

Oh, and Ethan Fraser kissed me.

Every time my mind wanders back to the present, or to the shoot, or to what the hell I'm going to do once I'm back in London, memories of the kiss creep back into my brain, making my stomach knot and my pelvis ache: his hands in my hair, his lips on mine, the smell, feel and taste of him . . .

Oh my god, it happened. Ethan Fraser kissed me.

I want to accept how I feel, but I don't know what that is. Am I actually falling in love with him? When I think back to all the great times we've had over the years – the best ones usually ending with us getting drunk, falling over and vomiting in a bush – our past and present don't match up. Ethan and I goof around, do daft things, tease each other, bicker over whose turn it is to choose our favourite takeaway and laugh until our sides split. We're best friends – just friends.

Maybe I should just be straight-up honest with how I'm feeling and how confused I am. I should tackle this like any other problem needing to be fixed. Maybe I need to put up some kind of a fight for him. But not yet. Wow. "Not yet" . . . that's solid progress from "never". When did that scary thought get inside my brain? Maybe a time will come when fighting is a far better and less risky option than shutting my feelings away, but I don't think that time is now.

***

I skip breakfast and frown at my overnight bag, which seems to have skipped sensible clothing. What weather was I expecting? I grew up in rural Yorkshire, so I should have known better. Yet, an hour later, here I am, standing at the summit of a mossy hill wearing thin jeggings, a cotton shirt and a jacket selected for a London summer – as opposed to a halfway-up-a-mountain-in-northernmost-England summer.

I choose to walk with Wendy to the shoot location while everyone else piles inside the vomit van. It only takes twenty minutes; the fresh air and beautiful scenery is welcome, but the cold isn't. I perch on a drystone wall and watch the tech guys battle the elements to set up their equipment. It feels like the wind is going to blow me Humpty-Dumpty style off the wall at any moment, and the jagged stones are biting into my behind. You could say I don't enjoy working on location. I was raised a country girl, but give me the city any day. My nipples are so stiff and raw I could hang a wet raincoat and a bag of shopping on them.

As the sun breaks through a fluffy white cloud, Wendy, Ethan and Daniel set up a great shot with Delfina, who is refusing to make eye contact with me, while Chip tries her best, given the wind, to straighten Alyssa's hair. When Delfina jumps in the back of the vomit van to change into another outfit, I try to have a word with her, but she won't even look at me. I tell the van door that I'm sorry about yesterday after she slams it in my face.

Ethan has been working with Wendy all morning, entirely engrossed in our project, and although he's given me a wink and a couple of smiles, we haven't had the chance to speak to each other. To be honest, I'm feeling like a bit of a spare part this morning. As a copywriter, it's useful to watch TV shoots and I've scribbled a few copy ideas down on my notepad, but this is Ethan's baby. He knows exactly what he wants the ad to look like, and he knows how to work with Wendy to make it happen.

Daniel slides up next to me. "Have you seen Stuart this morning?"

I hop down from the wall and give my arse a discreet rub. "No, not a word. Did you have breakfast together?"

Daniel nods, just as his phone buzzes. He takes it out of the pocket of his jeans. "Ah, speak of the devil. It's Stuart," he says as he answers the call. "Hi Stuart, where are you? . . . Uh-huh . . . What do you mean you need help? . . . Look, mate, calm down. Don't you have another pair of shoes? . . . Uh-huh . . . Okay, well the production assistant can go to your room . . . No, he can't go to your room if you have the key. You'll have to come up . . . Don't be silly . . . Look, they're just shoes and they can be cleaned. See you soon."

He puts his phone back in his pocket as a large grin spreads over his face, making his cheeks round like apples. "Trouble?" I ask.

Daniel starts to laugh. "He was on his way up the hill when he trod in some shit."

"Oh." I imagine how horrific this will be for Stuart's Italian leather shoes, not to mention his vanity. "That's too bad."

We laugh as Ethan approaches. "What's up?" he asks Daniel, his eyes briefly fleeting to meet mine.

"Stuart trod in some shit," says Daniel.

"Jesus Christ, is that all? Can he not rub it off on some grass? We've been waiting over an hour for him to review our film. How long is he going to be?"

"He's on his way up now."

Ethan heads back over to Wendy, who is straightening a sparkly halter-necked dress on Alyssa. Wendy has arrived on location in Hunter wellington boots, a canvas jacket and layers of sensible clothing. You can tell she's a mum – always prepared. I pull my much thinner jacket around me and rub my still-stinging nipples to make sure they haven't dropped off. There is nothing on earth like nip-freeze. Nothing.

"Oh my fucking god, it's Bigfoot!" Ethan shouts suddenly.

I turn around and gasp as everyone else breaks into howls of laughter.

Stuart makes it up the hill, and we're all horrified to see that he hasn't just trodden in your regular everyday animal poo; he's fallen into something a brontosaurus might have done. Thankfully his head and the top of his chest look clean, but from his abdomen down he's covered in shit. The wind blows waves of grass around his feet as he trudges towards us, bringing the overbearing aroma of fresh dinosaur dung with him.

"Jesus Christ, Stuart. What the hell happened?" Daniel asks.

"I told you I needed help," he moans, holding his hands high to stop himself from touching his body. This is pointless because his hands are covered in it too. "I lost my footing climbing a fence. Thought I'd fallen in mud, but I think it's sheep shit."

"You reckon?" howls Ethan.

"I don't think a sheep could produce that much," says the ever-practical Wendy. "And sheep excrement is usually darker and more solid."

"Thank you for your input, Farmer Giles," Stuart says, just as Delfina appears from the vomit van in an ochre knitted mini-dress.

"Oh my god, oh my god, oh my god!" she shrieks when she sees him. Her body convulses, then she starts to retch. "I will be sick! Why have you done this?" She shields her mouth and nose with her hands and dives back into the van.

"Don't you dare be sick in that van," shouts Stuart. "I have to drive back to London in that, and nothing stinks like puke."

"Erm, you might want to have a smell of yourself, Stuart." Ethan is clearly enjoying Stuart's predicament to the max.

"Cow!" Wendy shouts. "It's definitely not sheep shit. I'd guess cow shit."

"I don't give a fuck which animal's arse this stuff came out of." Stuart looks down at his ruined Balmain

208

jeans. "I just need clothes and shoes quickly. They won't let me in the hotel looking like this. The Hayfield is a five-star establishment!"

"I'll go and get them for you," I say, figuring I'll take the opportunity to put a vest on under my shirt and try to warm my nipples up a bit. They're in a climate zone all of their own at the moment.

"Erm, no thanks," says Stuart.

"Why?"

He looks a bit embarrassed, but all eyes are on him, waiting for an answer. "Well, I don't want you getting my underwear."

As if I haven't seen his underwear before – and the sorrowful appendage that dwells beneath it. "Are you being serious?"

"I'll go," says Daniel. "Come back with me, and I'll see if the hotel has something I can hose you down with." Stuart starts to follow Daniel down the hill. He's walking carefully, but he slips on some moss and lands on his bottom. "Ordinarily I'd help you up, but today I'm not touching you," Daniel says as Stuart clambers sorrowfully to his feet.

***

The shoot continues until late. When the sun starts to set over the vast landscape of green hills and navy-blue lakes, Wendy declares she's lost her light and we have all the shots we need for the ad. We finish up and have a late dinner.

Back in my hotel room, I reward myself with a muscle-tingling bath. The smell of grapefruit-scented bath bubbles cleanses the aroma of the outdoors from my skin, and I take a few soothing moments to think about today. Aside from Stuart falling into a pile of shit – hereafter remembered as "karma at its finest" – today felt totally normal. Ethan was naturally absorbed in creating the ad, and it's been a productive day. We worked together just like old times – or rather, like last night's kiss never happened. And I'm not sure how I feel about that. On the one hand, I'd be ecstatic if it meant our friendship could get back on track. But on the other hand . . . I want to find out if he really is feeling what I'm feeling. Could we have an even better relationship if we became something more than just friends?

I sigh. It's 11 p.m. and I know I could easily stay up all night asking myself these questions. I put on my pyjamas and climb into bed, twisting my still-damp hair up into a hairband. I switch on my Kindle and start reading one of the many books I seem to collect but rarely get a chance to read, determined to lose myself in someone else's love story.

***

Bang! Bang! Bang!

I climb out of bed to the sound of some twat with a death wish hammering at my door. I've never wanted to kill somebody so much in my entire life. I was enjoying a rather lovely dream involving Tom Hardy taking me on an adventure up the Nile. And no, that isn't a euphemism for sex, although if my dream hadn't been bulldozed I'm sure Tom and I would have ultimately explored our feelings for one another in a long-lost tomb of a forgotten pharaoh. Who says my passion for

Egyptology is dull?

I thunder my way to my door, leaving a cloud of angry mist in my wake as the knocking continues. My hair's a damp matted mess, my vest is erring towards indecent, and my stripy pink pyjama bottoms have a blob of orange body scrub stuck to them. I usually don't care what I look like, but when I open the door to reveal Ethan brandishing a bottle of wine and two glasses, I suddenly feel like the tail end of a donkey.

"Ethan? What the hell are you doing here? It's the middle of the night!" He cocks his head to one side and smiles a mischievously sexy smile, but it doesn't have the usual effect when my eyelids are stuck together with sleep. I still want to kill him.

"Firstly, I'm here because I want to talk to you. Secondly, it's only eleven thirty."

I gasp and run my hand through my hair, but stop when my fingers get tangled in a knot so large it would make the perfect home for a colony of ants. There's also something sticky in the knot. Ah, more body scrub. I pull my hair out of the hairband, attempt to smooth the ants' nest down, then scrape it up into a ponytail. "Only eleven thirty? It can't be."

"Yup, I'm afraid so," he says with a wine-infused slur.

"Well, what do you want?"

He twists his face at the abruptness in my tone. "I want to talk to you, but preferably not in the hotel corridor."

I roll my eyes then move aside. His eyes drift to my indecent vest top as he walks into the room. Or rather, they drift to what's underneath the indecent vest top. "I hear Malcolm Barrett isn't the only one interested in my tits," I say as I close the door behind me.

"Eh? Oh . . . sorry, they were in my line of vision, what can I say?"

I grab a cardigan out of my overnight bag, wrap it around me and button it across my chest. He sits down in an armchair, places the two glasses on the table and fills them both half full. I sit down on the edge of the double bed, deeply aware that the setting is probably – no, definitely – inappropriate. Ethan takes a drink of wine, his arm shaking slightly when he places the glass back down on the polished side table. I scrutinise his expression. There's a faint smile and a sparkle in his eyes, so I assume the talk isn't going to be serious.

"Okay, spit it out," I say, tucking one of my legs underneath me. "Is this about Delfina? Because I know I shouldn't have said what I said and I've already told her I'm sorry. Admittedly, she was behind a closed door when I apologised, but—"

"No, it isn't about Delfina, although . . . Okay, you did call an executive director of our agency a vile pig, so we are going to have to work out a defence to that when we get back to London. I admire your directness, Vi, honestly I do, but when you piss off the people we have to work with, it's bad for my career as well as yours."

I pause as Ethan's frustration with me sinks in. "I'm trying to work on that, but nobody's perfect. I've been trying to think before I speak for twenty-eight years without much success."

"Can we not do this again?" He rubs at his brow. His skin has developed a pink flush and his breath reeks of alcohol. "I didn't come here to talk about Ridley sodding Gates." He picks up the wine bottle and refills his glass. "Are you not drinking?"

I don't need wine. I need sleep. But I suppose wine

is the next best thing. I pick up the other glass and have a sip. Then a gulp. Maybe I do need wine after all.

"So . . . um . . . where shall we start?" I ask tentatively. His smile morphs into what I think of as "my smile". It's big and beautiful and makes his eyes glint in a way that I only see when he's talking to me. I confess the jury's out on whether I'm imagining the uniqueness of this particular smile, but I'm going to claim it anyway.

"We could start with 'I don't know how the hell to start talking to you'," he says. "Do you know where to start?"

The look of abject terror in his eyes breaks the ice and I giggle. "No, but I have to admit I'm feeling a bit scared."

"I don't believe you. Violet Archer is never scared. That's why I . . ." He pauses as the momentary ease on his face is replaced by terror again. "That's why I love you."

A swell of desire builds deep inside my pelvis, and my possibly-in-love heart squeezes tight when he says those three words. I can feel my pulse pounding in my head and . . . I *am* scared. Shit, I'm so scared I can hear my teeth chattering in my skull. But . . . wait . . . what kind of love is he talking about here? *Don't assume he means that kind and look like a fool.* All friends love each other, don't they? As in platonic love? What on earth do I say next? I dig deep, and all I come up with is . . . "Oh."

Words fail me again. I'm a twit – this year's winner of the world's most twittiest nitwit award.

"Was that a good 'Oh' or a bad 'Oh'?" he asks.

"It was an I-have-no-fucking-idea 'Oh', which I think means we have a problem."

213

"Well it doesn't sound good."

"Generally problems aren't good, but the first step in fixing a problem is realising there is a problem, so it might be more good than bad."

"Okay," he says with a nervous laugh. "Well, fixing stuff is definitely your area."

"Do you need to be fixed?"

His eyes meet mine and he holds my gaze for what seems like an hour. "I don't think so. Loving you just feels right."

I cross my legs on the bed, my feet tucking under my shins, and I try to ignore my heart thudding in my chest but I feel like I'm going to pass out. I take a deep breath, followed by a deeper plunge. "When you say 'loving me feels right' . . . um . . . what kind of love are we talking about here?"

His gaze becomes more intense, burrowing under my skin. "I haven't completely figured that out yet, but it was the kind that made me kiss you last night."

Suddenly I'm on my feet, but I've nowhere to walk, so I stand in front of him looking stupid, acting stupidly and thinking stupid thoughts. "Ethan, I . . . um . . . oh fuck . . . this really is a problem."

He stands up too. "Why?"

"You know why." I lean my back flat against the wall and stare up at the ceiling. My body is aware that he's just inches away from me, and it craves his touch. "Jesus Christ, Ethan . . . you're my friend! We've been best friends for three years. And you're pissed. Are you saying this because you're pissed?"

"No, I'm saying this because it's how I feel," he says with a smile that lights up his irises with specks of blue and amber. "I didn't plan this, Vi. I just started seeing you differently. I've always loved you. You're the best friend I've ever had, but I don't know what being in love with somebody feels like because I honestly don't think it's happened before. Not like this. You know the part I play – Ethan Fraser, the life of the party, the guy who always gets the girl. That's me, right? Except I've never got the girl. Not the one I wanted. Nobody has ever come close to making me feel like this . . ."

He makes a grab for my hand, but I pull away. "Ethan, I can't . . ." My voice shakes and I wish with everything I have that I wasn't such a wimp. Then I walk towards the door. I don't know where I'm going or what I'm doing – this is my hotel room after all – I just need to move away from him. "You can't love me, Ethan. Not like that. I'm nothing like the women you fall for. I'm not outgoing or exciting. I'm wrong . . . everything about me is wrong for you."

"You're not wrong," he says, frowning under the amber lighting. "How could you even think that? You're everything."

"You said yesterday that our friendship was everything. And then you ran away."

"I was scared yesterday, even though you kissed me back and it felt like . . . it just felt so wonderful." He moves closer and I push my back up against the door, my hand grasping for the handle. "I don't want you to be like anybody else. I want you to be you. I love you. And that's why I walked away last night. I can't help how I feel, but I'm shit scared of losing you because of it."

"You've been drinking, Ethan. How do I know this is real? This is what you do – you get drunk, then get needy, then shag the first woman in sight."

"That's not me anymore," he says, sounding wounded.

215

"It's barely been a week since Carly. A week since you vowed never to do this again."

His body stiffens and he rakes his hand over his hair. "So, this is about your law?"

"No, screw my law. This is about us." I turn the door handle and open the door. "I can't do this now. We can talk again when you've sobered up."

He walks into the corridor. He looks ready to say something, but instead he reaches out and sweeps an errant loop of hair from my face. I flinch instinctively, but then I let him tuck it behind my ear. "I was wrong yesterday. We don't have everything, but we could have . . ."

He leaves.

I text Daniel to say we're swapping our rides back to London tomorrow.

19

THE DRIVE HOME FROM CUMBRIA yesterday couldn't have gone worse. Delfina still hates me, Stuart still reeked of Eau de Cow Shit, Wendy bored us all about London's inadequate recycling facilities, and Dave Handcock (yes, his name is still hilarious) blessed the journey by developing the prostate of a pensioner. We had to pull over every half an hour so he could pee.

I got back to my flat by seven in the evening, and – somewhat miraculously given I couldn't sleep a wink for mulling – I was at my desk by eight o'clock this morning, far too wound up to eat. This means I'm starving, and nothing exacerbates my overthinking like hunger.

Ethan texted just after nine to let me know Stella and Ridley have scheduled a review of our location work at nine thirty. Not something I'm looking forward to considering I'm still totally consumed by visions of punching Ridley in the face. That's the other thing I'm overthinking about. What the hell am I going to do about Ridley Gates?

***

Just before the meeting, my stomach gets the better of me. I go to the kitchen to get a granola yoghurt, and Ethan's there. He comes over to the fridge and I'm overtaken by nerves. I want to say something, but as I mix around words to make sentences in my brain, the fear of sounding like a deranged lunatic, a heartless bitch and a needy drama queen all bundled into one super-scary package means I say nothing.

Ethan doesn't speak either. I watch him faff around in the fridge, but I can't imagine he has any food of his own in there. He always goes out for lunch.

"If you want a yoghurt, I have another one. Top shelf, right-hand side."

"You do? Oh, um, right. Thank you."

I pull the lid of my yoghurt pot open and a splatter of pale purple sprays up my arm, followed by a huge splodge which lands on my top. "Oh, crap. I loved this top."

"Here, let me get it," Ethan offers. I lick the yoghurt off my arm as he wets a piece of kitchen towel under the tap. He goes to dab it onto my top, stopping only when he realises the splodge settled directly on my left boob. He passes me the paper towel with a sheepish smile, and our eyes lock. He's looking at me in a way I don't like – there's a dash of frustration, a pinch of embarrassment, a sprinkle of longing and a large dollop of hesitation. I wonder what kind of cake I'd have to eat if I mixed that lot up and baked it in a tray for an hour or two. I'm sure it'd be the type that looks great but makes you sick after three mouthfuls.

"Ridley wants to see you after the meeting. Delfina told him about Vile-pig-gate. I tried to shrug it all off, but . . . well, you know how it is."

"That's fine." I dab at my top and get most of the purple off, but it will probably need a trip to the dry cleaners. I pick up a spoon and head back to my desk.

***

Ridley, Stella, Daniel and Wendy are assembled around a circular table in Conference Room C for a reveal of the material for the Quest ad. Ethan runs through Wendy's footage, detailing his ideas as images of Delfina and Alyssa wearing the best high-street outfits money can buy flash across a big-screen TV. He outlines the copy I wrote whilst having a drystone wall wedged up my bottom, and I watch as Ridley twists his creepy slimeball face at every single one of Ethan's ideas.

"I don't think you captured Delfina's best angle on that shot, Wendy."

"How could you let those outfits pass by the lens, Daniel? Stuart won't be pleased with those choices."

"Why did you shoot with only the hills as backdrop? You were sent to the Lakes and I can't see any lakes."

"The copy is wrong. It needs more work."

"The lighting is wrong. See what the CGI unit can do with that."

After he makes his twentieth negative comment in a row, Stella steps in. "Oh for fuck's sake, Ridley. The work isn't complete. We know what we still need to do."

"My arse is on the line here, Stella. I'm trying to save this account. I slogged my guts out to win this client." Daniel shifts in his seat at that news and I don't blame him – everyone knows it was Daniel who slogged his guts out to win Quest. Ridley showed up on contract-signing day with a champagne lunch catered by Ampersand and has taken full credit ever since. "Despite what you might think of our roles in this agency, we're *both* creative people, and I recognise crap when I see it."

"Ah, Ridley, I really wish you hadn't said that," Stella says. She's wearing a red, 1930s-style, figure-hugging sheath dress with a dramatic neckline and sleeves which ruffle at her wrists – like a modern-day Joan Crawford. "I could have let all this go if only you hadn't said that. You want to know why you don't *ever* get to describe yourself as creative? Because you're fucking not."

Ridley rises to the bait, his peroxide smile dazzling bright against his orange-tanned face. "Wow, is the great Stella Judd going to lose her cool over an adjective?"

Daniel clears his throat in a bid to draw the attention of the warring directors. He looks embarrassed, while Ethan looks pissed off and Wendy looks devastated.

"Let me tell you what a creative is, you ridiculously overly-Tangoed shitgibbon," says Stella, slamming her notepad shut and fixing her black-rimmed glasses to the edge of her nose. "A creative is someone who lives and breathes ingenuity, innovation and imagination. The people who designed this ad – my people – put in more hours than you every bloody day. Creatives are the engine that keep this whole machine running. I give no fucks if you disagree with me on that, but by all means come back to this discussion after you win an AdAg award or seven."

Ridley's grin doesn't waver. He's been playing the role of smug twat so long that he has it perfected to a fine art. "You lot may be the engine, but I'm the ignition."

Oh, dear lord. This could go on for some time.

"Come on, you two, you're acting like children," says Daniel.

"Nonsense. If I don't fight with Ridley, I'm not

doing my job properly. And if he doesn't fight with me, he isn't doing his. That's how things roll between creative and client services. Ridley just can't deal with the fact I beat him all the time." She peers through her smart reading glasses at her antagonist. "I do empathise with how I make you feel about yourself, Ridley."

"How about we review again later today?" Ethan says, successfully breaking up the bickering. "Wendy, can you do some post-production on the film and run some of Violet's narrative behind it?"

Wendy looks like she's been hit in the face by a force-nine gale, and I fight an urge to give her a hug. "Um . . . sure . . . I'll get straight on it."

"Maybe if we can see the Quest hashtag too," says Daniel. "It's always better to view an ad when it has all the correct branding."

"Great idea," Ethan says. "Violet, can you perfect your copy and get it to Wendy this afternoon?"

"Sure, we can get to work on that," I say, catching Ethan's eye across the conference room table. He gives me a smile which makes my insides flutter.

"No, it's not good enough. I'm not putting this in front of the client," says Ridley. "It doesn't scream 'adventure' to me; it screams 'tree-hugging leftie let loose with a camera.' How did you make Delfina look like a deranged Druidic wild-woman? Who did her eye make-up? She looks like she's possessed."

Wendy looks ready to explode, and I don't blame her. He's making this personal for no good reason.

"What the hell side of the bed did you wake up on this morning?" asks Daniel. This makes everyone in the room sit up and take notice. Daniel never loses his cool.

Ridley grits his teeth. "Watch yourself, Daniel."

"I don't need to watch anything. Stuart was with us

221

on the shoot – well, aside from the shit incident. He loves Wendy's work on this, and so do I."

"And so do I," Stella chimes in.

"Well, neither of you two are head of the Client Services department – I am," Ridley says authoritatively. "I get to decide if our product fits the client's brief – and it doesn't."

"Were you listening? The client has already seen the shoot footage and he likes it," says Stella dismissively. "By the way, what was the shit incident?"

"Stuart fell off a fence and landed in a mound of cow shit," Ethan explains, a glimmer of humour flashing in his eyes as he recalls the funniest thing that's happened since Max attempted to iron a t-shirt whilst wearing it and singed his chest hair.

"Oh my god, really? I'd have paid good money to see that. How much of the shoot did he miss?" asks Stella.

"A few hours. I took him back to the hotel and he had to be hosed down and stripped in the car park," Daniel says, laughing.

The mood seems to lift, but just when I think we're home and dry, Ridley reminds everyone he's a shit-stirring prick again. "Violet, just one thing before everyone heads off to see if they can salvage the thousands of pounds we've wasted on this shoot. I told Ethan I'd save this until after the meeting, but I think Stella should know. Can you explain the fracas you had with my wife?"

"There was no fracas," Ethan says abruptly.

"Now isn't the time or the place to talk about it," I add. What on earth is he playing at? Is he daring me to talk about everything I know about him and Carly and Malcolm in front of Stella? Or is this his way of making sure I don't?

"Wendy, Daniel and Ethan, you are excused." Stella's gaze is steely, but when she looks at Ridley's smug expression, I think the penny drops. "What's this all about, Violet?"

Daniel and Wendy get up to leave, giving me a supportive wink and nod respectively. Ethan remains seated.

"Didn't you hear me, Ethan?" asks Stella.

"I'd prefer to stay, if it's alright with you. I was there and—"

"No, it's not alright. I told you to leave, so get out."

Ethan reluctantly gets up and goes. I know he's trying to help, but if he thinks I can't face up to my responsibilities he's lost his mind. But, Christ, listen to me trying to convince myself I'm brave. Truth is, being in the same room as Ridley Gates makes me want to run away and hide under my desk until home time.

So I take the reprimand, all the while remembering that I have enough ammunition in Lucille's file to get him back one hundred times over. I apologise . . . again. I offer Ridley vomit-inducing fake gratitude for not taking my gross misconduct up with HR, and my stomach twists into a heavy knot of anxiety as I watch disappointment drain the colour from Stella's face.

There's nothing worse than showing the worst of yourself to someone you admire.

***

When I leave the conference room, Ethan is waiting for me outside. He pulls me into an empty meeting room along the corridor and shuts the door behind us.

223

"What happened?" he asks, an unmistakeable look of dread in his eyes.

I shrug. "I got my arse kicked. No big deal. I deserved it."

"No, you didn't deserve it. We need to tell Stella."

"Tell her what?"

"About Ridley and Carly. She's on our side; she hates Ridley. She'll want to help."

"She may be on your side Ethan, but she isn't on mine. She doesn't get me. Besides, I don't need any help with this."

"Oh, for Christ's sake. Ridley just played you in there. You know exactly what he's doing." He runs his hand through his hair, and his jaw clenches as he looks at me in exasperation. "Jesus, Vi! What's it going to take for you to let me in?"

I fold my arms around my body, my back stiffening at yet another dig at my coldness. "I can fix this myself, Ethan. Please trust me to do the right thing."

He throws up his hands in frustration, the veins in his neck bulging. Then he sighs, perches on the end of a table and looks at his feet. "If anybody should be sorting this out, it's me."

"Why do you say that?"

He folds his arms and drifts away in thought for a moment. "Because this has nothing to do with you. I'm involved. I was with Carly – Ridley knows, Malcolm knows, hell, even Stella knows. I'm connected to this, so I should be the one to fix it, not you."

I let out a sigh. I should be kinder to him. I know he's trying to protect me and that he still feels guilty about his alleyway dalliance with Carly. But I can't involve him in this. I don't want to dump a bucketload of mess on top of our relationship when we're both still confused about what's happening to us. I daren't let him know about the information Lucille gave me or what Ridley did to me, so I think up an excuse. "Ethan, can you remember when you tried to fix Sharon Taylor from Hexatex's problem?"

"Do you have to bring that up?"

"You know why I'm bringing that up."

"That was a one-off. I didn't know she had a thing for me."

"You didn't know she had a thing for you before she groped you at Hexatex's campaign launch party, or after?"

He screws his face up. "Before, obviously. I realised during the dance. And it's not funny – she practically violated me!"

"Yes, and you fixed it by snogging the face off her best friend half an hour later."

"I thought that would give her the message."

"It gave her the message you're a dick," I say, shuddering at the memory. "She cried on my shoulder for the rest of the night after I inadvertently ended up in the ladies' loos with her. Do you have any idea what that was like for me? I don't do women crying – empathy is not my area."

"Okay, okay, I take your point, but that was different to this. I just think Stella should be the one to handle this. She's an exec, you're not. You shouldn't have to put yourself at risk and take on other people's burdens."

"You forget I promised Malcolm I wouldn't tell anybody. He and Stella don't get on. That would be a really bad thing to do to him."

"Nobody gets on with Malcolm. Well, nobody except you."

He's having a dig again. He pretends he doesn't

mind that Malcolm has had it in for him ever since he started BMG as a graduate trainee, but every now and again his insecurity bubbles to the surface. Ethan needs to be liked, so if somebody dislikes him he takes it personally. He's yet to realise that Malcolm's visceral dislike of him says everything we need to know about Malcolm, and absolutely nothing about him.

"The fact that I'm one of the few people Malcolm likes – and trusts – means I'm best placed to help."

"So how are you going to do that, huh?"

"I have a plan."

His lips thin and he folds his arms again. "A plan you won't tell me about."

"It's not that I don't want to tell you . . . I just can't."

"Why? This can't be just about Malcolm."

I say nothing for a moment. Ethan's right – why am I taking on everyone's problems? Why did I just apologise to Ridley for calling him a vile pig, when only last week he had me pinned up against the door of his office, attempting to blackmail me into sleeping with him? Bravery would be pressing sexual harassment charges against him, not this . . . not whatever stupid plan I think I'm going to come up with to make everyone happy. And no matter how wonderful I think I am at fixing stuff, every now and then my ingenious plans go *BOOM!*

"Violet, please . . . let me in."

My heart aches in my chest. I want nothing more than to let him in. I feel my eyes begin to water and I try to force the tears back in with sheer willpower, but it's no use. I take a deep breath. "I want to," I say, flicking a tear from my face. "You have no idea how much I want to, but I'm scared . . ."

His expression changes from mild annoyance to

226

complete bewilderment. "Why?" he asks, lowering his voice to a whisper. "What are you afraid of?"

"Of doing the wrong thing." I walk to the door and open it. "If I don't get this right I could hurt a lot of people . . . so, please, if you care for me, just let me work through it."

20

I WORK ON MY COPY for the rest of the morning while Ethan is locked away in post-production with Wendy. I managed to push all the Ridley business to the back of my mind, but I know I haven't done my best work. In fact, when I make a trip to the art studio later in the afternoon, Max pretty much tells me his awesome graphics are wasted on the shit I've written. Max is usually more helpful than this, but he always says what he thinks, so by the time I leave him my mood has crashed through the floor.

Ethan, Will and Pinkie are all at their desks when I return in the foulest of moods. None of them look up as I thud myself down in my chair. I know I'm being a drama queen and I'd kick my own arse if it were physically possible, but today has been awful. This is what happens when I stop thinking rationally and let my guard down. I become unpredictable, volatile, terrifying . . . as unstable as my cranky boiler the second the temperature in North London dips below zero.

I switch on my computer and mindlessly faff around. I'm working hard at looking busy, but in reality I'm doing bugger all.

"I'm sorry for earlier," I hear from behind the cubicle wall that separates my desk from Ethan's, and my mouth reacts with an involuntary smile I couldn't disguise even if I wanted to.

"You're sorry for what, exactly?"

He peers over the separator. "I need to speak to

228

you."

"About what?"

"You know what."

"No, I don't."

I look over the cubicle wall at him. His short, choppy brown hair is brushed up off his face, and his eyes are wide and earnest. "I'm sorry for butting in, but it's impossible not to say something."

"I just want to find a way to help everybody, Ethan. I didn't want to leap in. I needed to think it through first."

"I know, but I wanted to help you, so I have."

"What?" The gigantic knot in my stomach tightens and I can't breathe. "What are you saying? Please tell me you haven't done something stupid."

He lowers his voice and his eyes scan our area. "Not here. We'll talk later."

Will and Pinkie mustn't have much work at the moment as they've been having Temple Run tournaments all day, whilst flying their gossip around the office. Yes, you heard that right – fly. Will likes to scribble down gossip, fold up the paper to make a paper aeroplane and then fly it across the office. The amount of times he's piloted his poisonous planes into the wrong hands is incredible, yet he never learns his lesson, and now he's recruited eager-to-please Pinkie, who has the sense of direction of a pissed seagull.

I turn to my side to see Pinkie has wheeled his chair so close in his attempt to eavesdrop that he's practically sitting on my lap.

"Get lost, Pinkie!" I yell at him. I think I could kill someone right now, I really do.

He tuts and shuffles back to his own space next to me. "Can't blame a man for trying," he says under his breath.

"Trying what? Trying to get my knee in your groin?"

Will sniggers. Pinkie turns very pink. I let it go.

Ethan stands up. "Come with me."

He leads me across the floor to Diego's vacant office. My palms are already sweating when I grab the handle to close the door behind us. I study his body language, my heart hammering in my chest. He's hanging his head and he can't make eye contact. "What have you done, Ethan?" He sits down on the sofa motioning for me to join him, but I can't. If I'm close to him it'll be far too easy to hit him.

The colour drains from his face – peach to pink to white. "I've been working with Stella all afternoon, and I told her."

"Wait . . . You've done what now?"

"I was worried about you. You said you were scared, so I told her."

My skin burns with rage and betrayal. How could he? "Ethan, I asked – no, I begged you. How could you do this to me?"

He stands up and walks over to me. "Look, it's going to be fine. Stella's our department head. She knows about Ridley and Carly now, so she's going to have a really good think about how to handle this so nobody gets hurt."

I can't process his words. All I hear is noise. "You had no right, Ethan. No right!"

He swallows hard. "I knew you'd kick my arse for this, but I'm not going to let you be scared at work. Stella has bypassed Ridley and sent the ad straight through to Stuart. Ridley knows she knows about Carly, so now he won't be able to affect our work. Look at what he did in that meeting earlier today. He was

230

playing games, and I'm not having him playing with my career—"

"This isn't about our jobs, Ethan. This is about somebody's life."

"Malcolm?" He shakes his head in disbelief. "Come on, Vi. You can't fall for his sob story."

I narrow my eyes. I hadn't once thought that Malcolm was being disingenuous. "You have no idea what you've done."

"If I have no idea, it's because you refused to tell me. What do you want me to say, Vi? I'm not sorry for putting us and our careers before Ridley sodding Gates. Stella knows Ridley is holding something over Malcolm's head, so she'll get together with Gordon Gray and the rest of the board and try to sort it out."

I feel like my lungs have exploded. I open my mouth and almost choke. "You . . . you told her about Malcolm too?"

"Yes, I had to." He runs his hand through his hair as if he's sweeping away his guilt. "Look, you have to work out your priorities here. Max is fine, I'm fine and you're fine. It's over."

"I'm not fine," I say, fighting the nausea that's threatening to engulf me. "I trusted you. I can't believe you've done this."

He looks at his feet, the toe of his shoe dipping into the burgundy loops of the carpet. "I'm sorry, but I had to." He raises his head. "I know why you did it, and I understand, but if he's making it so that people I love have to lie to me—."

"I didn't lie to you . . . I . . ." I stop talking and my breath catches in my throat. What the hell? Did he just say "people I love" again?

His face reddens as he realises he's just dropped the

L-bomb whilst sober this time. "I'm sorry, but I did this for the people who matter – you, me and Max."

In a perfect world, Ethan taking a trip to Blushing Meadows would draw us nicely into a discussion about our changing relationship, but it doesn't and it won't because both of us are afraid of going there. So up goes yet another row of bricks on that wall I'm building to protect myself from him. It's getting pretty high now, isn't it?

"Can you forgive me?" he asks, turning the page to a completely different chapter and leaving me stuck like a battered bookmark in the old one. "All this will be okay, you know."

I take a deep breath, knowing I'm about to take us to a place I don't want to go – knowing we're not heading over the rainbow. I'm not opening the door to a happy, Technicolor Munchkin-world. Instead, I'm taking us into the eye of the tornado, and I've no idea what will happen afterwards. "I spoke to Ridley again last week. Before we went to Cumbria."

"What did you say to him?"

I mentally click my heels together three times, but sadly I'm still here. "I confronted him about Carly and I told him to leave Malcolm alone, and . . ." My heart swallows my voice as he clenches his jaw.

"And what?" He stands and comes closer. "For Christ's sake, Vi, you're shaking. What happened? Just tell me."

I want to put the brakes on and call back the flying monkeys, but how can I when he's just told me he loves me? "Ridley . . . kind of . . . threatened me."

His eyes grow large. "He . . . threatened you? What did he say?"

Oh crap, why did I start this? What the hell was I

thinking? "I can handle him. He's just a horrible, disgusting slimeball. He doesn't bother me."

Ethan takes my hand in his. "Then why are you trembling?" He searches my eyes until I look away. "Violet, I'm going to ask you this once more, and I need you to tell me exactly what he said – word for word – and I need you to tell me the truth. If you don't, I'm going to find out from him, and I can't promise he'll still have all his teeth when I'm finished."

My stomach rolls. This is part of the reason why I didn't tell him in the first place. I've seen Ethan fly off the handle twice before – both times due to his brother getting himself in trouble, and both times he solved the problem with his fists. "He . . . um . . . propositioned me." His eyes pop and I can see his Adam's apple grind against his shirt collar. "He was awful. He . . ." I take my hands back and cross my arms in front of me as my vision blurs into watery shades. I curse myself for being weak, yet again. "I wish I hadn't said anything."

"Violet," Ethan says firmly. "What did he say to you?"

"He said he would back off Malcolm if I slept with him."

"He fucking what? He said what?" His face is burning so red I'm afraid to look at him.

"He was disgusting . . . horrible. When I close my eyes I can still hear him, smell him, feel him . . ."

"*Feel* him? Did he touch you?"

Panic charges through my veins as his face flames with fury. How do I backtrack out of this now?

"Did he hurt you? Violet . . . you have to tell me."

I nod and his entire body tenses. "He held me against the door and I couldn't get him off me." I push up my sleeve and reveal the line of faint purple bruises. "He gripped my arm tight – dug his fingers into me. Lucille heard everything, and if she hadn't interrupted him . . ."

No sooner have my words hit him than he unleashes the dogs of war. He bites down hard on his bottom lip until I'm certain I can see blood, his skin darkening to red and his eyes screaming havoc.

And then he's gone.

I call after him, but he's striding so fast down the hallway he either doesn't hear me or he's ignoring me. I have to break into a jog to follow him. I shout after him again, but I'd have better luck herding an eagle in sight of a rabbit, and I can't move fast enough in my stupid bloody heels. To make matters worse, everybody on our floor has stopped working. I suspect Will is building a hangar and terminal building for the amount of paper aeroplane traffic he's expecting to fly in.

Ethan disappears through the doors to the stairwell, and I know exactly where he's going. Should I follow, or should I get help? Who can I trust? Christ, I've never had so much shit happen in one fortnight. I kick off my shoes, pick them up and sprint down the stairs, practically jumping down the last few before swinging open the doors to the fourteenth floor. Ethan disappears to the right, but I go left.

***

Stella Judd is in her office with Malcolm, of all people, when I barge through the door, gasping for air as if I've run a half-marathon. "It's Ethan. He's gone after Ridley."

It takes a moment for Stella to process what I'm telling her, but Malcolm shoots straight to his feet,

234

bearing the expression of a man who's just been told his house is on fire. His moustache springs to action, followed by the rest of him, and he heads off in the direction of Ridley's office. Stella and I follow him, and my shoulders sag in relief when we spot Ethan in the hallway, striding headlong in the opposite direction.

"What the hell do you think you're doing, Fraser?" Malcolm yells as Ethan silently rushes past all three of us and slams into the men's toilets.

The stout frame of a terrified Lucille Monroe comes into view behind him, her dark face beaded with sweat and her eyes wide with concern. "Ridley's in there," she says between giant pants for air as she clutches her chest. "What the hell has that man done now?"

Stella doesn't hesitate before barging into the men's loos after him, Malcolm following behind her. I hang back for a moment. My pulse is rocketing and I feel like I'm about to drop to my knees. Lucille places her hand gently on my arm. "I gave you the power to bring him down," she says softly, yet so meaningfully it's as if she's speaking straight to my soul. "Don't react to him and don't let that young man react either. Just do what you need to do."

I follow the others into the toilets, bumping into an account exec who's obviously been interrupted mid-pee because he's still zipping up his trousers. I make an apology then clatter through the inner door to find Ethan pinning Ridley to the wall by his neck. They both look like they've had a swing or two at each other already. Ridley's face is red and swollen, and Ethan has a cut lip. His knuckles are cut too, and I don't know who has got the better of whom, but I suppose the guy with his hands around the other's neck is calling all the shots.

"Ethan, let go of him!" Stella's volume alone should be enough to make him back off, but he's in full action-idiot mode, hanging onto Ridley like a rogue FBI agent with a grudge.

"You fucking creep," roars Ethan, clutching Ridley's neck with one hand and punching him in the stomach with the other.

Stella raises her voice even higher. "Ethan! I said let him go! Or I won't be able to save your job."

Ethan releases Ridley by shoving him into the wall. Ridley falls to the ground, his hand clasping his throat. "What the hell . . . ?" he groans, wheezing for air.

I stare between each person, wondering how I'm going to explain this. Ethan straightens his tie and shrugs his jacket back onto his shoulders. I can't even look at Malcolm.

"Anybody mind telling me what the bloody hell is going on here?" thunders Stella. She fixes her ice-cold stare on Ridley as he staggers to his feet. "I don't know how out of the loop I am, but I assume this is connected to you cheating on your wife with a client, taking cocaine with her until she almost died, and then blackmailing Malcolm."

"I'll deal with this," interjects a nervous Malcolm, as if he thinks he can still try to keep the lid on his secret.

"The hell you will," Stella replies. She's standing with her hands on her hips, her red tailored dress the only splash of colour in the grey bathroom, surrounded by three men in grey suits.

"Unless you've forgotten, I'm CEO of this agency, and I've told you I'm dealing with it," he says.

Stella closes in on him, and all of a sudden I'm in the African savanna watching a lioness stalk an elderly gazelle whose survivor-brain doesn't work half as fast.

"Okay, let's see you deal with it then."

Jesus Christ, do we need a turf war on top of everything else?

Malcolm walks up to Ethan and glares at him. "Fraser, you're suspended until further notice."

Ethan just rolls his eyes and laughs, but I've had enough. "You call that dealing with it, Malcolm?" I snap.

"Miss Archer, this is absolutely none of your business." Malcolm is standing right next to me, but he isn't paying me the courtesy of looking at me when he speaks.

"Malcolm, you know this *is* my business."

"You want to do this now?" he scoffs, trying to front me out. "I thought you were smarter than this, but maybe Fraser has rubbed off on you." He turns to look at Ethan. "Get out of here, Fraser. Get out of my agency."

I can't believe what I'm hearing. "Malcolm, you don't know what this is about. You can't suspend him." He squints at me, and I can see the confusion on his face. I will him to realise what's happening here. *This isn't about your secret. Drop it, please, drop it.*

"This is my agency. I can do what the hell I like, and if you don't like it, I'll suspend you too."

Oh, shit. Okay, I wasn't expecting that. He's totally lost the plot.

"Malcolm, I wouldn't do this if I were you," croaks Ridley. He grimaces, rubbing his throat. "This is about her . . ."

Everyone turns to look at me. Stella's eyes narrow into a glare that could wilt freshly cut daisies, and I can feel Malcolm scrutinising me, looking between me and Stella and Ethan. I have no idea what he's thinking.

Malcolm turns to Ridley, whose swollen face is already blackening into bruises. "Oh, I get it. I see what's going on. I always thought Violet had good taste." His eyes lock onto mine with scorn. "Which one of these two are you screwing around with?"

Before I can answer, Ethan lunges at Malcolm, striking out with his already bloodied fist and delivering a blow to the side of his head which sends the older man crashing into the sink units, landing in a heap on his backside. Malcolm's hand shoots to his head. "You're fired, Fraser, do you hear me? Fired!"

"Ethan, get the hell out of here now!" yells Stella. I stand frozen in shock at the rapidly escalating bloodbath.

"He's not firing me because I quit," Ethan shouts, and I could kill him for acting so thoughtlessly. He walks straight past me without a word, his face burning with rage, and he leaves the room.

Stella helps Malcolm to his feet, but he practically shoves her out of the way with grumbles and more threats about what he's going to do to Ethan. "I have no idea what the hell this is all about," she says. "But Ridley, if this is down to you, I suggest you and Malcolm sort it out before the board gets to hear of it."

Stella ushers me out of the bathroom with her, leaving the two men to lick their wounds. The corridor has become home to a small audience, which, after a fierce glare from Stella, scatters to the four corners of the office. Will launches a paper aeroplane into the crowd and a group of interns rugby-tackle each other to the ground for it. Lucille – who has been guarding the bathroom door the entire time – receives a "Thank you" from Stella before returning to her desk.

Once we're alone, Stella leads me round the corner

to a quiet area of the lobby. "Violet, I want to know two things, and I don't want you to be offended by the first. Was Malcolm right about you having a relationship with either Ridley or Ethan?"

"No!" I say quickly, grossed out by the first option, but feeling guilty about the second. Does a kiss constitute a relationship?

"Good. Second. Did Ethan give them what they deserved in there?"

I want to give the right answer, but as I don't know what that is, I opt for the truth. "On balance, Ridley deserved more."

A look of quiet reflection sweeps across her face before turning into a faint smile and a slight raise of her eyebrows. "I see. Well, in that case, I think it's about time I sorted out this mess once and for all."

"You mean . . . sort out Malcolm and Ridley?"

"No, I don't actually. They can sort themselves out. I'm talking about what's best for me, and now's the right time to unleash the dragon."

21

I'M THANKFUL THAT THE TUBE ride from Bank to Piccadilly Circus only takes twenty minutes, because as usual on this line, the carriage is absolutely rammed. Annoyingly, I've no choice but to spend the entire journey holding onto a pole whilst standing directly under a fat sweaty man's armpit. For an added bonus, I also have an old lady's tartan shopping trolley digging into my legs every time the train jerks on its tracks.

To make matters worse, I don't even know if Ethan headed straight home after he was fired, so the battle scars – stench-induced nausea and bruised heels – could all be for nothing. I've texted him three times since I left the office but he hasn't replied. I'd ring Rory, but I know he's at a concert in Berlin. I'd start messaging his other friends, but Ethan is one of the world's worst Facebook-friend collectors. He barely knows who most of his thousand-plus followers are, so I'd have no chance of distinguishing a real friend from some girl he met in a bar once. I don't know how he finds the time to maintain such a huge fanbase. His timeline must be permanently clogged with drivel: football talk he isn't interested in, photos of people's kids he doesn't know and mindless, duckface selfies from the contingent of hangers-on he seems to attract. Why do women pull those ridiculous faces? Has any man alive in the history of the planet ever said, "I thought you were just okay before, but now you've contorted your face to look like a constipated duck, I can see you're the hottest girl alive?" Nope, never happened, has it? I need to have my finger on the pulse for my work, but I don't get this craze. In fact, I'm wondering if the RSPB should jump on the duckface bandwagon in order to raise funds for Britain's waterfowl when my train pulls into Piccadilly.

I get off the Tube and make my way to the surface via a succession of escalators to the tune of "The Scientist" by Coldplay. "Yes, I wish somebody had bloody told me it would be this hard," I mutter to myself as the lyrics hit home. I throw a couple of pound coins into a cap at the feet of a dreadlocked keyboard player. He shoots me a wink. I thank him (and Chris Martin) for the life lesson.

I make the ten-minute walk from Eros's statue, through Theatreland and up Lexington Street to Ethan's apartment on Broadwick Street. It's almost 7 p.m., so I'm walking shoulder to shoulder with hordes of tourists on their way to the West End's many theatres and bars. It's an exciting area on any night of the week, but tonight a new show is premiering, so some of Soho's backstreets have been cordoned off to make way for the celebrity and VIP guests and their entourages.

I take the lift to Ethan's penthouse and ring the bell. I'm not sure what's going to greet me – it could be nothing at all as I've no idea whether he's home. Sure enough, there's no answer, but I try again, and then again, hoping I haven't had a wasted journey.

And then he opens the door.

And I do my best not to laugh myself into the ground, because the last thing I expected him to be wearing was a bag of frozen peas.

I suck in my cheeks to stop myself from giggling. "I'm guessing that hurts a little."

"Yup." He grimaces and stands back to let me in.

I've already mentioned that Ethan's place is the size of a cupboard. It costs a small fortune to rent, but it's painfully tiny. In this city, if you opt for "location, location, location" over practicality, it usually means you have more money than sense and an ego that's writing cheques your body will have to run itself into the ground to cash. Sadly, this is Ethan to a T.

Still, I have to concede that his place is impressive. It has an industrial feel to it with exposed brick walls, original painted Victorian pipework and restored wooden ceiling beams. Like Max, Ethan has decorated every room white, but unlike Max, there are no paintings or prints on his walls – instead he has classic guitars and framed album covers: Fleetwood Mac (I think), the Rolling Stones (I'm sure) and Coldplay (of course). It's the epitome of cool bachelor pad and it suits him.

I go straight to his bathroom and rummage around in his cabinets for the box of medical stuff he produced when I was helping him build flat-pack furniture and I nailed my thumb to the back of a bookcase. Yes, there was blood. Yes, I cried. Yes, I've tried to blank out how much of a wuss I was.

When I find the box I return to the sitting room, taking a seat next to Ethan on his charcoal-grey corner sofa. "What on earth were you thinking?" I ask as I open the box and take out cotton wool and antiseptic cream. "Did you honestly think beating the living daylights out of Ridley Gates could ever end well?"

"No, but it felt great."

"Did it? Doesn't look too great from where I'm sitting. Give me your hand."

He puts the peas down on the table and cautiously does as he's told. "What are you going to do? I don't

242

think I want you to touch it."

I roll my eyes at him. "Don't be a baby." Men, eh? One minute they're Bruce-Willis-in-a-vest-style action heroes, next minute they revert to type and wimp out because of a couple of scratches. I manoeuvre his hand onto my lap and dab some antiseptic lotion onto his cut knuckles.

"Argh! Jesus Christ, that stuff burns like fuck."

"Oh my god, you're such a child. Just hold still. This will only take a second." I attach a few strands of cotton wool to his hand with some tape, hoping that will keep the antiseptic in and the cut clean, but I have no real clue how to do first aid. "Give me your lip."

"What? No way!"

"Seriously?"

"Yes, seriously. I'm getting a very distinct Nurse Ratched vibe from you here."

I put on my best attempt at an evil-nurse face. "Do you want me to sedate you?"

He shivers. "Okay, now you're scaring me."

I laugh and move closer to him. He flinches, and I raise my eyebrows just enough to let him know he's being ridiculous. He grudgingly gives in and braces himself for the sting. How the hell would he have coped in the trenches? I dab some cream onto his cut lip. "There, all done." I put everything back in the box and close the lid, snapping the metal clasps on each side. "Was that so bad?"

"Yes." He returns the peas to his cheek. "And I suppose I'm going to get a lecture now."

"You are, but I'm going to tell you you're an idiot first."

He pouts. "I already know that."

"So . . . ?"

"So what?"

"So, why are you such an idiot?"

He removes the peas again and draws in a deep breath. "I was angry."

"Yeah, so was I, but . . ." I look at him and can't help feeling a swell of gratitude, even if what he did was stupid. "Look, I would have loved to have slapped the shit out of Ridley Gates's smug face myself, but he's a director in our agency."

"It doesn't matter. I quit *and* I was fired, remember?"

"How could I forget?" My mood darkens as I realise that, for the first time in three years, I'll be going to work without him tomorrow. "So what are you going to do?"

His face bursts into a grin. "Get a new job, I guess."

"I'll come with you," I say in a flash. "Doesn't matter where."

He pulls me into a tight hug which sadly only lasts for moments because he shoots to his feet. "Looks like we're going to have a brand new future to celebrate. I'll get us a drink."

He goes to the kitchen and returns with two glasses and a bottle of whisky. I hate whisky. If evil had a taste, it would be whisky. If Satan were real he would live up a mountain in Scotland and whisky would be the flavour of his piss. I thank him as he hands me a glass, and I take a tiny, polite sip, but then I twist my nose and cough as my throat burns.

He laughs at me, but I don't mind. I love his laugh. "You enjoying your drink?" he asks.

I swallow and then giggle. "No, not really."

"Do you want something else?"

"No, I just want to talk to you." I put my glass down

on the coffee table and turn to face him. "What happened back there, Ethan?"

He takes a long drink and swirls the whisky around in his glass, the amber liquid lapping from one side to the other in waves. His face is etched with regret and his eyes seem to retreat. "I'm sorry I behaved like that. I couldn't help it. I was just so angry I couldn't even see straight. All I could think about was hurting him."

"I know Ridley's a pig, but . . . I've never seen you like that before."

He looks at me like there's a hundred things he wants to say, but I only hear silence. For once I can't read him. "You've never seen me like that because I've never felt like that."

"I was dealing with it," I say softly, a slight tremble in my voice.

He clenches his jaw. "You were upset . . . I . . ." He turns his attention back to swirling his whisky for a moment. Why is he finding it so hard to talk to me? I don't usually have to draw Ethan's feelings out like this. He isn't me. I'm the closed book – he's always been completely open and unguarded. "He hurt you and I have to protect you."

"I don't need protecting, Ethan, I'm—"

"The hell you don't!"

My breath catches in my throat and my heart leaps. I don't understand. I've never given him cause to believe I was fragile. At least I hope I haven't. We sit in silence again, intimidated by unspoken words.

"You're my best friend," he says at last.

"I know. And you're my best friend too."

"Remember when I said I thought we were more than friends?"

My stomach takes a sky dive. "Um . . . yeah."

245

"Well, 'friends' just doesn't seem the right word. It's not enough. It doesn't explain what you mean to me." He bites on his bottom lip, and there's hesitation in his eyes. "Do you think soulmates is the right word?"

Wait, aren't "soulmates" supposed to end up together?

"Maybe," I say. "I mean, I know we're great friends who know each other inside out . . . but sometimes I feel as though we're two strangers who don't understand each other at all."

"I understand you. I always have."

He looks hurt, and my instinct is to hold his hand, but I'm too afraid to reach out. "I know you think you understand me, but I don't think anyone ever has. Not really." I lean in close to him and whisper, "I'm pretty weird, you know?"

"You are, and that's why I love you. That's why I think we're soulmates, and I know that's a bit of a girly word, but I can't think of anything better." My eyes lock with his. The intensity in his gaze is drawing me in so deep that I panic and look away from him. I want to know what he's thinking, but at the same time I'm absolutely petrified. "Look, I'm just trying to tell you how much you mean to me, and that's why I did what I did. The thought of him hurting you . . . I just couldn't let him get away with that. I'm not sorry that I hurt him back."

My heart is pounding so fast in my chest I think it might shatter. The beat is like a drum, and the lyrics which keep playing over and over in my head match the rhythm: *Soulmates are friends, friends are platonic. Soulmates are friends, friends are platonic. Soulmates are friends, friends are platonic.* Da-dum, da-dum, da-dum.

"What are you thinking?" he asks.

"Hmm?" His question breaks my daydream, and my eyes are forced to meet his again. But I can't speak. I don't have the right words, and the words I do have terrify me. "Nothing really."

"I know we still need to talk about what happened in the Lakes . . . and last week in your apartment."

Oh. Shit. And. Hell. I said I wanted to talk but I'm scared stiff of talking about that. I'm not ready. I pull my legs up onto the sofa and tuck my knees in under my chin. I know, the body language couldn't be any more obvious – *leave me the fuck alone*.

"What happened in the Lakes surprised me," he says, his accent more pronounced than normal. He always gets more Scottish when he's angry, but when he's drinking whisky he may as well paint his face with woad and wrap himself in the Saltire.

"Why?"

"Because I knew how I felt about you, but I didn't expect anything to come of it. Then all of a sudden – when we were in the Lakes – I realised I wanted it." He closes the gap between us on the sofa, and my stomach cartwheels when I feel his fingers rest lazily against mine. "I can't really describe exactly how I feel, but I know I'm scared of risking what we have."

"I'm scared too. You're the best friend I've ever had, but you can't believe we're soulmates if you think we could be wrecked if we . . . um . . ."

His hand brushes mine. "If we tried to make it work?"

Is he saying what I think he's saying? I search his face for clues. His expression is blank, but intense, like a burning log in an open fire. "I honestly don't know if we could."

His face falls and regret lands in his eyes. "Since we made that stupid bet, I've realised I don't want to sleep with just anybody anymore. I want to wake up with the right person. Zoe and Erin and Carly and all those other girls . . . I thought they were what I wanted, but they weren't. They didn't come close. I look at who I am now, and all I see is someone who's been going from place to place, person to person, hoping I'll find something I like along the way. And then I realised that while I was doing all that, you were always there – by my side – with me."

"Ethan, I don't understand what you're trying to tell me. Please be clear." My heart thinks it knows. I can tell because it's leaping up and down in my chest, but my brain is furiously telling it to calm the fuck down.

"I just know how I feel when I'm with you. And that I know . . . you're different."

I want to ask him in what way he thinks I'm different. I want to ask him if he thinks I'm good enough, or special enough, or beautiful enough, or smart enough, or funny enough – all the things I want to be, but know I'm probably not. Am I good-different or weird-different? Do people like him ever end up with people like me? I want to tell him that despite having a best friend, I'm lonely. I am totally and desperately lonely because I think I've fallen in love with him, but I don't know if he can love me back. I want to ask if he's looking for someone different, anyone different, because he's bored – is that what he means? Is he just viewing me as something he's never tried before?

But I don't ask him any of those questions.

And I don't notice his touch at first, then suddenly it's there.

His fingers intertwine with mine, and I don't move. I

don't push him away. I don't tell him he should leave like I did last time. Every inch of my body tingles as I feel the sensation of our fingers weaving together. My skin goosebumps as his thumb traces light circles on my hand, following the contours of my palm in soft movements. His other hand glides through the length of my hair, allowing the ends to coil around his fingers. "I love your hair," he says as he sweeps it to one side and drapes it over my shoulder. My eyes are still lowered, but slowly I find the courage to look up and meet his gaze – the blue of his irises glinting under a veil of yearning that threatens to overwhelm me.

Then I feel it again. That same panic, just like before. I start to back away again. I shake my head. "We can't do this," I whisper.

"Why not?" He squeezes my hand just enough to reassure me. His other hand moves to my neck, slowly guiding me closer to him, massaging the base of my hairline and . . . I need to stop this. I should stop this. But this time I can't because this time I don't want to. My body doesn't want him to stop. I feel myself fall, and this time I'm not afraid, because I know he'll catch me.

"Is this okay?" he whispers into my ear as his hand moves in soft caresses down my back, all the way to the base of my spine. My body dissolves at his touch and I clutch his hand tighter. A faint moan escapes my throat as his warm breath drifts over my cheek. I inhale his cologne, his shampoo, the washing powder that lingers on his shirt and that special scent that is just the smell of him – his skin, his flesh and his bones.

His forehead touches mine again, and I look into his eyes and say, "Yes."

And then his mouth brushes against my mouth.

Subtle at first. Soft, like he's tasting the first strawberry of summer. I part my lips, allowing his tongue to brush wetness onto my dry skin. He tastes like whisky – bitter and strong – mixed with a tinge of antiseptic cream, but I don't care. I want more.

And then it's me who's kissing him. At least I think it is – it's hard to tell. I grab fistfuls of his hair and I let my tongue slide into his mouth with a demanding urgency. I can't remember the last time I felt like this about kissing anybody. Have I ever felt this way before, or have I just forgotten?

He pushes me back on the sofa and I melt into the cushioned fabric. Our bodies are pressed together, and the weight of his chest on mine crushes the air out of me until I feel like I'm alive only because I'm inhaling his breath. But I don't stop. I can't. I suck on his lip, my teeth grazing over his skin until he groans low in his throat. I remember his injuries and whisper "Sorry", but he doesn't flinch. His mouth trails my jawline with kisses, then my cheekbone, then that amazing spot under my ear which sends wild tremors rocketing through to my vulva.

It could very well be the best kiss I'll ever have, and as if to prove its worthiness a siren goes off. It's a loud and strangely familiar noise that rings in my ears, but as annoying as it is, it doesn't make me stop kissing him.

I plunge my tongue into his mouth as his fingers dance over my stomach and under my top. One of his warm hands dives under my bra and squeezes my breast until my nipple stiffens with longing. I let out a moan as his thumb rubs over the sensitive skin, and I hear the siren again.

And he pulls away.

The separation is agonising, as though my heart has

been wrenched from my chest.

"I should probably get that," he says, his voice punctuated by short pants for air.

"Get what?" I ask, my cheeks flaming.

"Um, the door. It sounds urgent." He looks at me with laughter in his eyes, and I realise the siren I heard was his sodding doorbell.

It buzzes again. He straightens his clothes and walks into the hallway. I tuck my grey top back into my pencil skirt and smooth my hair down by twisting it into a loop then letting it fall over my shoulders. It'll do. My hair is usually a tangled mess by the end of the day anyway.

He's out of the room for a few moments. I don't know if we can continue from where we left off. I don't know if we should continue. But when Ethan returns to the sitting room with our boss following behind him, I know I'm not going to find out.

"So, is somebody going to tell me what the fuck happened back at the office, or do I have to set this apartment on fire to find out?"

Looks like Stella wasn't kidding when she said it was time to unleash the dragon.

22

"I'VE JUST SPENT THE LAST hour persuading Malcolm and Ridley not to call the police. Tell me it was worth it."

Stella stands in the middle of Ethan's sitting room, her hands on her hips and her curved silhouette reminiscent of an expensive perfume bottle. Something by Givenchy – Eau de Fierce or Eau de Formidable or Eau de Fucking Pissed Off. I know a shitstorm is brewing, yet all I feel is the aftermath of that kiss, and that means I'm floating on the ceiling and my focus has gone to hell. I'm hearing words, but I'm feeling, tasting and thinking about nothing but sex.

Ethan offers Stella a drink, and she sits down on the corner sofa while he goes to his kitchen area to retrieve a third glass. I nervously sit down opposite her. Her lips are thinned to a narrow, angry line, and she's more pissed off than I've ever seen her – and yes, I'm including the time Daniel Noble lost her a ten-million-pound client because he drove to Cheltenham to close the deal instead of Chelmsford.

"Ethan told me about Ridley blackmailing Malcolm," she says.

I sink into the sofa. Her directness sets me on edge. "Um . . . yes . . . he said."

"You should have come to me sooner."

"Yes, I realise that now."

"Good."

Short and not very sweet.

We sit in silence until Ethan returns, looking more

than a little flustered. His hair is ruffled, and the memory of me grabbing fistfuls of it whilst I was burrowing my tongue in his mouth flashes in my mind and sets off waves of fizzing energy in every part of my body. Stella takes the whisky from him and takes a gulp, and then another.

Stella's eyes scan me from head to toe, and my stomach lurches. Does she know about us? My hand shoots to my hair and I try to smooth it down again as she watches me in silence.

"So, Ethan . . ." She leans forward and puts her glass on the coffee table. "I'm wondering if I've been wrong about you these past seven years. What I saw earlier has given me very serious doubts about your character. I'm doing all I can to get you your job back, but I don't know if I should be fighting for you."

Ethan rubs his sore face and I swear I can feel his temperature rise. "What do you mean?"

"I'm saying I don't want a thug in my department."

"This isn't Ethan's fault," I interject quickly.

"Really, Violet? Please do regale me with the very good reasons Ethan had for beating the living daylights out of Ridley Gates and punching the CEO of the city's largest and most prestigious ad agency in the face." She rolls her eyes and I know she isn't going to buy anything but the truth. "Tell me whose fault this is, Ethan. Malcolm Barrett might be a fucking prize prick, but he's also twice your age, and if you can't stop yourself lashing out against a sixty-year-old then I have to question what kind of a man you are."

Ethan sighs as if he's already defeated, and all I can think about is the fact I should have handled this better. If his career is over because of me, I will never forgive myself.

253

"So, what's the story?" Stella asks Ethan. Her voice is calmer and softer, but her expression is still unreadable. "Is this about Ridley and the Hayes girl? You told me about them this afternoon, but the gossip I heard was that you were the one who was with her that night. In an alley, I believe?"

He hangs his head. "The gossip was right."

"So you're telling me this was some kind of duel over her honour? Carly Hayes is going to be in rehab for the foreseeable future so I think that ship has sailed."

Images of Ethan with Carly invade my mind again – her lips on his, his hands pushing up her skirt, the look on her face as she threw her head back in ecstasy. The memory knocks the breath from my lungs. He said he didn't even like her. She was just "anybody". Has he really changed, or was I about to become his next "anybody"? *Ugh, how do I shut my stupid brain up?*

"The fight wasn't about Carly," he says.

"Well what was it about then?" she asks in an impatient tone of voice. "Look, you know how I feel about office flings. I don't like them. If you're letting your personal shit interfere with the running of my department, losing me clients and work, then I won't hesitate to fire you myself."

"We weren't having a fling. It was just once."

"I don't care." Stella tucks her long platinum fringe behind her ear. I can't read how she's feeling because her expression is stone cold. I'm learning that Stella never gives anything away. That's what makes the sting in her tail so deadly when she strikes.

She gets up from the sofa and pours herself another glass of whisky. She walks to the window, looking out over the theatres, bars and restaurants of Soho. The lights catch the gold in her hair and dance across her firm jawline. Slowly, she turns back to face us. "What did Malcolm do?"

Ethan and I share a nervous, silent look. I can tell his frustration with me is still present.

"What's going on?" she asks, noticing our reactions.

"Violet promised Malcolm she wouldn't tell anybody," says Ethan.

Stella turns back to the window, her hands on the gentle curve of her hip. "That ship has sailed too. If you want me to save Ethan's career, and stop him getting charged with ABH, then you need to come clean."

"He begged me not to tell anybody, and I promised," I say as I leap to my own defence. "I haven't even told Ethan."

Stella raises her eyebrows. "Okay, I admire that."

"You do?"

"Professional loyalty is priceless in this industry, but . . ." She moves back to the sofa and sits down opposite me. "If Malcolm has committed a crime, I need to know about it so I can protect you and help that idiot get his job back. Has he committed a crime?"

Should I lie, or shouldn't I? When in doubt, go for a half-lie. "Sort of."

Ethan stirs. "Sort of? Jesus Christ, Vi, why the hell are you defending him?"

I pause. Has this gone too far now? I hear Ethan's voice in my brain telling me we're soulmates and I sigh deeply because I know I have to break the promise I made to my mentor. "When Malcolm's wife, Emily, was sick, he borrowed some money from the agency to pay for her medical treatments . . . without telling anybody."

Both of their mouths fall open.

And I feel horrible.

"Borrowed without telling . . . you mean he stole it?" asks Ethan. I nod. "How much money are we talking about here?"

"I don't know exactly. Six figures. And then some."

"Shit," Stella says. "Does Emily know?"

"No. That's why he's so scared. He's paid most of the money back, but Ridley found out and he's been blackmailing him ever since."

Stella seems to lose her fire-breathing-dragon persona as she gets lost in deep thought. The change in the atmosphere is unnerving. "Okay, here's what's going to happen. Forget you know about this – both of you. This isn't your concern, and there's a much bigger picture in play. I have both of them exactly where I need them . . ."

Ethan clenches his jaw so tightly his neck starts to turn purple. "What's the bigger picture?"

"Leave that to me and forget about both of them."

Ethan shakes his head, but he's in no position to argue with her. "I can't forget, not yet. I wish I'd hit that bastard a hell of a lot harder than I did. And if I get another chance, I'll go for him again."

"Which one? Malcolm?" asks Stella.

"Ridley," Ethan replies. "That guy has a lot more coming to him."

"No, it ends here. Enough is enough," Stella says firmly. "Like I said, they're both exactly where I need them to be."

"But we haven't told you everything. Ridley threatened Violet and he hurt her, and if I was still in that bathroom . . . I don't know what you're planning, but he can't get away with what he did to her."

Stella's body stiffens as she turns to face me. "How

256

did he hurt you?"

I shrink into myself. I'm not cool talking about this, so I'm thankful when Ethan speaks for me.

"He told her he'd back off Malcolm if she slept with him." Stella shakes her head in disgust. "He forced himself on her and wouldn't let her go. Lucille had to intervene."

"Oh my god!" Stella turns to face me. Her eyes are narrowed and her jaw is clenched. "And to think I reprimanded you this morning for calling Ridley a vile pig. If I'd known about this I would have thrown a few punches myself. Why on earth didn't you say anything?"

"I thought I had it under control . . . it was important that I fixed it by myself."

"Okay, listen to me. This is separate to what I'm planning and you must act. If you make a formal complaint, then I'll back you." She stands and walks to the window again. I've never seen her so pensive. Stella says what she thinks, directly and assuredly, but tonight she's more cautious. She's also been alluding to something bigger than this horrific mess since she got here. As her silence wears on, I glance at Ethan. He looks as confused as I am. "Think about what I've said to you. We can discuss what needs to be done later, but right now I need to speak to Ethan . . . alone."

"Um . . . okay. Should I go home?" I ask.

"Yes, if you don't mind," she says, swinging around to face me. "The chess pieces have fallen into position without me having to play my hand. Which, if I believed in omens, would be the biggest and most beautiful omen I could have ever dreamed of. I told you it was time to unleash the dragon, Violet, and it is."

I stand and get my coat, leaving Ethan looking worse

257

than petrified.

"I'll . . . um . . . call you," he says as he walks me to the door.

Out of Stella's sight, I lift my hand to his face and softly cup his jaw, running my thumb over his cheek. "Goodnight, and good luck."

***

The upshot of yet another sleepless night is that I was able to read through all of the information Lucille – my plucky Fairy Godmother – gave me. In fact I read it ten times over. I didn't tell Stella about the files because I still want to help Malcolm find a way out of his mess, but I wonder if should. I wonder if whatever she's planning – her bigger picture – means I won't have to use it. I hope so. I love Lucille's give-no-shits attitude, but if I can keep her out of potential danger, then I will.

Work wasn't the only thing keeping me awake last night, of course. Every time my mind settled down to search for sleep, I felt him. Every time I closed my eyes, I saw him.

He kissed me.

I repeat:

He KISSED me!

And it was better than last time.

And I wanted it, because . . . I'm in love with him.

I'm totally, completely in love with him. I think. At least my heart thinks. My head isn't as sure because I'm not convinced he's feeling what he thinks he's feeling. It's true he has initiated every sexually charged encounter we've had over the past two weeks, but an army of nagging doubts are thundering into battle against my happiness. Why don't I trust his feelings? Simple answer is because I know Ethan. I have no idea if the fact he kissed me means anything or nothing. Strange, isn't it? How could a kiss mean nothing? I don't know, but allowing myself to think of that wonderful, breathtaking kiss in any other terms than Ethan making a play for the only female in the room would be tantamount to doing a backflip in the street, cracking my head open on the pavement and knocking myself out. And I'm not sure I want to risk brain damage.

***

I try to ignore the painfully obvious fact that all eyes have fallen upon me when I walk across the creative floor and sit down at my desk. It's after nine, I'm later than usual, so everyone is here and the atmosphere on the fifteenth floor is charged with gossip. I fear I'll snap the head off the first person who asks me about yesterday.

Less than a minute later, Will Thornton proves he has a death wish. "So, Violet, why did Ethan kick the shit out of Slimeball Gates yesterday?"

I give him the look of death.

"Come on, you've got to tell. Zoe told us Malcolm hasn't turned in today, Ridley is sporting two black eyes and people are saying Ethan got fired. I have a fleet of planes waiting for instructions from air traffic control."

"Do you think this is funny?" I snap. Pinkie sinks into his chair and turns his head away from me. "And if you even think about flying any of your stupid gossip planes around the floor with any of my business written on them I will personally fly you out the fucking window."

His expression shifts for a moment. Barely a moment. "You can't blame us for wanting to know what's going on, Violet. I've worked here for three years, same as you, and Ethan's my friend."

"If you want to know, you'll have to ask him yourself."

"He isn't here."

"Call him!" I yell, then I pick up my own phone and buzz through to Gabriel, Stella's executive assistant.

"Hi, Vi . . . Hey, that's funny, isn't it? Hi-Vi, like 'hi-fi'," he says in his delicious Catalonian twang. Gabriel Diaz is the proud owner of Barrett McAllan Gray's hottest accent. His voice has a luscious purring tone which radiates sex and desire. It isn't unusual for new female employees at BMG to fall at his feet the instant they meet him, totally oblivious to his gayness, despite his love of sparkly trousers and Versace shirts.

"I need to speak to Stella, is she free? It'll only take a moment."

He pauses far longer than necessary. "She is busy all today."

"Busy, where? It's quite urgent, Gabriel. I really need to see her."

"I'm afraid I cannot say where she is."

"Can't or won't?"

"Both."

"Thanks for nothing."

"I'm sorry, but I have my orders. Now, put the phone down – I have to keep this line open for sex."

Urgh. He doesn't deserve that accent.

I disappear to Production for the rest of the morning.

To say Wendy is a little alarmed that the Quest ad is due to be finalised by the end of next week and we've lost our art director would be an understatement. Unlike Will, Wendy doesn't pry, choosing to offer support and sympathy instead. Ordinarily, the touchy-feelies give me the heebie-jeebies, but Wendy mothers everybody, so I let her empathise with me about losing my partner and friend while we work.

I return to my desk after lunch to find a message on my iPhone from Ethan: *Meet me for lunch 12.30 @ The Hairy Lemon.*

I look at my watch – 13.15. Why didn't I take my stupid phone down to production with me? I quickly text him back: *Sorry, just got your message. Are you still there?*

Ten seconds later: *Didn't hear from you so didn't go. Few things to take care of. Meet there in an hour?*

I reply that I will. The second I put my phone down, my brain races with possibilities. Is Stella with Malcolm? Does Ethan have his job back? Can I report Ridley for sexual harassment without dragging Malcolm into it?

"And where the hell have you been?"

Max's angry German accent brings me out of my thoughts with a start. I've barely seen him since I got back from the Lakes, and I promptly feel guilty for ignoring him.

"I'm sorry, Max. I've been really busy."

He's standing with his hands on his hips, a very faded 1990s Ministry of Sound t-shirt clashing with a checked shirt and . . . what the hell is he wearing around his neck? A dog-tag pendant decorated with bling? Has he joined the hood since I've been away?

"Where's Ethan? Is he fired?"

"Yes."

He lets out a whimper. The kind of whimper you'd expect Bambi to have made when his mother got shot. "When . . . were you planning . . . to tell . . ."

I tenderly place my hands on his shoulders. "Stella's working on getting him reinstated. I think."

"What do you mean, you think?" His brow is pleated into tight ridges and his eyes are wild with anguish. "Why did he attack Ridley?"

I take Max away from Will and Pinkie's enormous, prying ears and walk him over to Diego's office, aka my second home. A paper aeroplane lands at my feet as I open the door. I glare at Will. He swings back in his chair, grinning from ear to ear.

Once we have privacy, I tell Max everything – well, everything except Malcolm's secret. He takes Ridley's involvement with Carly better than I expected, and he isn't even cross with me for not telling him before. But then the conversation moves on to Ridley's threats against me.

"I'd have done a much better job of beating up that piece of shit than Ethan. You'd have had to peel Ridley Gates off the toilet walls after I'd finished with him! Two black eyes? I would have broken every bone in his miserable body."

"Max, you're built like a scarecrow. Ridley spends an hour in the gym every day."

He looks hurt. "What are you saying?"

"Um . . . that you mightn't beat him in a fight?"

"Look, I might be tall and skinny, but I'm also fast and stealthy. I'd have thrown a punch and he wouldn't have seen it coming. Like, 'Whoosh . . . what the fuck was that?' I'm also crafty, so if he came at me, I'd nail him just by confusing him. I'm like a cross between the

Flash and the Riddler."

Oh, sweet Jesus. What planet is he living on?

"Wasn't the Riddler a bad guy?" I ask, trying not to laugh,

"No, he was misunderstood. The good people of Gotham, and later the residents of Arkham Asylum, were too biased to recognise his genius."

He sits down on Diego's sofa, right next to a giant fake potted palm which looks like it's been plucked from the Amazon. I take a seat next to him. All of a sudden he seems morose. He slouches low, his bottom barely hanging on to the end of the seat, his long legs criss-crossed in front of him so he looks like a knock-kneed giraffe.

"I'm bloody pissed off with you."

I fold my hands in my lap and let out a sigh. "I know. I'm sorry for not telling you, but you know me. I wanted to try and sort it out myself. I shouldn't have told Ethan about Ridley."

He inhales deeply and accidentally sucks a giant fake palm leaf onto his face. He bats it away, but I laugh. And then he laughs. And in that moment the tension disappears. "I'm not angry with you for telling Ethan, I'm angry you tried to handle this alone. For someone who is so smart, you can be so stupid, Violet."

"I know. I can't stop fucking up, Max. Ethan's lost his job, you went on a drink and drugs binge, and Malcolm . . . well, I dread to think what's going to happen there, and it's all down to me. Whatever you were going to say, just bear in mind that I hate who I am right now."

"No, stop right there. Don't you dare say that to me. I've seen you at your worst, I've seen you cry, I've seen you fail and I've seen you make the most godawful stupid choices, but this is who you are, and I love every bit of you – especially the fucked-up bits." Not for the first time in the last month, Max's kindness brings tears to my eyes. "This isn't your fault. It's Ridley's and Malcolm's and Ethan's faults. You may have screwed up a little bit, but they made the soup sandwich, not you."

"A soup sandwich?"

"Yes, a soggy, gloopy, totally unfixable mess."

I laugh at his perfect description. "I know you're right – partly right – but I should have put my friends first, just like Ethan said. If I had, he would still have a job. You've been mates since uni . . ."

"And we'll still be mates, but this isn't about us. It isn't even about Ridley. This is about you."

"Yeah, and I made this happen."

"Rubbish. You didn't make Ethan beat the shit out of Ridley yesterday. Everybody is talking about it, but that was his choice."

Tears flood my eyes. "Let them talk." I curse the crack that appears in my voice. Funny they call me the sodding Snow Queen when all I seem to have done for the past few days is cry. "Look, I have to go. I'm meeting Ethan in half an hour."

He stands and walks with me to the door.

"Will you promise to keep me in the loop?"

"Of course I will. Thanks for the advice."

"I didn't give you advice. You don't need it. You need love and understanding, so that's what I gave you."

23

THE HAIRY LEMON IS A gem of a pub hidden between St Michael's and St Peter's churches on Old Broad Street, not far from our office at the heart of the City. The building is a few hundred years old and is timbered in mock-Tudor beams. Of course, it isn't hairy and has no connection to lemons, so the name of the establishment remains one of many thousand peculiarities of London.

He's there when I arrive. I walk past the pub's window and feel his presence. I'm too nervous and too anxious about what news he's bringing me to smile.

The daylight ends as soon as I walk through the door. It's as if the dark wooden fittings and furniture absorb the light, leaving punters with the unnatural brightness of the amber chandeliers as they cast wild shadows on the burgundy flock-wallpapered walls. The whole place has a Dickensian feel – it's traditional and unique, which in this part of the city makes it cool.

My heels click-clack loudly against the tiled floor as I walk to his table. It's very private, almost secluded, and I'm immediately thankful I don't have to think about prying ears.

He stands as I approach. I wonder if last night is making me view him as hotter than ever . . . Oh Jesus Christ, am I even serious? Of course it is! My body clearly thinks so too – my skin tingles, my stomach somersaults and my thighs throb. He smiles "my smile" at me, and I feel like I'm either going to faint or explode into a ball of orgasmic glitter.

We sit in a circular booth with a round wooden table. He's already bought a bottle of red wine, which doesn't seem fitting for two fifteen in the afternoon, but as long as it's wet, I'll take it. He pours for me, and my eyes drift to the hard contours of his chest, outlined under a white v-neck t-shirt that's fitted like a second skin to his body. His hair is styled away from his face as usual, but the soft flicks have just the right amount of mess to add to the bad-boy vibe emanating from his bust lip, bruised cheek and cut knuckles.

After he pours my drink he drains his own in one go, then refills it. He's seeking courage, I can tell. Why is he seeking courage?

"Okay, I don't know how to tell you this, so I'm just going to blurt it out."

Oh sweet Jesus, what's he going to say? My stomach is suddenly assaulted by a strange fusion of fluttering-butterfly feelings and sinking, impending-doom feelings. This could go either way.

"This isn't definite yet, but . . ." He inhales a huge lungful of air as if he were a diver getting ready to plunge into the murky depths of the ocean. "I'm not coming back to Barrett McAllan Gray."

Fuck.

Fuck.

Fuck!

"Stella couldn't work Malcolm for you?" I manage to say as my heart sinks to my feet.

"It's more complicated than that. I've been offered an awesome opportunity elsewhere, and I'm almost sure I'm going to take it."

"Where?" He's just ripped my heart from my chest with his bare hands and I don't think he has any idea how much this is killing me. I stare down at my wine

266

glass and swirl the dark red liquid around in a rhythmic pattern, but I don't want to drink it. I want to drown in it.

"Stella's starting up her own agency, and she wants me to join her. She told me all about it after you went home last night. It's called Tribe. She has a fuckload of investment behind her already and she has premises in the Docklands. Millions of pounds are getting ploughed into this thing from all over the city, and from overseas too. Remember your ex-boss, Dylan Best, visited a few weeks ago? He's the major investor. Stella's going to be CEO, and they're merging with Lovett Ives and buying out Diablo Brown film studio. It's amazing, Vi. She's been building this thing in secret for months, but she's pushing forward now because of what happened yesterday. She's even got Quest to agree to give her their entire account when they finish with BMG next month."

"Oh my god!" Now I get why he's so excited. This is huge. But I can't help feeling put out that she asked me to leave last night to talk about this. Doesn't she trust me?

"It doesn't stop there, Vi. Stella hasn't asked me to come as an art director or a creative director. She's asked me to be a partner. Can you believe it? She wants me to buy in and oversee the entire creative department, so I'll be stepping into her shoes. Daniel Noble is going to be a partner too, as head of Client Services. I'm totally blown away. I can't even get my head around it. I'm going to be the youngest ad agency partner in the city!"

I take another drink of wine to steady my nerves. I can't think of anything to say. I can see how excited Ethan is and I don't blame him. This is his dream, and after seven years of being ignored by Malcolm he deserves every bit of it. But at the same time my own world has been completely blown apart. My head is spinning and I have a dull ache in my chest which is real and painful, and I realise it must be heartache – a real and literal heartache. I should be telling him I'm happy for him, but all I want to do is scream and plead and beg him not to leave me.

"What are you thinking?" he asks. His eyes are watching me in anticipation.

I force a smile. "When would you start?"

"Straight away. She told Malcolm her plans last night, and she's using what she knows as leverage to end her contract with BMG and take a couple of major clients with her."

"Wait, what?" I say, my insides suddenly burning with betrayal. "I confided in her and she used what I told her for her own ends? That is totally wrong."

The excitement fades from his face. "This was her big plan. Everything just fell into place."

"And I trusted her to help Malcolm, not to start blackmailing him herself!"

"It's not like that," he says, although I know he knows it is precisely like that. "Okay, maybe it's not the best outcome, but look at it this way. Malcolm's secret is safe, Stella has what she wants, Ridley is neutered, and I have a career-making job lined up."

"So you told her you're going to take the position?"

"I haven't told her yet." He pours yet more wine into his glass and takes a drink. He looks nervous and I'm sure his hands are shaking. "I told her I wouldn't work at Tribe unless you came too."

All I can hear is the rhythmic tick of a grandfather clock in the corner of the bar as a warmer, happier force creeps through me and starts to slowly repair my heart. "And what did she say?"

"She said yes. She likes you. Stella wants me to build the creative department, so I can choose to bring whomever I want anyway. Say you'll come. Please. You can't want to work in the same building as Ridley Gates whatever happens."

"I'll need some time . . . to think."

He looks a little bit disappointed, but I'm not sure why. Who'd make a decision like this in five seconds? "I didn't even realise I needed this until Stella gave it to me. I'd be a fool to turn it down. It's more than I ever dreamed of. But I don't want it unless you come with me."

Isn't life amazing sometimes? The only things I worried about last month were the five grey hairs I found on my head and my noisy neighbour's pervy sex life – my flat has very thin walls. And now? Everything that is familiar and comforting has been wrenched from me, and my world has been turned upside down in just two weeks. One shitty piece of luck after another has come at me from every direction and punched me straight in the gut. I feel lost and scared and it's a dead cert I'm overthinking all of this, but I can't control that either.

"If I came with you, who would I partner with?" I croak the words out into the room, my breath shaking at the thought of working with somebody who isn't Ethan. My head says that would be good for my heart.

"No, you don't understand. I want you to be our creative director, in charge of your own creative teams. You can steal whomever you want from BMG, or you can recruit – it's entirely up to you. I've already passed this by Stella and she's agreed."

"Me? A creative director, managing people? Oh, Ethan, I don't know. I'm not a people person, am I? You said yourself that I piss people off."

He pushes his wine glass closer to mine and scoots along the semicircular seat to narrow the gap between us. Our close proximity warms my blood and makes my skin goosebump. "That's not the way I see you. You're switched on and you understand people and you have a huge heart. You've mentored Ruby Sloan this past year and you were great. Where would Max and I be without you? You get me. You get him. Hell, you're the only person on the planet who gets him, so in my book that makes you a people person. You're not a stupid-people person and we'll have to work on that pissing-people-off thing you do, but you can totally do this. I know you can do it."

Is there anything more romantic than having somebody tell you they believe in you? I appreciate all of this, but my brain is throwing up doubt after doubt. "I don't know if I even want to manage people, Ethan. I'm a writer. I want to write."

"Then write. You can do whatever you want when you're the boss. Look, we've worked for this. We've worked our arses off together – as a team – for three years, and this is the next step. I'm ready to set the world alight, but I'll never be able to do that at BMG. And I can't do it without you. I need you to be in this with me. We're a rock-solid team. Just wait and see, we'll leave next year's AdAg Awards with armfuls of trophies."

"Yeah, that's not exactly selling it to me."

He laughs, and I can feel his breath on my skin. It smells of Spanish merlot mixed with courage and excitement.

"What about Max?"

"There's a job for him if he wants it."

"Really?" I can't help but grin as I imagine Max's reaction to this. He's going to be buzzing.

"Yeah, all three of us come as a package and we'll have the time of our lives."

I realise the only thing I'm fighting against is my own fear and self-doubt. I want to follow him. Hell, I'd follow him to the four corners of the earth, but there's still all this crap with Malcolm to deal with and . . . honestly? I don't deal well with change. It unsettles me. I need time to think. "When do you have to let Stella know?"

"She didn't say, but I don't want to leave her hanging. I think she was a bit surprised when I told her I wouldn't work for Tribe without you. I also have to find two hundred grand to buy in as a partner. I'm up to the hilt in debt, so short of selling my own body parts I have no choice but to ask my mum and stepdad for a loan. I'm sure my mum would stump up an interest-free loan if I begged her, but my stepdad is so tight I'd need a spanner to get a penny out of his hand. Selling a kidney to a Saudi prince would be more enjoyable than asking him for money."

I giggle at the analogy. Ethan's stepdad owns an estate agency specialising in executive properties in London's most sought-after postcodes. He's a good guy, but he has the personality of a chequebook.

Ethan flips a beer mat between his fingers as the sound of rain pebbles against the timber-framed windows. "I know this is a huge leap for you, but it's an even bigger leap for me," he says as he settles the mat under his wine glass. "I know everyone thinks I'm super-confident, but I'm not, not really. Partnerships

271

come around once in a lifetime, and Stella's chosen me. What if this is my one shot? If I don't take it, I could end up staying where I am forever, and I can't rot in the background at BMG, Vi. I can't and I won't."

"I'll let you know tonight." He looks disappointed again, but it's the best I can do. Ethan leaps without looking. I prefer to leap after I've assessed the risks, weighed up the pros and cons and then brought in independent expert analysis.

His face pales slightly as he registers my apprehension. His hands return to the beer mat, which I find funny. I've never noticed how much he fidgets when he's worried. What do we do now? This is hellish awkward. Should I venture into discussing our relationship?

His eyes return to me and I see the heat immediately. I love the light in his eyes – there's always a bright intensity inside the blue of his irises, but as our gaze locks, it's as if that familiar spark has flared into an uncontrolled flame. So much has changed, and so much is different about him.

I gather my bag and take a final sip of wine, leaving the glass a quarter full. "I should be getting back. Wendy is panicking because you're not there to see the Quest ad through post-production. I said I'd stay late to help her."

He says nothing.

All he does is stare at me.

And fidget with that bloody beer mat.

"Is there . . . um . . . anything else?"

"Hmm? Oh . . . okay . . . right . . ." He trails off, and his brow crinkles. "I'm sorry, there is something else. Stella's onto us."

"Onto us?" I ask, raising an eyebrow. I think back to

last night. Or rather I think back to what we were doing last night when Stella interrupted us.

"She asked me outright if we were having a relationship and if we'd ever . . . um . . . slept together"

"She didn't?"

"She did. And she was very direct about it. I told her we were just friends."

My stomach caves with disappointment, but I know that's unfair. He can't tell Stella what our relationship is when we don't even know. "What did she say?"

"She's slapping an inter-office relationship ban on her partners. No fooling around with clients or employees. The whole Quest fiasco stemmed from Ridley having an affair with Carly Hayes – and me too – so she's dead set on it. She's writing a clause in her partners' contracts: instant dismissal and a return of our investment if we ever – how did she put it? – 'land any personal drama at her feet'."

That's a humdinger of a get-out-of-jail-free card Stella has issued him with. "I guess it's just as well you already signed up to my celibacy law."

"Don't be like that," he says.

"What do you want me to say, Ethan?" I stand up and walk around the table to face him. "You started . . . whatever this is, and if you need to end it, then that's what you need to do. Like you said, this is a once-in-a-lifetime thing for you."

"Just tell me what you want. I have no idea what you're thinking. I don't even know how you feel."

My entire body sighs – a mixture of frustration and weariness. "I don't know what I want, Ethan. I don't know how I feel. I followed your lead and you took me here."

He stands too. I try not to notice how hot dressed-

273

down-casual-Ethan looks in his tight tee and relaxed-fit jeans, but it's impossible. "Do you understand why . . . ?"

"Yes, Ethan. I understand."

Easy words that do not in any way convey how totally muddled my brain is. Do I understand? No. Not even a little bit. I don't have the first clue what is going through his mind and I don't know what to say to him . . . No, that's a lie. I know what I want to say. I want to tell him I love him. I want to tell him he's everything to me. I want to tell him that when we're sitting at our desks and I catch him smile at me or wink at me or talk to me as if he knows me inside out, that in every single one of those random moments, I know I love him.

But I don't think he will ever be more than he is.

And if he goes to Tribe, we can never be more than we are – just friends.

"When will you let me know?"

"I'll call you tonight."

24

WHEN I GET BACK TO the office I head for the studio.

This is where Max and all of our other Maxes dwell. This is where paint meets paper, Photoshop doubles as a magic wand and Illustrator can turn mediocre artists into modern-day Rembrandts. This is the zone the corporate-suited account managers fear to tread. As if to prove it, there's a poster on the left-hand wall bearing the slogan "Here There Be Dragons", and it's a fitting analogy. The doorway to the studio symbolises the edge of the map, with the known world on one side, the murky realms of god-knows-where on the other.

Max is bending over his desk, the easel fixed upwards and an array of coloured pens and pencils scattered around him like sweets in a sweet shop. His bald patch dips as his arms brush strokes onto paper. I tiptoe over to him, careful not to break his buzz of creativity.

He raises his arm in front of him when he sees me, and I know to freeze and wait until he's ready. Interrupting Max when he's absorbed in one of his masterpieces is as dangerous as taking a bone from a hungry dog. I watch as he furiously scribbles away with a peach marker, adding layers of skin tone to the image of a woman in a 1970s-style string bikini for the Everdene & Hammond sun cream campaign.

He throws his pen down on the desk. "Okay, shoot."

I giggle at the abruptness of his greeting and give him a quick once-over. He still has dark circles under his eyes, but the grey of his skin is lighter and some pink has brightened up his pallor. "I've seen Ethan," I say with a smile.

His eyes widen. "What did he say? Is he coming back?"

"He has a new job already."

"What?" he asks, his face breaking. "Where?"

I pull him away from his desk and take him to a quiet area near the fifteenth-floor lobby. "He's starting a brand-new agency, as a partner . . . with Stella."

His eyes grow to dinner-plate size. "You're freaking kidding me?" He runs his hand through what's left of his hair.

"Stella's left BMG already. Daniel's going with her. And they want me and you too."

"Yes! Tell him yes!"

"Max, are you high again?" I ask, trying not to giggle. "Don't you want to know salary, benefits, job title, start date . . . ?"

He gives me his fake-hurt face. "Firstly, no I'm not high. I'm entirely compos mentis. Secondly, contract terms doesn't matter. I go where you go."

"I didn't tell him I was going."

He squints in confusion. "Why the hell not?"

"I guess I have unfinished business here and . . ." My thoughts drift as I wonder how much I should tell him. But I need to talk through my options with somebody and Max is the only person I can trust. "Okay, Max, I'm going to tell you something, and I need you to keep it to yourself."

"I am all ears."

"Remember when you accused me of being in love with Ethan?"

"I remember," he says cautiously.

"Well, back then, I answered truthfully when I told you I wasn't . . . but a lot has happened over the last few weeks and now I think I could be." My skin heats up with embarrassment as I reveal my deepest feelings. "And if I am in love with him, maybe it's best we don't work together, because . . . because I'm sure nothing can come of this."

"Why not?" he asks, his face creased with empathy. "I love both of you. I think you'd be great together."

I shake my head. "Ethan's messed up still. He doesn't know what he thinks or what he feels. He can't love me. He's never thought of me in that way before and I'm not the type of girl he goes for. I've always been firmly placed in the friend-zone."

There's a pause, and I know Max knows I'm speaking the truth. "All he needed was a huge event to make him see what was standing right in front of his stupid face." He grips me by the shoulders and delivers a beaming smile that makes my heart skip a beat. "And you can't move a mountain if you just sit on your arse staring at the fucking thing."

I smile at the analogy. I thought I was the wordsmith. "What are you suggesting?"

"Go where you'll be happy – with us – and see what happens with the rest. If it's meant to be, it's meant to be. But if you want him, you need to fight for him."

"The downside could be ruining the best thing I've – we've – ever had. Our friendship."

"Bollocks. That would never happen," he says, thudding his fist on his drawing board. "You're soulmates. You've been through everything together. Get off your arse and fight for him if he's who you want, but promise me we'll all be together."

"I have a few things to take care of before I can

277

promise that. If you're sure about this, I suggest you call Ethan, then make a start downloading all your files from the server – anything that's your intellectual property – and start packing up your desk."

"Everything I need is stored in my brain. Besides, I can't be bothered to do espionage. I'm not the MI5."

"You mean MI6"

"Don't be stupid. James Bond is make-believe!"

"But MI6 isn't make-believe. Their headquarters are just over the river."

Max looks at me as if I'm deranged, and – unusually for me – I decide to leave it. Now is not the time to argue with Max about whether the secret service is real or not.

* * *

I start tidying away Ethan's desk, boxing up stationery, photos, files and all the bits and bobs that have been collecting dust in his drawers over the past seven years. As I pack I realise that I have to leave. Of course I have to leave. How can I stay here if Ethan *and* Max are gone? I start uploading my own files from BMG's server to the Cloud. To be doubly safe, I copy our most important work onto pen drives. The disappointing news from my monitor is that my "espionage" is going to take over three hours to complete, so I leave it to work while I tie up loose ends.

First loose end is visiting Daniel and Gabriel, who look to be committing espionage of epic proportions from Stella's office. I knock on the half-open door and both of them look up and smile at me. I enter the room, stepping over half-packed boxes on my way. "You two look happy."

"That's because we *are* happy," says Daniel, packing a bunch of ring-bound files into a plastic box.

"Is Malcolm okay with you doing this?"

"What choice does he have?" Gabriel asks in his throaty Catalonian accent.

Daniel smiles again, and I figure he knows. *Of course he knows.* "So, are you coming along? I've put a great account management team together. Ethan needs you. And I'm guessing you need him."

There's something in his tone which unsettles me. I think back to how kind he was about that ridiculous date Ethan set us up on. He didn't hold a grudge or try to get his own back like many men would have done. But he did tell me he thought Ethan was "into" me, and I laughed it off.

"I haven't made my mind up yet. I was hoping to talk to Stella; is she around?"

"She flew out to New York with all the senior partners this morning. They're finalising the buyout and merger agreements. She's not going to be back until the middle of next week. I can talk to you though. Gabriel, could you excuse us for a minute?"

As soon as we're alone, Daniel manoeuvres his way around the obstacle course of boxes and paper piles to Stella's sofa.

I take a seat next to him and dive straight in. "I'm guessing Stella has told you everything about . . . um . . . Ridley and Malcolm."

"She did," he says carefully.

I sigh with disappointment. How many other people has she told?

"I already knew about Ridley's affair and it isn't his first. Ridley has been my boss for three years, and if the opportunity to work with Stella at Tribe hadn't come up, I'd have been looking for a new position anyway. I was taught to look for the good in all people and that's what I try to do, even though it's difficult to find it in some. With Ridley Gates it's impossible. The man is rotten to the core."

My stomach knots as Daniel reiterates what we all know about Ridley, confirming why I can't stay here. "What do you think will happen to Malcolm when we all go?"

Daniel leans forward, his face lined with unease. "We can't think about that, Violet. Stella said you've been trying to fix Malcolm's problems on your own, and you shouldn't have done that."

"He begged me, Daniel. He begged me not to say anything, but I did . . . and now look what's happened."

"You have nothing to feel guilty about. Malcolm did this – it's all on him. It was never your burden to carry."

I tell myself he's right. Part of my brain knows he's right – the smart part of my brain I always used to use. But then I see Malcolm's face begging me to keep his secret, and my heart slows to a pathetic "please kill me" beat.

I leave Daniel sure of what I need to do. One last thing before I leave the agency – the one thing that will hopefully make all of this right.

I wait until six, when my downloads are complete and I've finished clearing out mine and Ethan's desks. I take the stairs to the fourteenth floor, passing Lucille on her way up. She stuffs a note in my hand as she walks past. Fearing the worst, I immediately open the note and read it:

If there's a place for me at Tribe, I would be

honoured to join you. I've spent 24 years at Barrett McAllan Gray, but I'm done with these people. – Lucille x

I relax a little – thank goodness it's nothing bad. I can't help but smile as I read her note. I love and respect Lucille and I hope we can find a place for her. Actually, given what I'm about to do, I think we'll more than owe her a place.

Zoe greets me as I arrive at Malcolm's office with two sealed documents – one is in a large A4 envelope, the other is a letter.

"Violet?" she says with her eyes fixed to her computer. There's something about her tone I don't like. "Anything I can help you with?"

"I'd like to see Malcolm."

"And what could you possibly want, I wonder?"

She looks hurt. I assume it's due to the outcome of yesterday's bathroom brawl. "I take it you know about Ethan getting fired."

"I do," she says. Her red-lipsticked pout accentuates her movie-starlet face.

"And you know about Tribe?"

"I do." Her blue eyes flash me a look which says, "Come on, of course I know." She takes a sip of water from a pale-green insulated water bottle that co-ordinates with the objects on her desk – a delicate vase, a ceramic letter rack, a tissue box and a china rabbit ornament. I wouldn't be surprised if her knickers match too.

"Well, maybe there could be a place for you too . . ."

What the . . . ? Why did I say that? She's the last person I want to work with.

"I have absolutely no desire to jump ship. Why would I?"

"Um . . . I just assumed . . ."

"You assumed what? That I'd put myself in a position to have my heart broken by Ethan Fraser again?" She buzzes through to Malcolm to tell him I'm here, then she pushes her chair back under the table with a nerve-jarring screech. "Malcolm can see you now." My whole body convulses as I realise what I'm about to do. "Good luck at Tribe, Violet."

***

Malcolm glances up briefly from the stack of papers he's reading when I enter his office. He points his finger at me. "Is that what I think it is?" he asks. His pointed finger turns into a beckoning finger. I pass him the letter.

"Malcolm . . ." I say, drawing out his name. My anxiety is off the scale. "I'm not prepared to go into the ins and outs of why I felt I had no choice but to confide in Ethan, but I did not tell Stella. He did, and I'm upset with both—"

"Are you sleeping with him?"

"What?"

"I'm only asking because I can't think of any other reason why you'd tell my secret to that animal." He makes eye contact at last, and I notice a purple-grey bruise across his cheekbone. I feel responsible. Again.

"The answer is no, Malcolm. We are not sleeping together."

"Fine. One last question – do you feel guilty about what you did?"

"What *I* did?"

"Yes. How many people do you think are lurking in

282

the shadows, waiting to stick the knife into me now, because of you? I could handle Ridley Gates. But Stella Judd? She's a viper. She destroys anyone who crosses her. Don't think for one second you're exempt. Or Fraser. Oh, and don't think I don't know about you downloading every file you could get your hands on today. Why are you doing this? I've always been good to you, haven't I?"

"It's not about you. I've worked with Ethan for three years, he's my best friend and you fired him. I want to go with him. And Ridley has made it impossible for me to stay."

"Ridley?" Malcolm's shoulders roll back and he reclines in his seat, his grey eyes lit up with curiosity. "What has he done now?"

"Let's just say he has a talent for blackmail."

"Oh? What have you done to make him blackmail you?"

"Nothing, except know about you!" I shout. Malcolm looks shocked by my outburst, so I take a deep breath and proceed as planned. "Ridley said he'd leave you alone if I slept with him."

He looks horrified. I think. "Did you?"

"What? No! How can you even ask me that?"

"So that's why Ethan went after him?"

"Yes, it is."

He sighs deeply and his neck skin quivers against his collar. "I'm sorry. I doubt Fraser would want his job back now, so what's done is done. I'll just sit here and wait for the wolves to pounce."

"That's why I'm giving you this." I pass him the envelope filled with information. "This is only a tenth of what I have, but it's more than enough for you to keep the wolves from your door. For good."

He holds the document in his hand, not knowing quite what to make of it. "Thank you."

"I'm truly sorry for what's happened, Malcolm, and I wish you and Emily and all of your family well. I'll keep in touch."

He smiles faintly, but says nothing as I leave.

***

It's late as I make my way to the lobby with an enormous box containing mine and Ethan's belongings. I'm just about to press the button for the lift when that godawful thing I suspected would happen at some point during the day finally happens: I come face to face with Ridley Gates.

"Do you need any help?" he asks in his gut-wrenchingly slimy voice, eyeing the box I'm struggling to carry.

"I'm fine," I say, resting the box on the floor for a moment so I can stretch my fingers out in an attempt to get some feeling back into them.

"What's in the box?"

"Mine and Ethan's things." I look at him with disgust, but I feel a swell of satisfaction as I tally up the purple bruises and swollen cuts on his face. He definitely came off worse than Ethan.

"Well, I'll need to have a look inside to make sure you're not taking anything out of here that you shouldn't."

"Go to hell, Ridley."

He laughs and I want to colour his face even more purple than it already is. "Now, now. Is that any way to talk to an executive director?"

I raise my voice and look him square in the eye. "I've just resigned my position. You're nothing to me."

"Oh, I see. You're jumping ship too. Of course you are. I'd have bet good money on you running after Fraser like a bitch in heat."

I don't acknowledge him.

"Open the box."

I bang the lift button and pick up the box again. "Go. To. Hell." I repeat. My stomach lurches as I hear his creepy laugh.

He comes up behind me. He's so close I can feel his breath warming the back of my neck, and it's all I can do not to turn around and drop the heavier-than-a-baby-elephant box on his foot. "So what's Ethan Fraser got that I haven't?"

"Ethan is my friend," I say wearily. I am so tired of his games.

"Well in that case, I'm pleased you've got a grip on reality."

"Excuse me?" I say and already wish I hadn't. Why am I even engaging with him?

He leans in closer and whispers in my ear. "Carly was a slut and everyone knew it. I fucked her because she was easy. She'd spread her legs at the slightest whiff of cock – any cock."

"You're disgusting."

"I am, and so is Ethan Fraser. If you want him to fuck you, just spread your legs for him and he'll come running. Spread your legs for me and I'll come running too. I still want to fuck you. You'd be a nice upgrade after Carly."

I close my eyes in revulsion, then I take a deep breath and speak with as much confidence as I can muster. "You know, I've been thinking a lot about

September 2008 recently."

"What?" he says, sounding genuinely puzzled.

I stare at the lift doors, willing them to open. "September 2008. You billed Ellis Industrial an extra ten thousand pounds over budget and spent the difference entertaining god knows who."

"That's bullshit." He laughs, but I can see the anxiety start to build in his eyes, so I continue.

"March 2010, you paid a member of parliament a five-figure sum to lobby for your client Stennis Smith. August 2009, you paid Hilary McKinney yet another five-figure sum to drop the sexual harassment charges she made against you. You did the same for Sarah Cole in February 2012. October 2011, you overcharged Handy Industries over five different accounts, and . . . where did that money end up?"

I turn to face him. He's a shadow of his usual sneering slimeball self, his skin pale and drained of blood. "You can't prove any of that."

Revulsion burns throughout my body, but I keep my eyes trained on the lift doors and watch the electronic counter on the wall tell me my sanctuary is currently an alarming seven floors away. "I can and I will."

I'm still looking ahead, my heart racing, when I feel his body pressing up against mine. I manage to squirm away from him without dropping the box on my own feet, but he's back on me straight away, his chest pushed up against my back and his arm clutching my elbow.

"You're playing with fire. It would be such a shame if you got burned." He grips my arm tighter and sweeps my hair to one side, placing his mouth close to my ear. "Become a problem for me and I'll finish you."

I inhale a deep breath and steel myself. "I'm not

afraid of you, Ridley. I've just left a copy of the Ellis Industrial file with Malcolm, so you won't be blackmailing him anymore. I have another nine files in my possession – I can keep them, or I can send them to Delfina, or I can send them to the board of directors. It's entirely up to you how you want to play this."

And then the lift doors open.

And Max almost walks into me, grabbing hold of the box as I stumble.

I do my best to try to hide it, but my arms are shaking and I know my face is burning. Max offers to carry the box downstairs for me, but then he stops dead in his tracks, looking both of us over as his green eyes grow wider and wider. I can see the penny drop in agonisingly painful slow motion, and there's nothing I can do to draw him off the scent.

"What the hell just happened here?" The pupils of his eyes are angry black pinholes, and I know we're counting down to blast off.

"Just having a quiet word with Miss Archer before she leaves for the evening, Adolf," Ridley says with a smirk.

"What the hell did you just call me?" Max yells at Ridley's retreating frame. "That's right, walk away from me, you racist piece of shit!"

"Just let him go," I plead. I don't want a repeat of yesterday. I don't want punches to be thrown. I just want him gone. Forever. I never want to have to look at his face ever again.

"And for your fucking information, you greasy-headed cocksplat, I'm fucking German! Adolf Hitler was Austrian. Germany and Austria are two different countries!"

I would laugh if I could.

Honestly, I would.

25

THE RIP OFF TAXI FARE from the City to my flat is the final nail in the coffin of my day. Forty-five flaming pounds! It's usually thirty – thirty-five tops – but forty-five? I push my debit card into the payment machine and shoot the driver a look that could curdle milk. I've lived in Kilburn for two and a half years now, so I know he took more than a couple of lengthy diversions. Plus, there's practically a monsoon outside and he's stopped halfway up my street claiming it's the best spot to make a U-turn.

I snap my card back out of the machine, yank the taxi door open and pull my plastic box of belongings across the floor, snagging a fingernail in the process – the final of final straws.

"Don't help me with this, whatever you do," I bark at the taxi driver.

"Not my job, love. I charge for the ride, that's it. Plus it's pissing down."

"You charge for the longest, most convoluted ride possible, you mean. Think of that extra fifteen pounds you conned me out of as your tip for doing nothing."

"My pleasure, love. Hope you've still got enough money in your bank account for tampons, because it sounds like your time of the month is on the way."

"I beg your pardon?"

"You heard me. Hormonal, are we?" I lift the box and start walking, leaving the taxi door open. I hear the driver muttering away to himself as he's forced to get out of his vehicle. "Get fired today, did you? Boyfriend dump you, did he? You need to take a chill pill, sweetheart."

I spin around intending to flip him the bird, but thanks to the stupid box the only thing I can do is yell, "Go fuck yourself, you turgid bag of putrid flesh!"

Jesus, what's happened to my mouth?

The cabbie slams the taxi door shut and drives off, beeping his horn as he passes me. What a bellend. And could the universe be any crueller? I'm probably in the process of ruining my life, so serving me up a dollop of maggot-infested taxi-nightmare shit is the icing on the cake.

The rain gets heavier as I approach the entrance to my building. I try to walk quickly, but the box is too heavy. Who'd have thought the contents of mine and Ethan's desk drawers weighed more than an Olympic heavyweight boxer? My hands are already red raw and slippery, so I'm worried about dropping the damn thing. A plastic box full of crap landing on my foot would be a fitting end to my day.

I have to stop a few feet from the door. My arms feel like they're strapped to a medieval torture device. I put the box on the ground and rub away the pain in my hands. There are deep concertina ridges in my fingers, and two of them are entirely numb.

"Need a hand?"

My heart leaps into my mouth as a shrouded figure appears from nowhere, his hands hidden deep in the pockets of a black hooded top. In the space of one second, my shock is replaced by panic, then by rage as I recognise the idiot standing in front of me.

"Ethan! Have you lost your mind?" I gasp into the drizzly night air as I clutch my chest. I'd be having a heart attack if my heart wasn't broken already. An irritating laugh rumbles in his throat, and it's a good thing my fingers are crushed otherwise I'd be slapping him across his stupid face.

"I'm sorry. I didn't mean to scare you."

"Jumping out at women whilst being dressed like a rapist tends to have that effect." My heart rate starts to slow, but my temper continues to rise. I rub my fingers one last time and pick up the plastic tomb of death again.

"I was standing in the doorway because it's raining."

"How long have you been waiting?"

He looks at his watch and shrugs. "Almost two hours."

Shit, he's lost it. "Why?"

"I needed to see you."

"You could have called, texted, rung the office . . ."

"I needed to get my head straight, so I didn't mind waiting."

"In this weather? You're mad." The rain beats down so hard it splashes up the backs of my legs. I put the box down on the pavement.

"What's in the box?"

Surely he knows? I search his face again and I can't tell if he does or not. The rain is running down his cheeks, and his hood is soaked through. I can't even see his eyes properly because it's getting dark and the amber light from the streetlamp overhead is casting wild shadows. "Our stuff."

"Ours?"

"Yes, I resigned tonight."

He stares at me open-mouthed as the rain pours down his face. "Really? You're coming to Tribe? That's awesome!"

"I said I resigned, but I'm still not sure if Tribe's

going to be good for me." I watch his excitement fade in an instant, but although my heart is aching, I need to do what's best for me – whatever that is. "Look, you know me, Ethan. I'm great working on my own. I can work with you, but other people? Leading a team of people? That's not going to end well. I love copywriting. I've never wanted to be a manager or a partner – that's your ambition. It's just . . . I'm still not sure, so I've talked with Naomi Linus at TalentNetwork and she's going to put out some feelers—"

"What? I can't believe you're telling me this. Violet, please. You know how much I need you with me."

My eyes fill up, and I'm happy with the rainstorm because it's helping to hide my tears. "I know you *think* you need me."

"Violet. I need you. If it's the job, you don't have to be creative director. I'll back you in any position you want. You can stay as a copywriter – whatever it takes. Is that all you're worried about?"

"No, I suppose . . . it's not . . ." I bite my lip as the tears escape. I raise my face to the night sky and let the rain disguise my weakness. *You can't move a mountain if you just sit on your arse staring at the fucking thing* . . . "It's about us too, Ethan. When you told me about Tribe, you told me we had to forget what's happening between us in the exact same breath. That gave me the answer to every question I could ever have asked about your priorities. I can't go to Tribe knowing that you—"

"Violet, listen to me!" I suck in a breath at the sharpness of his interruption. "When Stella told me there could be no "us" at Tribe, there was nothing I could do. What do you want me to do?"

"This isn't about Stella. This is about you and me.

And since when does Stella Judd mean more to you than I do?"

"Since she's my boss."

"Apparently she's your partner, not your bloody boss. And I'm supposed to be your friend. Your soulmate, remember?"

He turns away. His trainers squelch as he walks over to the brick wall of my building and rests his frame against it. He looks to the sky as silver rain lit up by a streetlamp falls onto his skin. I start to walk away, tired of not getting a straight answer.

"Just tell me how you feel. Are you in love with me?"

His question stops me dead in my tracks. My pulse races, beating in unison with the rain and the sound of traffic swishing through puddles on the roads. "You know the answer."

He comes up behind me and I shiver as I feel my cold wet cotton skirt cling to my legs. "I didn't know for sure."

My stomach dies. It doesn't flip, lurch, sink or roll. It just dies. I know what comes next. I've heard it in my own head a million times, so I know the game is over and the count is in. Now would be the time to follow Max's advice and fight for him. I want to make the words tumble out of my mouth, and I want them to be brave and I want them to be honest and I want them to be beautiful. What do I have to lose now?

"If you want us to stay as friends, that's okay. I didn't want to fall in love with you. I didn't want any of this and I tried to stop it . . . I tried so bloody hard . . . because it frightened me so much. I know this isn't fair saying all of this to you now, but I need you to know that I didn't choose to feel this way. And I wish we could go back to the way things were, but I don't think we can now."

I leave him standing speechless as I walk away.

***

I don't expect him to follow me.

Whenever something major rocks Ethan's world, he goes into hiding and replaces the drama with silence until his brain is ready to come out the other side. I might hear from him in a week.

I practically hurl the plastic box to the floor as I reach my front door. I turn the key and kick the box into my hall, not giving a shit about the mail that gets shredded in the process.

But then he's there, behind me in the doorway. He lowers his hood and ruffles his hair, shaking off the water. His face is pale and his muscles are tense, yet he's still the most beautiful man I've ever laid eyes on. And I wish I hadn't told him. A minute ago, I didn't care. But now as I watch him take strained breaths, his mouth opening and closing as he stops himself from saying whatever is on his mind, I wish I could erase it all. I wish I could break out a DeLorean and go literally anywhere in space and time to avoid having to talk about how I feel.

I pull my hair over my shoulder and wring the dampness out. My top is sticking to my body and I know I'm soaked through to my underwear. It reminds me of those horrendous swimming lessons at school when Sister Annalise insisted retrieving a brick from a swimming pool floor whilst wearing pyjamas was a life skill everybody needed to master. Twenty years later,

I'm still waiting for a real-world opportunity to rescue a brick from a pond.

"Why are you here, Ethan?"

"I'm not going anywhere until we talk this through, and we're going to talk all night if we have to."

"There's no point. What's done is done. I need an early night – I promised to meet Naomi tomorrow morning."

He moves into the light and I finally see his face properly. He looks shattered – striking and gorgeous – but still shattered. "I can't believe you're thinking of working somewhere without me."

I shrug. "I'm not going to argue that finding a job with Naomi is a brilliant move, because it's a dumb move. But going to Tribe is also a dumb move. And if I'd decided to stay at BMG, that would have been a dumb move too. My life is a shitshow and you know what? I'm not going to blame myself anymore. I tried to sort everybody else's mess out, I tried really fucking hard, but none of this was ever my fault. Ridley Gates was not my fault!"

His eyes narrow, making the blue fade to grey. "I know that. Why are we talking about Ridley?"

"Because I finally sorted it tonight. I used some information Lucille gave me, and when he tried . . . when he tried it on again, I came at him with everything I had and I destroyed him – just like I told you I would. He won't hurt Malcolm ever again. And he won't hurt me again."

He freezes, and his face drains of colour. "Um, okay."

"Is that all you have to say?"

"I don't know, but I want to beat the shit out of him again."

"I told you before, Ethan. I appreciate that you care about me enough to do that, but I'm not a delicate flower. I may not have much in the way of brawn, but I'm astute – and maybe a little bit devious – and I *did* have this under control. I told you I could help Malcolm *and* deal with Ridley and I did it. You'll have to find a job at Tribe for Lucille though."

"I'll . . . um . . . sort something out for her," he says, looking a little bit shell-shocked.

"Good."

"And . . . I'm proud of you."

"Thank you."

"But speaking of jobs . . . Naomi Linus? I have to tell you, she'd do anything to get you away from me. She asked me out last year. Twice. I said no because Will shagged her a couple of years ago and she wouldn't stop calling him for weeks after."

"Oh for fuck's sake, really?" Just when I'd forgotten how self-absorbed Ethan Fraser is, he comes out with the most ridiculously conceited comment I've ever heard. "Are you going to let the sun know that the earth revolves around you now?"

"I don't mean she's helping you just because of me." I raise my eyebrows and he responds with a guilty swallow. "Okay, I did mean that, but you have to admit she's overly keen if she's meeting you on a Saturday morning."

"I need to find a new job quickly. I have rent to pay."

"So start at Tribe tomorrow."

All of a sudden I feel the weight of my drenched clothes dragging me to the floor. I back up against the door to my sitting room and place my hand on the handle to steady myself. It would only take a second to go inside. Just one second to escape him.

"It'll all work out," he says. "Please just give Tribe a chance."

I open the door and enter my sitting room, throwing off my wet cardigan before going to the bathroom to find a towel. I'm angry and I'm devastated and I don't know which emotion is controlling my actions because I also seem to have lost the ability to think.

When I return he's pacing the room. He looks like he's been put through a wash, spin and tumble dry cycle. He watches me as I towel-dry the ends of my hair. Neither of us speak a word.

"I'm really tired, Ethan."

"I told you I wasn't going until we'd talked this through."

"We've talked."

"You've talked. I haven't."

I sigh and sit down on my sofa, placing the towel over my lap. "Okay then, talk."

He fluffs his hair again then lounges on my armchair, one leg hanging over the arm. I toss him the towel and he sinks his face into it, seemingly breathing in the fleecy cotton for a moment before rubbing the back of his neck dry. The wait for him to speak is killing me – it's like I'm on trial and I'm waiting for the jury to come back with a verdict on whether or not I'm guilty of being a hopeless whiny wimp who had ten minutes of bravery this afternoon then promptly fucked everything back up again.

"These last few weeks, it's been like I'm living someone else's life. And now? The thought of you not coming to Tribe with me makes me want to walk in front of a bus. I know I'm being selfish. I know that, but I can't help it. Working with you? Well, it's

297

everything to me."

"Everything?" I repeat with a hint of sarcasm. Boy, am I tired of hearing that phrase.

"Yes. It's more than everything." He leans forward in the chair, his hands folded together. His elbows on his knees. His eyes firm and fixed and . . . damn my stupid stomach. It still somersaults when he looks at me that way. "There have been so many times over the past three years I've wanted to say this to you, but I didn't think you'd believe it. And I didn't want to ruin our friendship. None of this would have happened if I'd . . . if only I'd told you . . ."

He walks over to me, and all of a sudden I don't know where I am or who I am or what day it is. It's like I'm watching myself from across the room, like a modern-day version of Scrooge witnessing my life playing out in front of me. I will my alternate self to say something. I beg my alternate brain to start working. He sits down next to me, and I slide as far into the corner of the sofa as I can go. He reaches for my hand. I move it away, but I don't know what to do with it, so I start playing with my hair. "I'm sorry for all of this. I'm sorry for being me. I didn't know . . ."

"What didn't you know?"

His hand moves towards me again, but he thinks twice and pushes it down on his own leg instead. His jeans are patchy – dark blue on the bottom, paler blue where the thick denim has already started to dry out. "I thought maybe you'd started to feel the same way I did, but I didn't know for sure."

"How did you miss it, Ethan? For the three years I've known you, you've been addicted to making women fall in love with you. How didn't you notice that the woman you've spent every day of your life with had fallen in love with you too?"

He makes another grab for my hand and this time I let him. He locks his fingers in mine, and as soon as I feel the warmth from his touch I melt into him. "I love you . . . I'm in love with you. I fell in love with you the first day I met you, but I thought I couldn't have you, so I tried to replace you, with anybody, but it was always you. I never thought you'd love me back – never in a million years – so I settled for working with you and spending every day of our lives together. I fell in love with you, then I fell in love with being your friend – and the thought of not seeing you every day scares the shit out of me."

Every single part of me – mind, body and spirit – explodes with joy. I've needed to hear him say those words more than I've needed to breathe. I don't care what happens next. I just want to stay in this moment forever.

"What are you thinking?" he asks.

"I'm thinking you're probably crazy."

"I'm crazy for not telling you sooner."

"You're crazy if you can't see how wrong I am for you."

"Why do you say that?" We're inches apart. He takes both of my hands in his and holds them tight. "I love you just as you are, and I always have. I fell in love with you because you don't follow the rules. You're you and you're brilliant and beautiful and my god, never apologise for being you. Never." He releases my hands so he can cup my face and smooth my wet hair away from my eyes. "I want to show you how perfect you are for me."

I look up and slowly meet his gaze. "How?"

"I want you. I am in love with you, and I want you."

I open my mouth to speak – to tell him I love him too – but nothing happens.

Silence fills the air between us.

I try to talk again, but my words are blocked by his mouth on mine, the soft and urgent feel of his lips sending tremors through my body.

And then I'm kissing him back.

26

OUR BODIES PRESS TOGETHER AS we kiss and it's different to before. Last time it was more cautious; his kisses were soft and guarded because he was so unsure of himself. This time there's urgency and there's certainty.

It starts softly. A brush of skin against skin. Reassuring and tender. Only the slightest pressure at first, but it sends ripples of electricity buzzing through me until all I can think about is what it would feel like to have those same sweet, gentle lips visit every single inch of me.

I kiss him back, parting my mouth desperately, begging for his tongue, but instead he pulls me to my feet, his lips moving swiftly to my jaw, then my neck. He walks behind me and pushes my wet hair aside to trail kisses down my back, wrapping me up in his arms. And the nagging doubts about whether we're right for each other are silenced.

He releases me to unzip his hooded top, letting it fall to the floor with a heavy thud. He turns me around and we kiss again, this time stronger and more forceful. I move my hands through his soft, feathery hair. It feels different, smoother, the styling products washed out by the rain. His t-shirt is damp, and the cotton clings to the contours of his body as he presses against me again. I find the bottom of his t-shirt and snake my hands underneath to feel his warm skin. A deep moan escapes his throat as I run my fingers along the taut muscles of his chest, stopping to caress the spot where his heart is pounding under his ribcage.

He responds by pulling me even closer. I wrap my arms around his neck, grabbing fistfuls of his hair, and he clutches my waist tightly. I part my lips again and this time his tongue is there, exploring my mouth until I feel like I'm going to implode. I pull away for a moment to catch my breath. My forehead rests on his, my gasps merging with his more urgent pants. Our noses align, but our eyes are cast down, as if meeting each other's gaze would ignite an inferno that neither of us could put out. Would we even want to put it out? We stand locked together, frozen for a moment, yet swaying to silent music.

"Vi . . ." he mumbles breathlessly. "You have no idea how much I want this. I want you."

"I do too. I promised myself I would change . . ."

He cups my face and pulls me in close, his thumbs gently caressing my cheeks as he looks directly into my eyes. "I already told you. I don't want you to change a single thing."

"No, I mean I promised myself I would start to fight for you – that's what I'm changing. I don't want to hide my feelings anymore. I want to let you in." He smiles and kisses me, and heat pools in my belly. "But I admit I'm a little bit terrified. Are you?"

"No. Not in the slightest." His hand grips mine and he pulls it to his chest. "I've never been so sure about anything."

I grin. "But what about our bet?"

He looks confused for a moment, then the glimmer of recognition lands in his eyes and he laughs. His laugh is delicious. "You resigned and I was fired. We don't work together anymore."

"I'm still not sure about Tribe."

He leans into me again, claiming my mouth with his. He tastes of mint toothpaste – fresh and clean. "I don't want to think about that . . . All I want to think about is this" – he kisses my neck – "and this" – he kisses the base of my throat – "and most definitely this" – he kisses my lips possessively. He's making every moment last as long as possible and I hope I never forget how good this feels . . . how breathtakingly, astoundingly, brilliantly wonderful this moment is.

He starts to walk, but he doesn't let go of me, kissing me as we take a few steps towards the sofa. He guides me backwards and lowers me down, then he stands above me in silence, his eyes sparkling with the silver light reflected from my chandelier. He smiles "my smile", and I instinctively push my legs together as the throb in my thighs beats hard into my pelvis.

"You're so beautiful," he says as he sits down next to me. I feel myself blush, but I don't speak. I can't, because my heart has taken up residence in my mouth and if I tried to talk, I think I'd choke.

I lean against the back of the sofa as he reaches for the clip that's holding my hair back from my face. "I love your hair," he says, running his hands over the wet tangles.

I laugh. "Even if it's a bit messy?"

He brushes my hair from my face and lets it fall over one shoulder. "I love messy, because you're messy and I love you."

He rests his arm on the back of the sofa, his hand gently touching my shoulder, making lazy shapes with his fingertips. His other hand moves to my leg, sliding under my skirt, kneading the soft flesh of my inner thigh, then he takes me with a frantic, possessive kiss that lasts so long I feel breathless and light-headed. If I suffocate under him, it's fine. I can think of many worse ways to die.

He untucks my top from my skirt, and I raise my arms as he pulls the damp material over my head. My hair falls forward over my chest. I look down and mentally high-five myself when I notice that somehow – against insurmountable odds – I managed to put on one of my very few sexy bras this morning.

"Fuck," he gasps as he stares at the sheer, fuchsia-pink netting which encases my breasts but leaves little to the imagination. He reaches out and runs his fingers along the peach lace trim. "That's one hell of a hot sight," he murmurs. I grin at his reaction, then I grin wider as I recall putting on the matching pair of knickers this morning. Luck is on my side – that's definitely never happened before.

He moves in closer and kisses me again, moaning into my mouth as our chests crash together. I tug at the bottom of his t-shirt and he breaks off to impatiently yank it over his head. I spread my palms over his chest, and he mirrors my movements, brushing his fingers over my bra and thumbing my nipples, already hard and protruding under the see-through fabric.

"Oh . . . my god . . ." he says as his hands become moulded to my tits, his fingers rubbing roughly at each hard peak. Each time he breaks off from kissing me, I'm captivated by how wide his eyes are and how spellbound he seems to be. "You're so amazing . . . why did we wait so long for this?"

I can't help but smile with pride. Don't get me wrong – I know I can pull off "sexy" when I try, but tonight I seem to have managed it with absolutely no effort at all. Given I've also been rained on for half an hour I figure he must like the drowned-rat look. "Wait until you see my matching knickers," I purr into his ear.

"Oh my god." His voice is strained with heavy panting breaths that persistently remind me how completely into this he is. Shit. He's completely into me, isn't he? His throat vibrates as he kisses the tops of my breasts. "You're killing me," he groans.

"I know I am," I say with a teasing giggle as I change position suddenly to sit on my knees, taking him by surprise. He falls back into the corner of the sofa and watches me reach for the zip on my skirt. I don't feel shy or embarrassed or insecure at shedding more clothing because I can see the longing, the raw desire, embedded in his face. He's looking at me as if I'm everything he's ever wanted, and I don't think – although I might be insane – that he only wants sex. I believe he's picturing his future with me in it.

I let my skirt fall around my hips, then I stand up and let it drop to the floor. I step out of the floral cotton at my feet and manoeuvre myself between his legs. I wish I could kick off my heels, but sadly they're strapped to my ankles. He pulls me forwards, his fingers hooking under the elastic of my underwear, his palms warm against my hip. He kisses my stomach, his tongue dipping into my navel, and it feels amazing. I pull his head into me and run my fingers roughly through his hair, desperately needing . . . begging for . . . more.

He pokes off his trainers with the back of each foot, followed by his socks, and then he grabs my behind, pulling me into his lap. I position myself so I'm straddling him, and I gasp as I feel his hardness beneath me. I meet his mouth with mine again, rubbing against the damp fabric of his jeans, making him groan as I press down onto his cock. I'm determined to make this the best sex I've ever had. I can't vouch for it being the best he's ever had given his colourful history . . . but the way he's already responded to me is making me feel like I've got the bedroom skills of a high-class escort. Is that even a good thing? Oh, who cares?

"Shall we go to the bedroom?" I ask, rocking gently on his groin, soft throaty gasps escaping into the space between us.

"No . . . I want you . . . here . . ."

"You want me right here?" I say with a giggle.

"Yes, so don't you dare think of going . . ." He moves his hands to my back and fiddles with the clasp of my bra. His trembling knuckles jerk and dig into me as he battles to undo the hook, cursing under his breath. I pull my hands behind me to help him out, but he's won before I get there, the peach lace straps falling from my shoulders. I let him peel away the remaining fabric and he surprises me by immediately taking one of my breasts into his mouth. I arch my back and moan as he pulls at my nipple with his teeth.

"If we're staying here, we need to get protection. I have some in the bathroom . . ."

"My . . . wallet . . ." he says with difficulty, his mouth full of breast.

He lifts his behind and I raise myself up so he can pull his wallet from his jeans pocket. He throws it down on the sofa next to him and unbuckles his belt. His fumbling is manic, and impossible with me straddling him, so I get up and take the opportunity to unstrap my heels.

"No, leave them on."

"What?"

He pulls his jeans off one leg. "I like them on. Heels are hot . . ." Then he loses his balance and topples over as his other leg gets tangled up in half-dry denim.

"Shit . . . I'm stuck."

"Calm down," I say with a chuckle.

"No chance of that." He pulls the errant jean-leg off the end of his foot and reaches to pull me back. "I have no idea how long I'm going to last, by the way . . ."

"So, I'd better speed things up," I say as I push my hands down the front of his shorts. My god, he's hard. Forget pocket rocket, think cock-a-saurus rex. He inhales a sharp breath as I take him completely into my hand, stroking him until his face is so flushed he looks as if he's been out in the sun for too long. He raises himself up so he can push his shorts down. I groan as his cock presses underneath me. Shit . . . I don't think I'm going to last much longer myself. I am more ready than I've ever been in my entire life when I feel his hands push the fabric of my underwear aside.

"Oh my god . . . that feels . . . please . . ."

I sense that the tidal wave of pleasure is about to course through my body, so I try to block it out. I don't want it to happen yet. I dive for his wallet and hand it to him, both of our hands trembling during the exchange. He pulls out a black foil wrapper, rips it open and rolls the condom on. I reposition myself on top of him, but he pushes me back to my feet. "Not like this. I want you naked."

I stand in front of him as he pulls net and lace down over my hips and legs, then I inhale sharply as I feel his mouth on me. He grips my behind and pulls me in close to his face. I grab his hair and moan wildly when he licks my smooth skin. Thank the gods, fate, luck, karma and whatever else that I mowed the lawn in the shower this morning. My legs feel weak as he takes me into his mouth, and I grip his shoulders as I feel the ripples course again. I'm nearly there, but I want more . . . I'm aching for more, and my god, I know I have every right to be selfish.

I push him back against the sofa and straddle him again, groaning when I feel his cock rising up under me. I lower myself onto him and we both groan deep in our throats.

We start to move together, building a beautiful rhythm, one that feels like more than just sex, like a choreographed dance I've always known every step of.

"Oh fuck, Vi . . . Jesus. That feels so fucking good. God, I love you so much."

I pick up the pace and he responds by pushing upwards into me. The sound of our lovemaking is glorious . . . if a little squelchy, but I don't care, and I know from his breathless moans that he's finding the noise a massive turn-on. His mouth teases my nipples and he bites down lightly but sharply, the pain shooting into my arousal and intensifying the rumblings that are starting to build once more. I feel his hand pushing between us to find my clit, and it happens moments later. I feel myself contract around him and the ecstasy erupts from my core and trickles in smaller waves through the rest of my body. I fall forward onto him, crying my release into the warmth of his neck. It's mind-blowing – astonishingly, unbelievably mind-blowing – and I don't want it to stop. "Oh my god . . . that was awesome," I say as the shudders eventually dim and my body slowly recovers.

He's still inside me, so I start riding him again, but he stops me and rolls me onto my back, my head resting on a cushion. He enters me again and I suck in a breath. I lift one leg high onto the back of the sofa while the other dangles towards the floor, giving him scope to plunge deep. My heels dig into his back as his

308

pace speeds up, each thrust threatening to be the last, but he manages to hold on.

Our skin is wet and sticky with sex and sweat as our bodies slam together. He starts to pant in rhythm with his movements, stopping briefly to look at me. His gaze sweeps over my chest, my hair, my lips, and then settles on my eyes. "I love you," he says innocently, as if I'm the first woman he's ever fallen in love with. And then I bite down on my lip and tears fill my eyes as I realise I might be.

"I love you too," I say as a tear escapes. His face momentarily crumbles. Just for an instant. And then he's buried into my neck, screaming my name and clutching me tighter than anybody has ever held me before.

We lie together, our arms wrapped around each other, for several minutes. I wonder if he's as stunned as I am. I wonder what comes next.

We don't speak a word when we finally separate.

Instead, he takes my hand in his and we go to the bedroom.

And then . . . somehow . . . we do it all over again.

27

I didn't sleep until the sun came up.

I was too impressed by the number of times we'd managed to do it. It was the banging session to end all banging sessions. A shag-a-thon of such epic, gargantuan proportions that the night probably fractured the space-time continuum (I learned that term from Max and his love of Star Trek). I might be bragging, but I've had more sex in the last twelve hours than I've had in the past three years, so I'm going to allow myself some swagger. It was amazing. He was amazing and I was amazing.

I don't think I'll ever forget that first time though. I figure that's what sex feels like when you're in love, and I realise I've probably never been properly in love. We managed a repeat performance in the bedroom just a few minutes afterwards. Then, he sneaked into the bathroom while I was showering and sealed the deal on an amazing third time.

A jaunt to the kitchen for a snack in the middle of the night somehow resulted in an impromptu escapade on my kitchen worktop featuring some whipped cream, a lemon and half a punnet of strawberries. After that, I think I fell asleep before he did, and I don't know how many hours have passed, but when I open my eyes and yawn into my pillow, I notice that the sun is high in the sky and my room is lit up with bright sunlight.

The next thing I notice is that I'm alone.

A swell of panic knots in my stomach as reality hits: he's left me.

I call out his name, and my heart thuds in my chest when there's no response. He's really gone and done what he always does.

I sit up in bed, my face burning with the realisation that after everything – after the most amazing night of my entire life – he's reverted to type, shit the bed and run away. Why? I imagine a little red devil sitting on my left shoulder, sticking a pitchfork into my skull. "*You should have known this would happen. You knew he'd never commit. You fell for his patter hook, line and sinker. You knew all along you weren't his type. You're such an idiot.*"

And I'm supposed to be meeting Naomi from TalentNetwork this morning. I look at my clock and force my eyes wide open to make sure I'm seeing what I think I'm seeing. 10.36 a.m. Oh my god! If I got dressed and left home now I wouldn't be in the City until lunchtime. What the hell? The bastard not only sneaked out of my flat and left me with a screwed-up love life, he's also left me with a screwed-up career.

I give in to the tears. There's no point in keeping them in. Nobody can see me and nobody can hear me. I sob for a good five minutes. Then another imagined character with wings and a halo distracts me with kinder words: "*He told you he loved you. He said you were everything. He said he doesn't want to change a single thing about you. He made love to you like you were the only woman he's ever fallen in love with.*"

I remember every word he said to me – I believed them all – and this makes his abandonment ten times more hurtful. I decide the only thing that would help me now is a) alcohol or b) a gun, so I choose the more pleasurable option and get out of bed, pick up some grey yoga pants off my bedroom floor and a lime-green vest top from the ironing pile, and get dressed. I make a beeline for the half-full bottle of French red I know is in my kitchen cupboard.

I stop still as I pass through my sitting room. The cushions are neatly stacked on my sofa and . . . what the hell? My clothes have been folded neatly and placed in a pile on the coffee table. Bra and knickers sitting proudly on top. What kind of masochistic prick tidies up before he does a moonlight flit? He's even stacked my clothes in size order. What's up with that? Does he think that's the least he could do? Is he on the phone with his brother, laughing about humping and dumping some chick but feeling bad enough to give her flat a quick tidy-up first?

I go to the kitchen, find the wine and pour myself an enormous glass. It's full to the brim, but there's still a splash left in the bottle so I take a sip and refill. And there's still some left. Fuck it! I tip my head back and pour the dregs straight down my neck, the warm liquid burning my throat as it rushes into my stomach.

"Jesus Christ all-fucking-mighty, is this the effect I've had on you?"

I almost jump out of my skin, and I lose a mouthful of wine down my front in the process. "What the hell . . . How did you get in?"

He rests in the doorway and dangles my keys in the air.

"You took my keys with you when you left? Did you lock me in? You knew about my meeting with Naomi."

"I assumed you'd have a spare set somewhere." He's grinning, and I have no idea whether I want to kiss him, scream at him or punch him. "And . . . it's kind of a bit late to start thinking about your meeting. Have you just woken up?"

"Yes, and that's your fault too!"

He opens his mouth to speak, then stops himself. He rolls his eyes and smiles at me in that patronising way men do when you're epically spitting-feathers-grade pissed off with them but they think you're cute when you're angry.

"Don't you dare look at me like that!" I yell. He walks towards me and I take a step back. "And don't you dare come anywhere near me either."

He does as he's told, and we stand at opposite ends of the kitchen. I think of last night. The memory of strawberries and whipped cream and what we did with that lemon just a few hours earlier invades my mind.

"I had to pop out for something. I'm sorry. You were sleeping; I thought I'd be back sooner."

I sigh and shake my head. I know this is my fault and I hate myself for being so insecure. "I thought you'd just . . . left me."

The humour in his face is replaced with regret. "I would never do that. How could you even think it?"

Is he for real? "Because I woke up and you were gone."

"I couldn't sleep. I didn't sleep all night. I just got up and had a few things to take care of." He walks towards me and his eyes are drawn to my chest.

"Seriously?" I look down and see I'm smuggling more than a couple of peanuts. Think hazelnuts soaked in red wine. I reach for a towel to dab at the splashes, but obviously the vest is ruined.

"Sorry, line of vision."

"Line of vision if you're looking. Did you not get enough last night?"

"I can always make time for more . . ." he says. I roll my eyes at him and he shrugs. "What? You're hot, I'm

313

completely and madly in love with you, and you're not wearing a bra. I mean, give a guy a break here!"

"Give you a break? You left me and you let me sleep in, probably on purpose." He twists his mouth to stifle a grin. "Oh my god, you did do it on purpose, didn't you? Jesus Christ!"

I barge past him and head back to the bedroom, pulling my vest over my head and throwing it on the floor as I pull my drawers open. I dig out a bra – my most comfortable and least sexy one – and pick out a t-shirt. When I turn around he's in the doorway. He's smirking. I feel the corners of my mouth twitch upwards, so I suck in my cheeks and turn away. I get dressed with my back to him.

"I think you look better without a bra on. Especially that bra. Did your grandmother knit that thing?"

I look behind me and scowl at him. "Where have you been?"

"Oh, a few places."

I put my hands on my hips. "Let's start with the first place then, shall we?"

"Why are you interrogating me? You were much more fun than this last night."

I roll my eyes again. "God, you're such an idiot."

"Yeah, I know. That's why you love me."

"That's why I'm going to knee you in the balls if you don't answer the question."

He winces. "I don't like the sound of that."

"Better start talking then."

"Okay, come with me."

He walks back into the sitting room. I heave a sigh but follow him. He picks a box up from the coffee table. It's plain white, letter-sized, flat, and fastened with a red satin bow which reminds me of a graduation scroll. Not that I attended either of my graduations. I couldn't bear being the only person without a supportive family cheering them on. He hands me the package with a huge, satisfied grin on his face.

I pull the ribbon free and pop open the box. My stomach goes into freefall as pangs of dread stab at the back of my brain. What the hell is he trying to tell me? "I'm a patron of the Royal Opera House?"

"Yes."

What the hell . . . ? He's smiling about this? Is he kidding me? This was our bet. He's telling me he failed to keep his promise not to sleep with a client or colleague and he's smiling about it?

I slam the box lid down. "Who is she?"

"Eh?" he says as I practically throw the box back at him.

"Who is she? Do I know her?"

"Vi, what's wrong with you? Jesus, it's one thing after another. She's you, you dipshit."

"We don't work together anymore, Ethan. We discussed this not affecting our bet last night – in this very room – before we . . ."

"Before we had amazing sex a shitload of times?"

"Yes, before that." I should be feeling pretty stupid, right? Embarrassed, maybe? Yeah well, I don't. Since I woke up this morning all I've felt is completely weak, pathetic and out of control.

"Okay, think about the happy sex memories when I tell you the second thing I did this morning." His eyes retreat and his skin reddens. "I had to give Stella an answer, so I told her we were both coming to Tribe. And I know what you're going to say, but I don't care. I need you. I don't just think I need you, I *do* need you. You totally own me, you're my everything, and if I

315

can't work with you, I can't work at all. I can't be a partner at Tribe without you by my side . . . but if you really want to work somewhere else, I'll understand. I'll even call Naomi myself and rearrange your meeting."

I don't know how I feel. My instinct is to stamp my foot and tell him he doesn't get to decide what I do, but at the same time I'm overwhelmed by the enormity of the gesture – and the gift, which I know came with a six-grand price tag.

"Did Stella say anything about . . . us?"

"No, she didn't. But we'll cross that bridge when we come to it."

He places the box down on the coffee table and I smile at my neatly folded pile of clothes. I remember how I wanted to kill him when I saw that pile earlier this morning, but now I'm already back to loving him with every single cell in my body.

But I can't shake off the sinking feeling that's clawing at the pit of my stomach, hooking my throat into my chest. It's accompanied by the worst kind of nausea and fear of impending doom. For no real or rational reason, I'm certain this isn't going to end well, and I can't seem to free myself from these crippling emotions. I've lived with them for most of my life, after all. They came in words said by others. They came accompanied by hate, resentment, jealousy and spite. They were spoken into the air and I breathed them in and they've been living inside my brain ever since – nagging at me, reminding me I'm hopeless, ruining my happiness: *"You're not good enough"*, *"You're unpopular"*, *"You're unfriendly"*, *"You always say the wrong things"*, *"You're too quiet"*, *"You're unlovable"*, *"You'll always be alone"*, *"You're nothing"*.

"What is it?" he asks with concern in his voice.

I sit down on the sofa and wait for him to join me. I inhale a steely breath. "Remember when I told you I thought I was wrong for you?" He nods and our eyes lock. "Well, I still don't feel right, Ethan. I'm not ready to believe this is real."

He reaches for my hand and I let him hold me. "It is real, but I understand. I know this is huge . . . and it's huge for me too. I'm going to help you, and you know what? Despite being an idiot, I know how I'm going to do it."

"You do?" I ask with a gentle laugh.

His cheeks dimple as he smiles. "Yeah, I'm going to help you by loving you." He smooths my hair with his palms and kisses me on the cheek. "We're going to have everything we've ever wanted and more."

"I know you *want* to help me by loving me, but you don't know how hard I am to love and . . . god, I want nothing more than to make peace with the parts of me that are dark and lonely. It would be great if you could fix me by loving me, but I don't think you realise how enormous that task is going to be."

"We've all got dark inside of us, Vi. All of us. You said that to me once before, so you know that already. But I don't care about your dark because I only see your light." He leans forward and kisses me. It's a different kiss again. One that is composed of trust and tenderness instead of lust and passion, but it's the one I need in this moment. "I told you I loved you exactly the way you are. You question yourself with honesty and you worry about your faults like nobody else I know, but you know why that is? Because most of us are afraid to admit when we're floundering. I may not worry about my demons, but that doesn't mean I don't

317

have any. It just means I'm not as brave as you."

"I'm sure I'm not brave, Ethan. I don't feel very brave. I feel like I'm falling apart."

"Well, I'm going to hold you together." He puts his arm around my shoulder and pulls me into him. My head tucks into his neck and I smell last night's rainfall on his clothes.

I run my hands over his chest and nuzzle into him. "If I work at Tribe, what are we going to do about the clause Stella's put in your contract?"

"Play it by ear," he says, then he starts to chuckle.

"What's so funny?"

"I'm just wondering why the irony fairy decided to magic your stupid law into a real law." He gives me a squeeze and kisses the top of my head. I hug him tighter, and I start to realise that this is real. A revolution has taken place. I opened myself up, fought for what I wanted, and I won. Finally, I won. I love him and he loves me.

"Vi," he says softly, his arms still wrapped protectively around me. "When did you first realise you were in love with me?"

"I think it was at the AdAg Awards. When you held my hand. But maybe deep down there's always been something. I've always loved your humour, your ideas, the way you talk, the way you look at me . . ."

"I am pretty awesome."

I whack his chest playfully. "Note, I didn't mention your modesty."

"Yeah, I'll have to work on that," he says with a huge grin.

"What about you then? Did you really love me at first sight?"

"Yes, on the day Stella and Diego brought you onto

the floor. You were wearing a green dress with a little black belt. You wore your hair down – the way I like it – but you had this little silver comb pinning it off your face. I thought you were the most beautiful woman I'd ever seen. Then, as we got to know each other, I discovered you were smart and funny and brave and kind, and I've never had a better friend. Even though I've never stopped wanting more, I never thought you'd believe me and I didn't think you'd trust me."

"Why on earth wouldn't I trust you?"

"Because I'm me. The office player – the guy who fools around all the time because he's too chicken-shit scared to tell the woman he loves how he feels about her. I hated that guy and I never wanted to be him. That's why I adopted your law. I wanted to prove to you that I wanted something better . . . that I wanted you. Women like you come along once in a lifetime."

"Soulmates?"

"Fucking right, we're soulmates."

We snuggle in for a few more minutes, then he strokes my hair, kisses me on the cheek again and releases me. "I have to meet Daniel, Gabriel and a team of lawyers at two, so although it's going to kill me to leave you here, I need to go. But it's Saturday, so tonight I'm taking you out on a proper first date."

"Ooh, where are you taking me?"

"It's a secret."

"You have absolutely no idea, do you?"

"None whatsoever. But I'm going to think about it all afternoon and I guarantee it's going to be awesome." He stands and picks up his phone and keys from the coffee table. "Now I need to get out of these manky clothes, get my arse to the Docklands and try not to think about you while I'm in that boring meeting." He takes my hand, kisses me and walks through to the hallway. "I'm going to be counting down the seconds until seven thirty."

I kiss him back. "Me too."

"There's something else in that box I gave you."

"Oh?"

"Yeah. You didn't get around to asking about the third place I went this morning."

He kisses me again, opens the door and leaves.

And it's going to be an extremely long afternoon.

I walk back into the sitting room and pick up the box, removing the glossy brochure and documents from the Royal Opera House. At the bottom of the box is a black velvet pouch. I'm reminded of the silver pendant necklace with the engraved laurel branch that Ethan gave me last week. It was just after I'd told him about my sister, and I've worn it every day since. I pull the drawstring fastening open, and another coil of silver falls into my hand. It's a bracelet with three circular charms.

Tears form in my eyes, and I'm glad I'm alone because I feel like a total wuss. The first silver disc is engraved with a flower – a violet – and it's beautiful. The second is inscribed with yesterday's date – as if I'm ever going to forget about yesterday.

The last silver charm is engraved with two hearts. They're not perfect hearts. They're scratched, scribbled, not-quite-complete, complicated hearts.

But that makes them perfect, because they're ours.

THE END

A WORD FROM GUNTHER
(Max's cat).

If you enjoyed this book, then *purr-lease* would you consider leaving a positive review on Amazon?

Reviews help other readers find Elizabeth's stories and open up different ways of marketing to all the millions of humans out there who will love her books.

She says I (or rather my idiot owner) might get my own story if I can *purr-suade* you. I personally don't know how this will work. Max is a liability. He still hasn't realised that I'm the one who steals the Serrano ham out of the fridge. I've been doing it for seven years! Seven!

Mee-ow

Ready for the next chapter in Violet and Ethan's turbulent relationship?

Secret Summer is a FREE! short story available from all leading online retailers.

It's Complicated – Book 2 in the agency series – is
available now as an ebook or paperback.

How it all began . . . a short story from Ethan's POV. FREE! from all major digital outlets.

THE AGENCY SERIES
Short Story 0.5

Elizabeth Grey

He fell in love with the one girl he couldn't have

ALWAYS YOU

"A smart romantic comedy about unspoken love."
Grace Jolliffe - Author

THE SPIN-OFF ☺

The Agency Book 3
2019

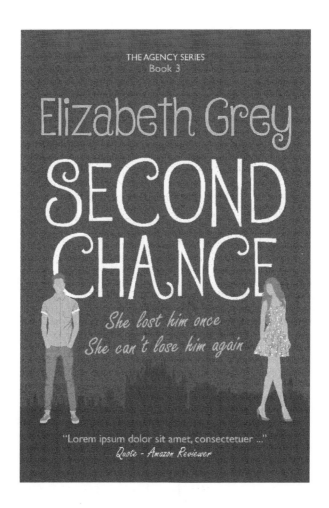

THE AGENCY SERIES
Book 3

Elizabeth Grey

SECOND
CHANCE

She lost him once
She can't lose him again

"Lorem ipsum dolor sit amet, consectetuer ..."
Quote - Amazon Reviewer

CAST OF CHARACTERS

Barrett McAllan Gray is based on several real life advertising agencies. Here's a quick reference guide to help you figure out the organisation of the company:

SENIOR PARTNERS

Malcolm Barrett	Partner & CEO
Sylvie McAllan	Partner (silent)
Gordon Gray	Partner & Chairman

CREATIVE DEPARTMENT

Stella Judd	Head of Creative Services
Diego Vega	Creative Director
Ethan Fraser	Art Director
Will Thornton	Art Director
Violet Archer	Copywriter
Pinkie Pinkerton	Copywriter
Ruby Sloan	Junior Copywriter

PRODUCTION DEPARTMENT

Wendy Smith	Film Producer
Max Wolf	Graphic Designer

CLIENT ACCOUNT MANAGEMENT

Ridley Gates	Head of Client Services
Daniel Noble	Client Account Director

ADMINISTRATIVE

Zoe Callaghan	Executive Assistant
Lucille Monroe	Executive Assistant
Gabriel Diaz	Executive Assistant

ABOUT THE AUTHOR

Elizabeth Grey spent a sizable chunk of her childhood in North East England locked away in her bedroom creating characters and writing stories. Isn't that how all writers start?

Following a five year university education that combined such wide-ranging subjects as fine art, administration, law, economics, graphic design and French, Elizabeth entered the business world as a marketing assistant before moving into operations management.

Marrying Chris in 2007, Elizabeth now has three young children and runs a small, seasonal business selling imported European children's toys and goods. She is active in local politics and campaigns tirelessly to improve the UK's education system.

During her time as a stay-at-home mum, Elizabeth rekindled her love of writing and thinks herself lucky every day that she is now able to write full time.

When not working, Elizabeth finds herself immersed in her kids' hobbies and has acquired an impressive knowledge of Harry Potter (thanks to the big boy), Star Wars (thanks to the little boy) and Barbie (thanks to her daughter). She loves European road-trips, binge-watching Netflix series and doing whatever she can to fight for a better world.

She's been told she never loses an argument.

Elizabeth's top quotes:

"Real courage is when you know you're licked before you begin, but you begin anyway and see it through no matter what. You rarely win, but sometimes you do." – Harper Lee

"In this life, people will love you and people will hate you and none of that will have anything to do with you." – Abraham Hicks

"Be who you are and say what you feel. Because those who mind don't matter, and those who matter don't mind." – Dr. Seuss

"I am no bird and no net ensnares me. I am a free human being with an independent will." – Charlotte Bronte

"I am not afraid of storms for I am learning how to sail my ship." – Louisa M. Alcott